A Muto's Pron
The Guardia

ISBN: 9781791804343

FIRST EDITION.

<u>Dedication</u>

I would like to thank my husband Darren, for your patience and helping to make this book possible. For being my light at the end of the tunnel and being there when I need you the most.

My parents, Cynthia and Desmond. You are both truly amazing. Your love, guidance and support has made me who I am today. This book is for you.

My Children Joshua and Samuel, I love you both.

To a very talented young Illustrator and Artist Jaime Cook, you saw my vision and created something magical.

A very special thank you to Steve Tomlinson who read the story first.

~ Chapter One ~

The Beginning

The stars began to fade as a golden hue of light crept through the canopy that warmed the highest precipices of the redwood trees. Morning dewdrops draped the branches like chandeliers; creating a prism of diamond lights that illuminated the very needle tips that nimbly revealed each shaft of light. Each sparkle reflected the natural spectacle of the birth of the new day; that reawakened from the gloomy slumber of night. Stood proud and rooted on guard with armaments of branches encased in an emerald carpet of moss; the mighty wooden warriors were prepared to protect its inhabitants that snoozed in its undergrowth from the evil that threatened to destroy the land.

Assembled high - elevated above the forest floor, two bright, blue, sapphire eyes pierced through the forest flora. It gazed at the last astronomical pin pricks that pebble dashed the heavens. Crouched on four lean limbs, it breathed deeply against the icy morning air. Heavy, hot mist encircled its creator that got ready to retreat for its breakfast.

It slowly stretched every sinew in its body to anticipate the decline. It knew it needed all its strength and agility to reach the bottom of the trunk, to where a meal lay to fill the empty space in its belly. It carefully wrapped its limbs around the colossal trunk. Suspended in mid-air it savagely clawed the loose scraps of shelling bark that detached itself from the shaft of the monumental structure. It clenched the skin of the tree trunk and swiftly peeled towards the terrain below. The blue-eyed creature silently touched base with gravity.

It felt that it was being watched. It cautiously looked around and stepped forward not wanting to alert anyone of its presence. It stared at the base of the redwood tree and readily spied at the human inhabitants that resided within. The perpendicularly pillared roots were large enough to house a whole family. The creature drooled and licked its lips as it sniffed the air and caught the aroma of its breakfast from within the household. Unable to control its hunger any longer, it dashed towards the arched doorway and burst its way inside.

It stood still, panted and quivered with hunger as it cautiously scrutinized the surrounding area. The room was dimly lit with a single candle that flickered causing shadows to dance in the warm orange glow. A small pot of porridge simmered over a tiny fire. In an oak crib wrapped tightly in a soft woollen shawl it spied; three small human infants that slept soundly snuggled together. Carved on the foot of the crib were three distinctive marks: the mighty bear, the watchful hawk and the spiritual wolf.

It sniffed the children; it knew immediately which infant it was destined to take. The creature's stomach groaned in anticipation when suddenly a scream pierced through the air from behind. A young beautiful woman in a crimson dress stood, frozen to the spot. Her long blond hair cascaded over her lavish gold velvet cloak. She looked on with horror at the creature that was between her and the safety of the children.

From across the room an enormous brown bear gazed at her. It stood on its hind legs with huge paws and claws large enough to mutilate her and the children in one swoop. She noticed the bear's blue eyes; she had seen them before, she collapsed to the floor and sobbed. Her cloak draped over her body that showed the same imprint as the oak crib: the mighty bear, the spiritual wolf and the watchful hawk all entwined within a shield, stitched in red thread on her left lapel.

The bear stood still, silently gazed at the crest, retreated from its hind legs and began to shake. All of a sudden, it unexpectedly disappeared and an odd-looking man with tanned buckskins and a decorated bandolier bag slung over his shoulder stood in front of her.

"You're a Shape Shifter?" she mumbled and cried in relief as she clutched her dress.

"Yes, my Lady, but I prefer if you use Muto, because that is what I am."

"I remember you; you were there with Tycus that day we…"

"Yes I was," he interrupted her.

"You are the one they call Ursus?" she sighed with relief.

"Yes, that is what I am known as to a select few, but my family call me Healing Paw."

She looked at his weather beaten skin and noticed how much thinner he was without the fur.

"I know why you are here," she croaked. Ursus nodded in politeness. "You must be hungry. I don't have much, but what I do have I will share with you."

His blue eyes twinkled and he smiled at her generosity. He had hoped she would offer him some porridge; after all, it was the aroma of porridge he could smell from the top of the redwood tree that tantalised his taste buds. He licked his lips in anticipation; it is well known that porridge is a bear's favourite food?

"I was hoping you would find us Ursus, I was told the aroma of porridge would draw you out of hiding. It is time that you and the others fulfil your promise. But first we must eat, we will talk later." She scooped two large dollops of steaming porridge and heaped them on top of one another into a bowl and handed it to Ursus. He cradled the bowl in his hands, took a huge sniff, and smiled as the aroma entered his nostrils.

"Ahh, de-licious, ab-so-lutley de-licious," and smacked his lips together in contentment.

They sat in silence as they ate. He scraped the last remnants from his bowl ready to lick it clean but stopped and glanced at his host and remembered, it had been a long time since he had shape shifted into a human. Even longer, since he had been in their company and after all, he knew he was not in the presence of an ordinary human. He reluctantly left the remaining scraps on the side of the bowl.

She looked away from Ursus and whispered softly, "It's all right; I don't mind if you want to lick it clean, I will not punish you for your crude manners."

"I am sorry, please forgive me," he murmured, as he bowed his head low.

"There is nothing to forgive; I am the one who is sorry, for putting you and your tribe in this dangerous position. If he ever found out...." she sobbed unable to continue the conversation further.

Her face was red and swollen from crying, the anguish of the last couple of days had had its toll on her strength. She slumped to a dishevelled heap on the ground. She gazed at her lap and spoke slowly.

"Do not be alarmed Ursus, but I sense a visitor waiting outside and they know you are here."

"Yes, I know. I felt their presence watching me when I arrived," he acknowledged.

"I do not want any hostility Ursus... please promise me. I am aware the tribes blame one another but they shouldn't. I need your help to make a truce with each other."

"I will try but, but it will not be easy.... do...do you know what you are asking?" He stammered in anguish and trepidation.

"I do Ursus, but remember you made an oath to Tycus. This is important; not just for the people of the land, but for them." She glanced at the sleeping infants in the crib and smiled.

He silently nodded in agreement as he now understood why she had sought him out of hiding. This confirmed the purpose of their meeting as he had suspected when he first glanced at the crib and the sleeping infants. What she requested was the only solution. His thoughts were suddenly interrupted with a long howl, followed by a high pitched whine and an impatient scratch at the door.

"Please Ursus, you promised," she pleaded.

He nodded and considered to change his form back into a bear. He wondered if he changed his form it would seem offensive and realised that would not be a good start to encourage a truce, so he thought against it. He promised to try after all.

"I will try my lady, but I cannot speak for the others," he sighed.

"That is all I ask of you Ursus."

"I think you should move back just in case," he warned.

He breathed heavy, not knowing what type of greeting he was going to receive. He gingerly placed his hand on the doorknob, what will he be faced with, man or beast? A long howl, then a growl answered this question. His heart pounded in his chest as he opened the door.

Stood at the threshold, was a grey and white oversized wolf with matted fur and black, onyx eyes that bared its teeth and snarled ready to pounce. It entered the room and slowly circled the tight space. It looked for the bear that it had witnessed enter earlier. A low growl rumbled in the pit of its throat. The wolf could smell him but could not see him.

"For heaven's sake Nubilus stop pacing around me, you are making me feel sick... I am here. And hold your tongue, remember whose presence you are in," demanded Ursus.

The wolf stared at the lady dressed in red and noticed she wore the crest of the mighty leader Tycus and immediately stopped both his pacing and growling.

"And change your form; we need to talk, you know I cannot bark," he snapped.

The wolf stretched its limbs and gently scratched. With a quick shake of the head the wolf disappeared and in its place stood a young man. His bronzed body shimmered in the candle light, reflecting the outline of his perfect, muscular form that clung to his skeleton. His long black hair was just as matted as his fur and his black onyx eyes twinkled like large, black diamonds.

"What makes you think that I Nubilus will do what YOU want? I do not take orders from you. I am not part of YOUR tribe!" he exclaimed

"Listen to me Nubilus," pleaded Ursus.

"Listen to you? Are you being serious, LISTEN TO YOU? Are you asking me to make *another* mistake? It is because I listened to you in the first place that has now put us all in danger," he argued, and he raised his hands above his head in frustration.

"We all made that decision Nubilus, have you failed to remember that it was a three-way decision," Ursus reminded him calmly.

"Oh yes, I remember - I also remember that Altaira disagreed with you. I should have agreed with her, but no, I went along with you. It is a mistake I will never repeat," Nubilus furiously spat.

Ursus bowed his head and looked at the floor. He had always thought of Nubilus as being the son he never had. Nubilus's hatred for him had now torn them apart.

"I am sorry you feel that way. I really thought it was the right decision," Ursus mumbled,

"What was that? Sorry! Am I hearing right? The mighty Ursus admitting he is wrong!" Nubilus laughed.

"No! I never said I was wrong. I said I am sorry that you feel my decision was wrong," Ursus corrected him. "I still stand by my decision and the reasoning behind it. I hope in time both you and Altaira can understand and believe the decision we all made was the correct one."

"I doubt that will happen; you now know how I feel. I don't forgive easily Ursus. As for Altaira she refuses to speak to either of us. She feels that we have betrayed her, and we have," Nubilus was looking straight at Ursus. "Can't you understand what we have done to her? She has lost all confidence in her ability to see beyond what is in front of her."

"I do regret that Altaira feels betrayed," he solemnly acknowledged. "And umm... I know... I know how close you were with each other," he softly spoke trying not to anger him further.

Unable to control how he felt any longer, Nubilus let a low growl sound through the air, followed by an unhappy sniff as he wiped his tears from his eyes with the back of his hand. He blinked hard to control his tears and sauntered to the opposite corner of the room. He leant against the wall and rested his head on his arm. The room fell silent as Nubilus fought against his grief as he mourned his lost friendship with Altaira. Slowly, he stood up straight, sniffed and let out an enormous sigh as he turned to face Ursus.

"You have no idea how close we were - or the guilt I feel for not supporting *her* decision. You have no idea how much I despise you or how much I despise myself for betraying her," he groaned bitterly.

Ursus walked towards Nubilus and gently placed his hand on his shoulder, "Old friend please," he whispered.

"Old friend! Old friend," he spat. "We - are - not - friends Ursus by any means. Get your hand off me, GET IT OFF! I will not be responsible for the consequences. I swear. I WILL NOT BE RESPONSIBLE!" Nubilus screamed.

Ursus held both his hands up in the air as a gesture of peace and slowly backed away to the other side of the room and sat down. He frowned as he placed his head in his hands. Ursus closed his eyes and sighed. He started to think twice about his promise of a truce. It was impossible he thought. Nubilus is far too angry to reason with. His mood is too threatening and he is impulsive; he is incapable of yielding and forgiving. How could he ease Nubilus's pain and convince him that they were right. He realised he needed Nubilus if he stood a chance to gain Altaira's trust; let alone convince her that they have not betrayed her. Should he give up and go back on both his promise of a truce and his oath to Lord Tycus? Lord Tycus, that is it he thought, that is the answer, Lord Tycus is the solution.

Ursus lifted his head out of his hands, smiled as he looked at the sleeping infants. Why was he so blind? It was so obvious, the infants, it all made sense now he thought. They were right after all. They were right; he just needed to convince Nubilus now he thought, as an idea came to mind.

"My lady, when I arrived I introduced myself to you, but please forgive me, I do not seem to remember you telling me who you are," Ursus pretended to quiz her as he knew from the beginning exactly who she was.

With a puzzled expression, she looked at him; confused as to why he asked this. After all, they had met before and she knew he was aware of whom she was. She decided to play along with Ursus; she wanted to understand his motive for the question. Ursus stared at her and nodded his head toward Nubilus. Nubilus had never met her. He had no idea who she was. She pondered for a moment and wondered how much she should disclose. She decided that it was best not to completely reveal her identity. It was acceptable that Ursus had known her, because he had been there with her and Tycus. He was aware of their secret.

"I am and will always be a friend," she cautiously answered, not knowing where Ursus's thoughts were heading, or how much she could trust Nubilus.

"Yes, but a friend to whom?" Ursus asked. This he was curious about; he didn't fully know where her loyalties lie, now that Tycus was dead.

She began to realise where Ursus was directing the conversation and why. "A friend to you both," she looked from Ursus to Nubilus. "A friend to the children and a friend always to Tycus," she choked, as she fought back the emotion when she said her lord's name.

"My Lady, you said you hoped I would smell the porridge and come out of hiding. Why did you want me to come out of hiding?"

"It is important Ursus; I need all three of you. I knew if you came out of hiding, Nubilus's hatred for you would also lead him here," she confessed.

"All three of us? What do you mean; you need all three of us?" Nubilus asked.

"You see, I also made a promise. A promise to see the children safely delivered to your care Nubilus. Delivered safely into the care and guardianship of the three loyal Muto's that Lord Tycus trusted."

"What? Us!" Nubilus exclaimed.

"Yes Nubilus, as you *all* promised; Ursus, Altaira and you," she smiled a half-hearted smile. "You all swore an oath," she reminded him.

"I did not! The only oath I promised was years ago, if the time came, I would help guide Lord Tycus's off-spring. Tycus is dead, he died without an heir, so my oath is…… void," he uttered and stopped in mid-sentence and looked at her. "Hang on, am I hearing right did I hear you say children?"

Nubilus scanned the room and silently in the corner for the first time he noticed a crib. He gasped as he observed at the foot of the crib were the three distinctive marks of the loyal Muto's. Why did he not see them before? He realised it was his hatred for Ursus that blinded his senses.

He stood still and took a moment not knowing the best course of action. He could hear the rhythmic breathing from the crib. He slowly approached and found three beautiful infants, snuggled together sound asleep. Realisation hit Nubilus; he now understood who they were. And what part he was expected to play.

"This cannot be! Are these children the off-spring of our Noble Tycus?"

"Yes," they both answered in unison.

Completely confused and lost for words, Nubilus gently stroked the face of one of the sleeping children. An overwhelming feeling came over him. He felt hope mixed with despair. Hope, as he knew that they were special. Despair, as he now knew he needed to fulfil his promise. A low murmur was heard; from whom it was not clear.

"I… umm…I need some air," he spluttered as he sprinted to the door.

Outside he paced back and forth from one tree to another as he kicked the ground and sent the leaves in all different directions. He ignored the icy air and the sharp wind that attacked his bare skin. His thoughts were after all elsewhere. It was not possible that *he*, Nubilus was expected to care for a child, he thought. What were they thinking? Teach a child to fight and hunt, yes, he could do that, he admitted. But care for a child, no - it was impossible.

He glanced up towards the sky, the morning started to wake. Streaks of sunlight bounced through the tree top canopy that captivated and enthralled its occupants. He listened to the harmonious dawn chorus; their fertile melodies injected a sense of wonder that instinctively carved the natural launch of daybreak.

He crouched on all fours to feel the soil that pressed between his toes; hard, sharp and coarse to touch, not at all as it should be for the time of year. He slowly scooped up a handful of dirt, inhaled the aroma and deliberately rubbed it in his hands. He repeated this ritual several times over and over again.

Sat cross-legged, he gently raised his head, sniffed the air as the wind elevated the leaves that circled around him. He raised his arms in the air to feel the full force of the breeze. He closed his eyes to meditate and touch the spirits from within. He breathed peacefully; gradually he lowered his arms and opened his eyes. He still methodically controlled his rhythmic breathing and fixed his conscience on his surroundings, hoping the spirits would help guide him.

He slowly got to his feet and cautiously moved toward the stem of a redwood tree. He placed his head against the trunk to smell the sweet bark to help regain his senses. He expected the sweet aroma to fill his nostrils and took an enormous sniff, but for some unknown reason he was greeted with a foul stench of rotten wood that burned his nasal passage and caused his eyes to tear.

"Argh, what on earth," he choked and spluttered screwing up his face with disgust. Alarmed, he frantically ran his hands up and down the trunk, he could not feel or see anything different; the tree seemed fine, but still, he could not smell the sweet bark. How peculiar he thought. Something was not right; the land was changing this he was sure of.

He sank to the floor and hugged his knees and thought about the elders of his tribe; who foretold a horrible tale when he was much younger of a terrible plight that was to befall the land.

"When the earth is sick the animals will begin to disappear, when that happens, the warriors of the rainbow will come to save them," he muttered to himself.

No, it cannot be, it was not possible he thought; these were just legends and stories he told himself. But he knew with all stories told within his tribe there was an element of truth to the tale no matter how big or small. He got up and examined a further five redwood trees. All the same, the smell of rotten wood. He could find no evidence of decay on the outside. He stood still and gazed at the trees. How very odd, he pondered. It was almost as if the spirits were telling him the very heart of the land was dying but the body continued to live. Was the land evolving? Was it adapting to survive the evil that began to envelope it? he questioned.

What could he do about it? As soon as this thought entered his mind, he knew. He had no choice but to accept the task and fulfil his oath. Stunned into realisation Nubilus whispered to himself,

"Maybe Ursus was right after all."

He stood still, listened to the wind that howled around him. He watched the branches dance and sway as the gusts advanced upon them that forced them to rock side to side and backwards and forwards. He scraped his feet in the dirt and proceeded towards the door. He scratched his forehead and let out a heavy sigh and waited outside the door to compose himself before he quietly entered.

He stood in the doorway and viewed the sleeping infants. An aura of spirits hovered above the children's crib that created a rainbow prism that reflected and danced. It soon became clear to Nubilus that their destinies were linked to the elder's stories.

"The land is changing," he spoke in a worried tone. "Time will tell if our decision was right after all Ursus," he reluctantly admitted. "It does not change how I despise you or how Altaira despises both of us," he reminded him.

Ursus smiled but only for a while as he knew Nubilus was right. The hardest task was ahead and it was not going to be easy to approach Altaira. There was so much hostility; but it was clear they must approach Altaira, no matter what danger they faced.

The flame from the candle wavered as it caught the arms of the wind that followed Nubilus into the room. He closed the door behind himself with a gentle click. His heart raced and his legs trembled. Nubilus wandered forward towards the crib in the corner of the room. He gripped the edge of the solid oak cradle. Silence filled the room as he smiled with great fascination at the sleeping infants as the auras danced overhead.

Ursus anxiously observed but kept his distance, not wanting to interrupt Nubilus endow the protection of the spirits that hovered in the air. Ursus flinched as he watched Nubilus unsheathe his knapped flint blade. He sliced through the flesh of his right arm that revealed a flow of scarlet liquid. He clenched his right arm in his left hand to stem the flow and whispered, "Nakoma with my blood I consummate and accept the gifts you bestow. The Great Spirit is our Father but the Earth is our Mother. She nourishes us, that which we put into the ground, she returns to us."

With his index finger smudged in blood, he bent over and marked the forehead of each infant to perform the ancient ritual to both honour the spirit warriors and the Earth Mother. The rainbow aura of spirits separated and hovered over each child and swayed back and forth before they settled above to combine their precious gifts onto all three children.

Ursus gave a heavy sigh as he looked upon the blood stained infants. So, this is it he thought, this is the beginning. Our fate and the fate of the land lie with three small sleeping children.

~ Chapter Two ~

Healing Paw

The children wriggled and murmured in their crib. Six small delicate arms and legs punched the air for attention and sent their shawl in all different directions. Nubilus chuckled as one infant got their arms and legs caught in the fabric that immobilised them from moving and aggravated them further. Their little cries filled the air and commanded the attention of those around them.

Ursus quickly approached the crib; he placed his hand on the head of each child and gently stroked their cheeks to calm them. The infant in the middle calmed to his touch, then immediately ceased crying and wriggling. A huge grin appeared on Ursus's face as he bent over the crib and gently lifted the infant out into his arms.

"My Lady, have the infants been named?" Ursus asked.

"Yes Ursus, you are holding Ryder and he is a boy."

Ryder was the biggest of the three children. Ursus looked at the child and wondered where his head finished and his neck began. There was so much baby fat it was difficult to see. She walked over to the crib and lifted another child out.

"This is May and she is a girl, she is named after the month of their birth."

"That is always a good omen, she will always be at her strongest during this month," he informed her.

This child was much more delicate and smaller than the other two. She held her close to her chest and rubbed her nose gently on the side of her cheek. Ursus could see it was clear that the bond between them was very strong. Nubilus lifted the remaining child out of the crib and asked.

"And this one?"

"He is called Ezra," she chuckled.

Ursus glanced at Nubilus as he cradled the child in his arms and chuckled.

"And what is so funny?" Nubilus demanded.

"It's just, that if I didn't know any better I would have thought that you were the father of the child," he laughed. "The resemblance is uncanny," he continued.

Nubilus looked down at the child and began to laugh with them. He was not as big as Ryder but like Nubilus, he also had a huge mass of hair that stuck out in all different directions. Nubilus placed the child back into his crib.

Blood dripped from Nubilus's elbow onto the floor and it soon became clear that his wound needed attention. Nubilus's sight became blurred and he blinked several times to try and clear the haze that was now began to cloud his vision. He wiped his arm with his other hand but just managed to smear the blood without restricting the flow. Without warning Nubilus slumped to the floor with a thud.

"I think your arm needs attention Nubilus, here let me help."

She handed May to Ursus who was now trying to balance two infants in his arms. She grabbed her cloak and ripped the hem off in one stroke. She gripped the fabric between her teeth and continued to rip the cloth into several parts. She believed that, first she would need to clean the wound before attempting to staunch the flow of blood; that now showed no sign of stopping. She looked around the room for her wash bowl and noticed it was on the other side of the room directly beside Ursus.

"Ursus can you pass me that wash bowl please," she asked without looking at him.

Ursus looked down at the two infants in his arms then glanced at the bowl. He couldn't put the children back into the crib as Nubilus was sprawled out in front of it. He couldn't pass her the bowl either as he already had his arms full with two infants and one of them was so heavy that his arm was beginning to ache.

"My Lady, um… I… um," he calmly spoke.

31

"The bowl Ursus, quickly, the bowl," she interjected without looking at Ursus who now struggled to hold both infants. "I can't stem the bleeding without cleaning it first."

Ursus looked at Nubilus who began to lose consciousness as he closed his eyes.

"URSUS THE BOWL NOW!" she bellowed as she pressed down onto the wound. She wondered why he hadn't passed her the bowl and looked around then realised he had both children in his arms.

"Put the children on the floor Ursus, it won't harm them and then pass me the bowl please."

Ursus did as she asked, placed the children on the floor and passed her the bowl. She dipped the cloth into the water and began to clean the wound. Every time she wiped the blood off his arm more poured out from the crevice of raw flesh. Panic started to envelope her and tears started to flow down her cheeks.

"My Lady, please let…"

"No Ursus, I know what I am doing," she interrupted him. She continued to clean the wound but was still unable to stop the flow.

"No Ursus, I know what I am doing," she interrupted him. She continued to clean the wound but was still unable to stop the flow.

Nubilus slowly opened his eyes and whispered. "Please."

Unable to hear what he said she leaned in further to him and placed her head nearer to his. Nubilus raised his blood soaked hand and smeared the scarlet liquid across her forehead and marked her in the same way as the children. He closed his eyes and uttered, "Ursus," then he became still and silent.

She looked at Nubilus; it was obvious that he wanted Ursus to attend to him. Bewildered, she staggered to her feet and gazed at Ursus, then moved away and left him to bleed on the cold floor. Ursus seized his arm, raised it in the air and grabbed another piece of cloth.

"You have done well my Lady, but it is clear the bleeding is not going to stop." He grabbed her arm, "keep his arm up in the air, I need to find a stick." He rushed outside and left her there alone, holding Nubilus's arm in the air.

"A stick, why do you need a stick?" she asked in complete bewilderment.

"You will soon understand why," he answered.

Outside he immediately found a small stick that the wind had detached from the tree that had now become part of the forest floor.

Perfect he thought, not too big and not too small either. He hurried inside to be at Nubilus's side.

"My Lady, I need you to support his arm so I can wrap the cloth around it," he instructed her as he began to wrap the cloth several inches above the wound on his upper arm.

"Ursus you have missed the wound completely."

"Yes, I know; it is important that I go above the wound and not on it. If I do he will be in an extreme amount of pain and it will not stop the bleeding," he answered.

She carefully watched him wrap the cloth several times around Nubilus's upper arm and tie a single knot in the cloth to hold it in place. She curiously observed as Ursus placed the stick on the recently tied knot and secured it with another knot. He very slowly began to turn the stick that gradually twisted and tightened on Nubilus's arm. Ursus could see her frowning and he knew she did not understand what he was doing.

"This will stop the blood pumping from his heart reaching the open wound," he advised her. "Once I have stopped the blood, then we can clean the wound and dress it," he explained further. She showed she understood and nodded in agreement but felt foolish with her lack of knowledge.

"Now, I would like you to wash his arm and put something on it, so I can see if it works," he ordered her.

She gently washed the blood off and placed a fresh clean piece of cloth from her cloak on the open cut.

Gradually she could see the blood was starting to reside. Satisfied, Ursus stopped twisting the stick and tied it in place to stop it from unravelling. He knew it would need to be in place for a little while. If he removed it too soon it would be dangerous to Nubilus, and if he kept it on too long this would be as equally dangerous; he needed to time it just right.

He slowly stood and stretched his back in to an arc; two slight clicks from his spine were heard as his vertebrae shifted back into place. He grinned with satisfaction and relief. He noticed on the other side of the room there was a make shift bed, slightly elevated off the floor with a large deer hide for a cover. Nubilus needed to be kept warm. He quickly pulled the cover off the bed and without any effort scooped him up off the floor. He gently placed him on the bed and secured the deer skin over his shivering body.

He glanced at the fire that radiated very little heat and noticed a small pile of kindling stacked haphazardly nearby. He seized two large pieces of timber and carefully placed them horizontally on the dying flames. He hoped to restart the remaining embers. Slowly a wisp of smoke curled and snaked its way around the smouldering firewood. A tiny flicker of orange, hungry to ignite a blaze, sparked to life. It began to dance and sway then rapidly captured its prey and forced it to surrender to the coils that began to engulf it. Ursus smiled with contentment as he listened to the sound of the wood spit and crackle under the strain of the fresh raging heat.

Slung across the chest his beaded bandolier bag hung beside his hip, weighted with a variety of herbs and ointments. Wrapped in individual pockets of animal hide was an assortment of leaves and seeds. Ursus carefully unfolded and placed them in a ceremonial order. He pulled out a small animal bone that had a rounded bulbous end. He dropped several seeds into a handled pan and positioned it over the heat of the fire. With no time to waste, he placed several leaves on a piece of kindling and used the bulbous bone to pound the leaves together until they became a pulp of green and brown mash. Ursus continued until the room was filled with a pine and sage aroma. He cautiously looped a piece of kindling under the handle of the pan and lifted it out of the burning structure. He tipped the contents on top of the mashed leaves and continued to crush the seeds to produce a salve buttery substance.

Nubilus's breathing became very shallow. Ursus glanced and groaned at the heroic sacrifice that his friend had made to endow the gifts of the rainbow warriors. He hoped that the sacrifice was not going to claim his life. He knelt beside him, rested on his heels and mumbled a healing prayer. He gradually released the stick on the top of his arm; checked with each turn that the flow of blood had ceased to ooze from the self-inflicted gash. He very slowly unravelled the remaining cloth that had helped to restrict the flow of blood. Nervously, he glanced at the gaping hole on Nubilus's upper arm and smiled with relief. He did it, he thought, the bleeding had now thankfully stopped.

Ursus scooped up the freshly made paste of seeds and leaves and smothered it over the wound as he muttered an incantation; calling on the Earth Mother to heal her humble servant of the forest. Ursus continued to chant as he placed a large dandelion leaf over the top of the freshly pasted arm. He secured the leaf with the animal hide that had once enveloped it inside the medicine bag.

"What did you put on his arm?" she curiously asked.

"What the earth mother has provided from the forest," he answered.

"Yes, I could see it was vegetation from the forest, but what type of vegetation, what was it?" she continued to probe. "I could see that you used a dandelion leaf, but what else did you use?" she enquired again.

"My Lady, I cannot tell you my tribal secrets. Some have been passed down to me, some I have discovered for myself. The healing properties I use are sacred. They are sacred to my tribe and the next healing servant of the land that is chosen to take my place," he answered. "The properties I hold in my bag are sacred only to me; it is my most valued possession. I will never part with it. I will take it to the holy resting place with me," he stated.

"But what if they do not choose another within your tribe, what happens then?"

"My knowledge dies with me," he answered solemnly.

"Surely your knowledge of the land should be passed on Ursus, don't you agree?" she spoke slyly. She hoped that Ursus was going to yield and confide in her what ingredients he had used in his healing balm.

"No, I do not agree. Knowledge of the medicines of the land is poison in the wrong hands and this is very dangerous.... Very dangerous," he stated. After all, he knew who she was and parting with his knowledge of the plants to her would be very foolish.

"Please do not ask me again my Lady, for I will never part with the knowledge the Earth Mother has entrusted me with," he ended. This was his final word on the matter. She snorted at his lack of cooperation to share his knowledge and began to feed three hungry mouths that screamed for her attention and their nutrition.

Ursus knew he had one last ritual to perform to help the healing process. He pulled out a small braid of dried sweet grass. He placed the tip of the braid into the flame of the fire and began to wave the burning braid slowly in wide circles in the air as it smouldered. A strong scent of vanilla took hold of the room. Nubilus unknowingly breathed in the healing aroma that filled his lungs. Ursus had hoped that this would cleanse and restore his soul.

"Do you think he will survive Ursus?" she asked.

"It is difficult to tell, he has lost a lot of blood and he is very weak," he replied. "He needs to rest now. I have done all I can; he is in the hands of the spirits. If they believe he has a purpose in life, then he will survive and follow that path. If not, he will return to the Earth Mother and nourish the ground," he calmly spoke.

A Muto's Promise
The Guardians

Exhausted and drained they sat in silence for many hours and took respite from the frightening ordeal of Nubilus's self-infliction. Hypnotised by the dancing orange and yellow blaze of the fire, they slowly closed their eyes and snoozed in the warmth. A concord of snorts spluttered through the air with each inhaling lungful of sweet grass they took from their surroundings.

A small grey mouse scurried and meandered across the floor in hope of a tasty meal. It searched for any remnants of seeds that Ursus dropped during the healing process. It sniffed the air, caught the scent of seeds inside Ursus's medicine bag, and cautiously scuttled up the leather hide. Ursus twitched as the mouse's whiskers brushed the hairs on his skin that alerted his senses. With one foul swoop, he swiped the mouse off his bag and sent it scuttling across the other side of the room.

Half asleep, Ursus gazed at the fire as it popped and sparked. A wisp of smoke snaked slowly upwards as a pair of emerald green eyes appeared through the cloud of embers.

"Altaira!" a stressed voice spoke from behind him. "I am coming."

Ursus looked over his shoulder as he recognised Nubilus's strained vocal cords. His patient was still fast asleep. He was completely unaware of his verbal outburst. Ursus glanced back at the emerald eyes and the fire hissed as tears fell and hit the burning cinders. Her voice rang in his ears,

"Help me!"

"I am coming Altaira," Nubilus repeated.

Ursus knelt beside him and wiped his brow, unsure if Nubilus was hallucinating with a fever, or if he too was responding to the vision he had seen from the flames. Slowly the eyes in the fire began to fade, but her voice still rung in his ears. Ursus sat on the floor, crossed legged, with his hands placed on his knees and closed his eyes. What did it mean? Is Altaira in danger? No, Altaira is a great tactician of war, *she* cannot be in danger, he thought. Then why did she ask for help? This vision was a concern.

A hand squeezed Ursus's shoulder that disturbed him from his meditative trance.

"Altaira," a voice spluttered as Nubilus strained to sit up. "We need to go," he gasped trying to catch his breath as he spoke. "I heard her Ursus, in my head, she needs us – we have to leave." He continued to gasp as he stretched his hand out to Ursus to grab his arm.

"Shush Nubilus," he whispered and put his hand over Nubilus's mouth as he glanced at the sleeping woman. "Shush," and mouthed the words; "I do not trust her and neither should you. Do not mention the vision of Altaira in front of her. I will think of a way to leave, just be patient," he reassured him.

Nubilus nodded his head and understood; Ursus must have his reasons for the secrecy. He knew not to question Ursus's motives and slumped back down onto the bed exhausted and wondered who exactly she was.

"What happened to me?"

"You passed out like a Tiqala," Ursus sniggered. "You, who are meant to be of Mala, slumped to the floor like a Tiqala."

Nubilus glanced at his arm and then back at Ursus. "Is this your handy work?"

"I had to do something you were making a right mess on the floor," and pointed to the mass of red residue stained across the ground.

"Besides, someone could slip on that if they were not careful," he laughed, and disturbed the sleeping woman from her slumber.

Nubilus nodded his head as a gesture of appreciation and respect to his friend for saving his life and snuggled back down amongst the deer hide to keep warm. Nubilus kept thinking about Altaira, why had he heard her voice in his head? He tried to understand what it could mean. All he did know was that she was in trouble and she needed his help. He noticed Ursus boiling water and watched as he sprinkled several pips into the potion. Ursus let it simmer. Occasionally he added more pips to the concoction for a stronger draft. He poured the steaming brew into three beakers and handed them out to the eagerly awaiting consumers.

"Here you go Tiqala," he sniggered as he helped Nubilus sit up.

"Tiqala, what does that mean?" she asked

"It means strong and powerful one," Nubilus lied.

"It means, little one," Ursus corrected him as Nubilus frowned with embarrassment of being called, 'Little one'.

She laughed, then looked at Ursus and looped her arm around him and smiled as she sipped her herbal brew.

Late afternoon advanced as Ursus continued to tend to Nubilus's wound. A rustle of material was heard from across the room as the person wearing it paced back and forth, diagonally from one side to the other. She clenched her hands, anxiously folding them into one another and then unfolding them. She touched the children's cheeks each time she stepped near them. Her footsteps became heavier with each visit as she dragged her feet away from the cooing infants. She ceased her pacing and let out an enormous sigh, her eyes began to swell as the weight of leaving the children loomed within her. She knew that she had no choice. To keep them with her would condemn them and her to death.

"Ursus the sun will soon fade and night-time will be upon us, I need to leave. I cannot stay any longer. They will notice my absence, if they have not already. I have fulfilled my oath to Tycus. I leave the children in your guardianship." She tore off her cloak, ripped it into three pieces and swaddled each child in the gold velvet keepsake. "I will go immediately, before it gets too hard to leave them."

She wasted no time and kissed each child tenderly. She sniffed with trepidation as she tried to ease the sharp pain radiating in her heart. She held each infant in her arms and snuggled them close to her chest. Tears cascaded down her cheeks as the grief absorbed her soul.

"I, I ccan't do it Ursus, I can't," she sobbed.

"You must. You are doing the right thing," he reassured her.

"Am I? Then why do I feel so bad, if it is the right thing?" she cried.

Ursus took the children from her, placed them back into the crib and held her close while she sobbed on his shoulder. She gently pulled away, slipped a bracelet off her arm and handed it to Ursus.

"It's not much, but can you make sure they have a stone each, it was their father's. I know it is what he would have wanted." She handed the stringed bracelet with three different coloured stones to Ursus and placed it gently into the palm of his hand.

"Time will heal your pain, in more than one way. Search inside your soul for peace and you will find it." He reached inside his bag and placed a hematite stone in the palm of her hand. "This is to replace the ones you have sacrificed to the children; it will give you the strength and protection you need."

"Thank you Ursus." She wrapped herself in a black and silver cloak and fastened a pebble necklace around her neck. Nubilus gasped as he saw it. Who is she? He now understood why Ursus was careful. All he could think was that she was one of them... She was one of them and they were helping her, he did not understand. Why did she make an oath to Lord Tycus when she is clearly wearing the colours of the King? Mouth wide open, he continued to stare at her in confusion. She walked towards the door and slowly opened it. Then stopped and pressed her head against the frame.

"I am glad you are better Nubilus," she turned around to look at him, "I didn't think you were going to make it." She looked at Ursus and smiled. "You truly are Healing Paws," she sniffed and fought back the tears.

"My Lady, what of their mother? We know nothing about her, what do we tell the children?" Nubilus asked.

"The truth Nubilus... she died the same day that Tycus was brutally murdered. Yes Nubilus, he was murdered," she hesitated, glanced once more at the children and whispered, "Thank you. Don't worry your secret is safe with me, I will not disclose who you both are, I owe you that at least."

With a heavy heart and a tear stained face, she shut the door firmly behind her.

~ Chapter Three ~

The Journey

Ursus and Nubilus both stared at the door, half expecting her to come back and reclaim the infants. She had fulfilled her oath and now she was gone. Gone from the infants' lives forever. Ursus began to scout around the room looking for food for their journey. Time was now their enemy; there was no more food for the children. They needed to travel quickly to make it back to his tribe where nursing mothers would feed the younglings. He knew the best time to leave would be at night, when the land was quiet from human spies; ready to ambush them and kill the children and torture both him and Nubilus. He was aware they would not be alone as they travelled. Night time was always a busy time for wild animals hunting for their prey. He just hoped they would not fall victim to the bloodthirsty voracious beasts and he prayed for safe passage.

Ursus knew they needed to make haste. He thought about Nubilus who was still too weak to make the journey by foot, this he was sure. Although he knew, Nubilus would disagree and insist he was fine to make the journey unaided. Without speaking, he quietly went outside. He looked all around and could sense no sign of their host. Like a phantom, she and her black cloak had disappeared. Ursus looked back at his patient and sighed. He needed to gather some branches to make a travois to transport Nubilus and the children to his tribe. He looked up at the heavens and noted it was getting darker with each passing moment. Bright pinpricks started to cover the leaden sky. He detected several large branches buried amongst the fallen leaves. He ran his hand along the branches and lifted them up off the forest floor to check their weight. He casually threw them back down on the ground with a heavy thud. No good he thought, far too heavy for him to drag. He continued to search the forest floor but to no avail. He could not find branches that were to his satisfaction. Some were long enough but they were too heavy. Ursus knew he was strong, but not strong enough to pull those hefty branches with three infants and Nubilus in tow.

Disappointed, he made his way back to his patient and three charges. He dragged his feet across the room and plonked his body on the bed next to Nubilus.

"Ursus we need to talk, I have lots of questions that need answers," Nubilus cautiously spoke.

"I know you do, the answer to the first question is - yes, the answer to second question is - yes and the answer to the third question is – I'm working on it," he answered without even looking at Nubilus's bewildered face.

"But I, haven't said what the questions are yet," he spoke in bewilderment.

"Nubilus, I know you better than you think, did I answer them?" Ursus asked.

"Well, yes you did…but."

"But nothing Nubilus, please just rest and leave it to me. You are now aware of whom she is and *that* little secret must not be shared with anyone, do you understand, no-one must know who brought the children to us and how important they are. I know you are eager to talk about it, but not yet," Ursus softly spoke. "Yes, I am worried about Altaira too and yes we will be going back to my tribe and it is this that I am working on," he confessed.

"What do you need? Maybe I can help…. you know, give you some ideas…maybe," he cautiously spoke not wanting to take over and anger Ursus. He knew Ursus could be stubborn and often refused help when offered.

"Well unless you have a secret stash of timber to make a travois that is suitable for me to transport you and the children on, I don't think there is much you can do," Ursus sighed.

Nubilus scanned the room and shook his head. He shivered, wrapped the hide tighter around and perched himself on the edge of the bed.

"I could always walk and we could make a papoose for the children that you could carry," he suggested.

"I don't think you are strong enough to walk all the way back to my tribe Nubilus, but we may not have a choice," he solemnly spoke as he looked at his feet.

"Well Ursus as you said, we have no choice do we. I will make a papoose and secure the children on your back," he proposed.

Slowly, Nubilus gathered the cloak and the blankets from the children's crib. He twisted and turned the material wrapping the younglings into a tight secure cocoon. He pulled the final piece that held all three children in their papoose, tied it in place around them and secured it in place on Ursus's back. He bent down and placed his hands on his knees; drops of sweat gathered on his forehead. He gasped for air and breathed heavy as he swayed from side to side. He slowly stretched his body and raised his hands in the air to open his diaphragm hoping to get more oxygen into his lungs. Nubilus struggled to stand, flopped onto the bed and heard a loud creak as the wooden timbers took his weight.

"Ursus!" he shouted. "What about using the bed frame to make a travois?" He lifted the bedding up to reveal the wooden structure below.

"This is perfect for a travois, absolutely perfect," he announced with a beaming smile.

Ursus ran his hand up and down the wood as an enormous grin appeared across his bronzed face.

"Brilliant, this will certainly make a travois. Not too heavy and still strong enough to carry you. Fantastic, you're right…. absolutely perfect," he agreed.

Ursus began to dismantle the frame and stacked three lengths of wood, two of a similar size and one much smaller on top of one another. He lifted and dragged them outside. Within a few moments, Ursus had finished constructing the travelling vehicle and threw the deer hide over the A shaped frame. It was now ready to trek across the open wasteland and transport Nubilus and the infants back to his tribe.

Ursus walked back inside the dwelling and carried the wooden crib outside.

"Surely we are not taking that with us," Nubilus asked.

"Of course not, we need to destroy all evidence that the children exist, it's safer that way. It has the Muto's inscriptions
engraved on it, some may guess and make a connection to us and start asking questions."

He went back inside with a twig from the forest floor and took a light from the small fire that was still burning before stamping it out. He gently blew on the twig and the embers began to burn. He flicked the small twig on to the crib and watched it devour all proof of the children's existence. He looked at the tiny pile of ash: just a few tiny embers were left. Ursus tipped a pot on to it to smother the ambers.

"We need to go now Nubilus," he demanded as he lifted the papoose off his back and gently handed the infants to him.

Nubilus carefully balanced himself with the sleeping children on the travois and gradually moved his body in to a secure and comfortable position.

"Are you ready Nubilus?"

"Erm, yes, I think so. Are you ready? Are you sure you can do this Ursus?" he answered in a doubtful voice.

"Well, we'll soon find out," he responded.

He bent down, lifted the protruding wooden lengths and balanced them on his shoulders. He stood still for a moment as he panted and blew out his cheeks. Then he suddenly sucked in the air and gradually began to walk with small, slow, steps dragging his cargo behind him.

Nubilus closed his eyes and listened to the scraping noise of the travois as it churned through the rough terrain beneath him. He began to feel guilty that Ursus was exhorting all his energy on him, especially as he remembered how he treated him moments before, when they first met inside the redwood tree. Then, his thoughts moved to Altaira. With heavy eyes, he closed his lids and fell asleep.

The journey was slow and arduous as Ursus struggled to trek across the wide-open wasteland. Ursus staggered as he stomped his feet one in front of each other stirring clouds of dust in his wake. His face contorted and strained that showed the bulging veins in his forehead and neck. Sweat glistened over his face as his body strained to pull the weight. He dragged his heavy load that etched tracks in the soil that marked the distance he had travelled. Many hours had passed, and he felt he was no nearer his destination. He knew time was against him. The children would need nourishment and Nubilus needed tending. He had no choice but to stop. He gasped for breath, he stooped over with his hands on his knees, taking huge mouthfuls of air to regain his oxygen levels and rest his aching limbs. He glanced at his patient who began to stir.

"Is everything alright Ursus?" Nubilus whispered with a strained voice.

"Yes, I am just resting to catch my breath," he answered. Ursus slowly stood up and arched his aching back and then gently rubbed his bony shoulders. He winced as he touched the blistered indentations on his skin from where the travois had rested. Suddenly he noticed two, yellow, eyes in the scrubland watching and waiting. This was what he feared. The night-time scavengers were patiently laying low to ambush its prey. Two yellow eyes blinked, suddenly turned into four, then six and then eight. Ursus gave out a heavy sigh; this was not what he wanted to run into. A posse of Garchy were gathering forces to bring down their prey and he knew they were the prey.

Ursus quickly became aware he must hide Nubilus and the children and he would need to change his form. From what the elders of his tribe had told him, Garchy were frightened of bears. Their superstitious beliefs stopped them from harming a bear. They feared that ill-fated consequences that could befall them and their tribe.

"What is it Ursus and don't lie to me, what is it?" he asked as he tried to sit up.

Nervously, Ursus spoke, "I, well, umm, I don't know how to break it to you," he announced.

"Just spit it out. I'm a big boy. I can handle it," he winced in pain as he spoke and tried to prop himself up a bit farther to listen.

"A posse of Garchy!"

"WHAT! I was wrong Ursus, I can't handle that. Why the hell did you tell me that? You could have told me something else," he shouted.

"Shush, well what did you want me to do? LIE to you. Is that what you want? Oh, it's okay, it's nothing to worry about - it's just a pack of wolf cubs heading our way. Is that what you wanted me to say? You need to calm down, they will hear you," Ursus advised through gritted teeth.

"Hear me! Hear me! It's not hearing me I'm worried about," he hissed through clenched teeth. "Just look at me. They will smell me. I have blood all over me. They are hardly going to come over and say, oh, hello and lick my wound better and then say bye, are they. They have teeth. Bloody sharp teeth too and they know how to use them. What the *hell* are we going to do Ursus?" he panicked.

Nubilus looked up at Ursus for an answer but none came. Ursus stood still, he remained silent and looked down at the floor of the gravelled wasteland. Nubilus continued to stare at him and waited for an answer, but still no response. He understood it was up to him now. It was his turn to become the mighty warrior. He looked up to the stars for an answer, but they too were as silent as Ursus. He looked at his wound, if only he had not made that sacrifice, he would have been strong and a posse of Garchy would have been a huge challenge but a great story to tell the tribe none the less. In his heart, he knew what he needed to do as he forged a plan in his head. But yes, there was a but; and a big one too, did he have the strength to do it or the courage to follow his plan through? Yes, he thought - it might work, or at least he hoped it would. He had heard many stories from the tribe's leaders, but one stood fondly in his memory and he was hoping it was true. He was counting on it.

"Right, okay, right, this is what we are going to do," Nubilus announced. "You are going to take the children to safety and I will distract them, they will be after my blood and hopefully they will not smell you or the children."

"No, Nubilus I can't let you do that, they will tear you apart. I am not letting you sacrifice yourself, you will die. Just give me a minute and I will think of something," he pleaded.

"No!" Nubilus shook his head and repeated, "No, we both know we have no choice, now go. Go on before it is too late. Go on, go!" he demanded, as he lifted himself off the travois to stand.

"You are not strong enough to fight a whole posse of Garchy, you will die."

"We all die eventually, that has been decided, but how and when, ah, that is yet to be decided. If it is my time to go then the spirits can have me, but they will not have me without a fight." He spoke nervously trying to convince himself he was doing the right thing.

"Go!"

Ursus began to stretch his arms in the air and paw the floor with his feet like a dog. He twisted his neck and jaw and instantly his human features changed. His animal senses suddenly became very alert and all he could smell was the sweet scent of blood that radiated from Nubilus's wound. He knew Nubilus was right, it was his odour that alerted the Garchy and they would stop at nothing until they consumed its source and human blood was their favourite nectar. He understood his prime concern was to protect the children. His razor sharp teeth bit into the papoose that tightly bounded the infants and he pulled them off the travois into the hedge and hoped they would be safe.

The Garchy had caught the scent for sure and raced towards them with haste. They were one of the fiercest hunters of the wasteland. They were known for their speed, agility and perseverance. They never yielded once they caught the scent of their prey. Sometimes they would feast immediately or take their prisoners back to their lair to torture and eventually consume after they had their fun. Their yellow eyes grew closer and closer. Ursus stood over the children, his chest became tight as his heart constricted and began to beat faster and faster until the sound saturated his eardrums.

Slowly, out from the darkness he saw a single Garchy cautiously approach and sniffed the air around him. Half animal and half human, it was one of nature's mysteries. It was known for being a creature that had no purpose but to consume from the land without giving anything back. It made a clicking sound and signalled to the others to join him. They began to circle the area, constantly sniffing and snorting. Ursus stood very still and guarded the infants. He knew that Nubilus was completely exposed and very vulnerable. He was grateful he could only hear them clicking, it was the high pitch cry of when they were about to attack that he feared. He could see their battle scars on their distorted faces and the horrific stench of rotten flesh entered his nostrils. Dry, stale blood was splashed across their bodies from their victims. Bits of sinew and gristle were still stuck to their skin from their previous meal. The scars and blood were not just from attacking their prey, no, they thought nothing about eating each other after they challenged one another to move up the ranks of their tribe. He watched, not knowing what he was going to do. Did he risk leaving the children unguarded and unprotected to save Nubilus from being ripped apart, or did he leave Nubilus to the jaws of one of nature's freaks?

Nubilus stood waiting, the blood on his bronze body radiated in the moonlight and the odour curled its way in the air towards the Garchy's nostrils. The clicking immediately stopped and silence fell. Suddenly, a high pitch shrill was heard from the lead Garchy and the others followed in unison with a reply. The sound was deafening as it echoed across the wasteland. They had spotted the source of the aroma. The creatures licked their lips and surrounded Nubilus. They stood snarling, drooling and showed their sharp teeth, as they got ready to pounce on Nubilus to rip him apart.

Nubilus crouched down and rubbed his hands in the soil to ask the earth mother for protection. At top speed, two Garchies ran towards him, with wide eyes and saliva that dripped from their gums. He quickly got two hands full of soil and threw it in their eyes. As quick as a flash Nubilus skidded through the dirt and sent clouds of dust up in the air to confuse the Garchy further. He plunged his knapped flint blade in the belly of one of his pursuers and slit him from naval to neck without letting go of the blade. Exhausted, he twisted his body round. He threw the blade at the other and buried it into the eye socket that pierced straight through to its brain. Both

Garchies slumped to the floor. Dead. Two down he thought, as the remaining Garchy began to scream and hoot in anger. Nubilus scrambled to his feet. Breathing heavy. Not knowing how much longer he could defend himself. He had exhorted all his energy. His adrenalin carried him through as he quickly ducked when another Garchy jumped at him to tear him from limb to limb.

Suddenly, the sound of a crying baby was heard, as it echoed through the night air. This was a sound that both Nubilus and Ursus did not want to hear. Nubilus closed his eyes and let out a heavy sigh as one of the children continued to cry. The two remaining creatures immediately stopped. They started to hoot and their shrill got louder and louder as they began to search for the noise.

Ursus gingerly moved forward. Silently he placed his large paws on the ground in front of him. His out-stretched claws scraped and crushed the soil as he prepared himself to fight. He could see Nubilus struggling to stand, he knew he could fight no more, but he still tried to distract them from the children and to focus on him.

"Come on!" he shouted breathlessly as he fell to his knees.

"What are you waiting for? Come and finish me off. Cowards!" he baited.

It was no good; they now had another source they wanted to kill. A source that was defenceless and less likely to put up a fight. Or so they thought.

Ursus knew it was only a matter of time before the Garchy would smell Nubilus's blood on the fabric that wrapped the children.

He left the children unguarded and unprotected from the jaws of these foul creatures. Silently he hid himself and waited for the right time to ambush and ensnare his foe. Cautiously, the Garchy moved, they looked back at Nubilus who was now slumped on the floor and no longer a threat. They would kill him after they feast on their new prey. They sniffed and snorted as they did before as they moved through the wasteland bushes. They found what they were searching for; but this time no high pitched scream was sounded. The three tiny children would not put up a fight. Their battle cry remained silent.

The baby continued to cry as a Garchy picked it up. It held the infant in the air and blew its toxic breath on the child. The child immediately stopped its crying and became limp. The other Garchy did the same to the remaining two children. He replaced the once crying child back with its intoxicated siblings. Ursus, waited and watched. The bigger of the two Garchy sat on the floor and gave out a sound similar to a chuckle as he picked one of the children up and dangled them in the air by a foot. He licked his lips and the drool off his chin. He opened his mouth wide, ready to swallow the child whole. Ursus knew he could not wait any longer and got ready to attack.

On all four paws, Nubilus also charged forward; howling at the top of his voice. He pounced at the Garchy and sent the unconscious child skidding across the floor.

Ursus emerged moments later from his hiding place. He stood on his hind legs, roared and showed his deadly fangs as he swiped at the creature with his claws. He sliced through the creature's flesh and sent him tumbling backwards to the ground. The terrified Garchy scrambled to his feet and tried to run but Ursus stood on him with all four paws and pinned him to the floor. His heavy frame slowly squeezed the air out of its body. He lowered his head and swiftly ripped the Garchy's head clean from its body and spat it out like a piece of dirt.

The last Garchy watched in horror as he saw the head roll towards him. He twisted his body and tried to run. Stood in front of him, was a huge wolf growling and curling his upper lip, baring his teeth and gums. The Garchy began to shake. Nubilus knew; it was not going anywhere as he leapt in the air sinking his fangs into its throat and forced the un-naturally large body to the ground. Its body twitched uncontrollably as the remaining ounce of life escaped its dying corpse. Then, it stopped. It too was dead. The bear and the wolf panted, breathed heavy and collapsed to the floor with exhaustion and relief.

Ursus mutated back into his human form and he carefully wrapped all three intoxicated children back inside their papoose. They would be asleep for a while, he thought. Smelly Garchy breathe can knock a man out for hours let alone a small infant. He gently patted Nubilus on his huge wolf head and said, "Well done Nubilus."

The wolf just lifted his head, let out a low whine in acknowledgement and closed his eyes.

Ursus's eyes began to burn and tear as the smell from the Garchy's dead bodies began to radiate in the air. He knew he needed to burn the dead corpses to stop the horrific smell and other unwanted visitors. He dragged the bodies and piled them on top of one another. He could see the remnants of Garchy organs scattered on the floor from where Nubilus had sliced one in half. Such accuracy, very impressive and he nodded his approval. He pulled the knapped blade from the Garchy's eye socket and wiped it clean on its clothes. Ursus rubbed two flints together to create a spark to light a small pile of twigs. A tiny, bright flicker caught hold and the twigs began to glow steady as Ursus poked and prodded the small fire. Gradually, the fire began to build stronger and stronger as he added dry grass. Ursus took a light from the orange inferno and dropped it on the pile of bodies. Slowly their clothes began to glow and shrivel as the flames took hold. The smoke curled its way up in the night sky as the blaze licked and consumed the flesh of its victims. He stood watching a while as the blaze soared out of control, disintegrating the bodies wrapped in its coils.

Ursus sluggishly walked to where Nubilus and the children were resting. He took the remnants of the red cloak that wrapped the children and threw that too into the flames. All evidence of the children's lineage was now gone. Ursus touched his bag and felt for the bracelet. In time, he would give the stones to the children. For now, the stones were safe in his medicine bag, waiting for the right time to be given to their rightful owners. He decided he would give Nubilus a little while longer before he would wake him to continue their journey. He plonked his exhausted frame beside Nubilus. He sat in silence as he stared at his brave friend. He began to grin as he watched the wolf dream. All four legs began to jolt; his eyes and ears started to twitch as he gave out the occasional outburst of a growl and a very low howl; then a tiny put, put noise as he blew out the side of his jaws. He showed his teeth and gums as he growled and curled his lip. He waited, mesmerised by his companion's animal instincts. If he had not known any better, he would have thought Nubilus was all wolf, instead of being human.

He began to pat Nubilus's head, but suddenly darted backwards as Nubilus quickly scampered on all four paws and pressed his nose to Ursus's face, growling and not at all impressed he had been disturbed from his slumber.

"It's me, it's all right it's only me," he reminded him. But he continued to growl and show his teeth. Something was not right. He slowly backed away hoping that may make him calmer. He growled louder and became more aggressive as he jumped over Ursus's head. Ursus flinched and cowered, raised his hands to his head then cautiously turned around. Lying on the floor pinned by the wolf was a man screaming his head off.

"Healing Paw, Healing Paw it's me, it's me, Dak," the man shouted. Ursus looked at the flattened man on the floor and instantly recognised him.

"It's okay, he's from my tribe," he announced.

Nubilus looked at Ursus and then at the man and lowered his head to his to sniff him. The man closed his eyes and held his breath, not really knowing if he was about to be eaten or not. Nubilus continued to pin the man to the floor, breathed a hot slobbery breath and panted over him.

"P ...p please Healing Paw," he stuttered.

Nubilus looked at Ursus, who nodded to let him go. Nubilus lowered his head again and let his cold, wet, wolf nose touch the man's face. Before he got off his body, he gave the man an almighty lick with his rough, smelly tongue and left a thick residue of drool on his cheek.

"Argh, that's disgusting," the man said as he used his sleeve to wipe off the saliva.

"You are lucky," Ursus said. "You should have seen what he has just done to three Garchy. I bet they wished he only licked their face," Ursus chuckled.

"What! Garchy... here?" He scuttled to his feet, twisted his body around to search for them.

"Relax, they have been taken care of," he advised.

"How many?" he asked, still looking around nervously.

"Three small Garchy and one enormous one. I think he was the lead as he was giving the orders," he answered.

"And you killed all four?" he enquired with admiration.

"Yes."

Nubilus stood up, looked at Ursus and gave out a small yelp in protest.

"Well, actually the wolf killed three and I killed one. But I killed the biggest one and it was like killing three." He looked at Nubilus and said, "What? Well it was; he was enormous compared to the three little ones you tackled."

The wolf huffed in protest and walked away in disgust. Three little ones... still two sets of teeth more than he had dealt with, Nubilus thought. He plonked himself beside the children; stared at Dak and growled. He didn't like him very much. There was something about him. He had an odd smell that Nubilus had smelt before but could not recall from where.

Dak tried not to look anxious as he noticed the wolf surveying him and looked away nervously to speak to Ursus.

"So, um, why are you out here on your own?" he enquired.

"I'm not alone, I have Wolfie with me," he sniggered.

Nubilus looked up and let out a low growl. So, that's it now, he thought. I am Wolfie, not Nubilus, but Wolfie. He was too tired to mutate back to human form and argue. He felt much better staying as a wolf. He stood and stretched his paws, scraping his claws into the soil. He yawned, showed his sharp blood stained canines and began to strut around the children. He dumped his huge, heavy body down with a thud. Nubilus placed his pointed nose on his paws and continued to stare at Dak.

"Who are they?" Dak curiously asked and pointed to the children.

"No idea, I think the Garchy had already killed their parents before I got here. I have just burned several half eaten corpses along with the four Garchy we killed," he lied.

"What are you going to do with them?" he enquired with curiosity.

"Not sure. I thought about taking them back with us, nobody deserves to die out here." Ursus replied, not entirely convinced that Dak believed him. But it didn't matter, that was the story he was going to stick with. He knew he could not trust anyone.

"So Dak, why are you out here on your own?" he quizzed him, eagerly awaiting his reply.

"I saw the smoke and to be honest, I was looking to see what I could take and then sell. Then I saw you and the wolf. There have been frequent assaults in the area and I thought I would try my luck."

"What do you mean assaults.... by whom?" he asked with a concerned voice.

"We don't know who is leading it, but it is happening all over the land. Many villages and tribes have been slaughtered and they have taken many prisoners," he said. "There are only a few tribes that have not been touched."

"What about our tribe?" he anxiously asked.

"No, no, we have been lucky."

Nubilus immediately staggered to his feet and stood beside Ursus.

"I know what you are thinking," Ursus said as he patted Nubilus on the head. He was thinking of Altaira too. The vision in the fire's flames made sense now. She *was* in trouble and she needed them.

"What is it Healing Paw, was it something I said?" he asked.

"No, no it's nothing you have said, it's just that we need to get back. I'm worried for our safety." Ursus lied. He knew he needed to seek counsel with his tribal leader urgently.

"If you noticed the smoke how many others detected it, we need to leave before we have any more unwanted company. Are you feeling strong Dak?" he asked.

"What?" "Am I feeling strong?"

"Yes. Are you feeling strong?" he repeated.

"I don't think I can pull that travois over there on my own." He pointed to the travois that was haphazardly lying up-turned in the dirt.

"I thought we could put the children on the travois. I don't think Wolfie is able to walk very far either, looking at the wound on his leg. He must have sustained that injury fighting the Garchy," Ursus lied. The less Dak knew about Nubilus and how he got his self-inflicted wound, the safer the children would be.

"Why would I want to pull that thing, when I have my pony with me?" he announced.

A broad grin broke out across Ursus's face and he patted Dak on the back; then glanced through the shrubs to see a pony tethered in the distance. Perfect he thought with relief as he rubbed his shoulders
then winced in pain. He knew his strength had left him and he desperately needed to recover. Ursus stumbled as he lifted the travois from the wasteland floor. He desperately tried to hide his fatigue from the others and tried to shield his fatigue from the others.

"Dak can you get the children and secure them in place please," Ursus asked, as he staggered and tried to steady himself as he harnesses it onto the beast.

Dak moved towards the children but was greeted with a fierce warning growl as Nubilus harnessed his protective instincts. Dak stopped in his tracks and the growling also stopped. He slowly moved his foot forward and Nubilus growled once more; keeping a guarded watchful eye on him. Dak flinched and immediately stopped moving. Once again, the growling ceased. Ursus grinned as he knew Nubilus was deliberately teasing him. However, Dak didn't know that.

"I cccan't he wwon't let me near them," he nervously stuttered.

"Yes, I forgot, old Wolfie is very, very temperamental, perhaps I should get them," he added. Ursus pretended to be afraid of Nubilus as he collected the children and placed them on the travois. Nubilus had great fun as he pretended to nip his heels.

"Come on old one, your turn to get on too," Ursus announced.

Nubilus stopped and glanced at Ursus, WHAT... OLD ONE! Who is he kidding he's the OLD one not me, I'm, I'm just a... just a PUP, he thought. He limped and slowly climbed up with his sore aching limbs and cramped muscles, desperate to rest. Yes, just a pup, he tried to convince himself, but the darkness of sleep immediately consumed him.

~ Chapter Four ~

In The Dark Bowels Of The Castle

Silence was broken, with the sound of a scurry, followed with a high pitch squeak. Two green eyes blinked through the darkness; trying to make out what had broken her solitude. No, it is no good she thought; it was far too dark to make out what had taken up residence in her cell.

She sat on the chilly, stone floor and pulled her legs up close to her chest as she shivered. The cold iron manacles around her ankles dug into her already torn flesh as she moved. She hugged and rubbed her injuries and tried to keep warm as the damp cold air enveloped her. The darkness had taken her sight, but all her other senses were perfectly alert. She could hear the sound of metal keys jingle through the torch lit corridor as the sentry paced up and down outside her cell. The rancid smell of diseased human flesh radiated and hung in the stale air.

She sat in silence and put her head on her knees. So, this is how I am going to die, she thought. Not in battle or of old age but in a cell manacled to the floor; starving to death. She knew if the lack of food did not kill her then the cold or her injuries would. At least the King had left her alone and stopped torturing her. That was something she was grateful for.

She shuddered at the thought of being whipped, stretched and deprived of going to sleep again.

She had lost all sense of time since she returned to her cell after her gruesome encounter with the King. She had no idea how long she had been asleep or how long she had been held captive - or if it was night or day.

She closed her eyes as the nightmare of the King's barbaric attack on her forced its way through and once more consumed her thoughts and forced her to relive the brutal abuse.

"I know who and what you are," he spat. Change your form, you are a Muto, admit it," he accused her.

"I don't know what you mean. Change my form? What is a Muto? What do you want from me?" She wept.

"Do not pretend that you do not know what I am referring to! You know exactly what I want. Change your form," he spat with venom in his voice.

"No! Are you sure you are not going to give me what I want? Rack her Riend," he ordered.

Riend grabbed her by the hair and dragged her along the floor. He tightly twisted his hand amongst her hair; taking clumps out of her scalp as he yanked her to her feet and dragged her once more toward the rack. He slammed her already bruised body violently against the brutal structure. He tightly secured rope around her wrist, ankles and neck. Slowly at first, the rope tightened and suspended her several inches off the floor. He twisted the frame so she faced downwards and the ropes began to stretch her body. Her screams vibrated off the walls.

"Admit it, you are the Muto that they call Altaira and you can change into a hawk. SO, CHANGE!"

"I cannot change into a hawk. I am not who you think I am," she continued to sob and scream out with a burning pain that hit all the sinews in her body.

"Do not lie. I know who you are. You are one of the three Muto's that my stupid DEAD brother trusted. ADMIT IT… GO ON, ADMIT IT!"

"Ahh. Please. Please, stop," she screamed as the rack continued to stretch her limbs.

Riend stopped turning the spindle of the rack and Altaira's body slumped with relief.

"Had enough?" The King spat, as he pressed his face down to hers.

"Yes," she answered barely audible.

"Admit it and change your form," he sneered.

"I... I c..can't I am not who you think I am. You have it wrong. I cannot change into a hawk. I can't," she sobbed.

"Can't or won't?" he spat with annoyance.

"Can't, I am not a Muto. A Muto is a myth. They don't exist, they are just in stories," she answered in defiance.

"We'll see," he nodded to Riend who began to turn the rack once more, tighter and tighter.

Altaira screamed as she felt the sting of a whip lick her bare flesh. The rack continued to pull, then …. it stopped. The lash of the whip quickly followed as it cracked through the air and fiercely sliced her skin. Riend continued this assault on her body until she lost consciousness. She could just make out muffled voices as the King ordered her release. Her body quivered as the tight hold of the guard's hands gripped her under the armpits lugging her upper torso along the corridor. The hard floor tore strips of flesh from her feet and knees as

her lower body dragged exhaustedly behind. They opened the door to
her dank cell and brutally threw her broken body back in the confinement of the fortified chamber and attached the cold iron braces to her ankles.

In the icy cold surroundings of her cell, she slowly opened her eyes; she shook as her mind broke from the awful recall of her dreadful memories. A small sliver of light peaked through the tiny elongated slot in the cell door. More light flooded as the slot opened further and a handful of bread was thrown in.

She staggered to her feet. Her daily challenge had begun. Unable to move her feet forward, she crouched back down to lay on her front. Her outstretched arms fumbled to seek her rations. Everyday had become the same. Sometimes she was lucky and found them, other days she did not. She moved her arms in a sweeping motion hoping to find her bounty. She suddenly stopped as she felt something touch the tip of her finger.

"There it is, found it," she muttered to herself. She stretched her body further and tried to get her hand closer. The manacles pressed deeper into her already torn flesh and she screamed out in pain. She could just touch it.

"Just a tiny bit more," she told herself, as she once again pulled on her manacles and tried to stretch a little further. She suddenly stopped as the searing pain engulfed her. She laid still,
gasped for breath as the soreness continued to rage and pulsate through her.

"NO, NO, NO!" She shouted as the sound of scurrying feet advanced towards her.

"This is mine," she spat as she quickly struggled to secure her feast. She felt the bread swiped out of her reach as the rodent rushed away with her bread. She became still as she buried her face into the cold stone floor, too exhausted to even weep.

Moments later the larger square slot in the bottom of door tilted upwards. This time a bowl of water skidded across the floor towards her. She immediately started to feel the floor to recover the liquid. She reigned supreme as she quickly tracked her reward. With shaky hands, she drew the vessel toward her mouth and gulped.

She closed her eyes and thought of Nubilus. She was sure he would try to rescue her if he knew she was imprisoned. She thought about the last time, they had spoken and that it was in anger. That seemed like a lifetime ago now and she gave out a heavy sigh. She opened her eyes and starred into the dark without blinking, still thinking of Nubilus.

"Help me Nubilus, oh please…. Nubilus; I am sorry. Please, if you can hear me, help me," she chanted as tears cascaded down her cheeks. She just hoped that somehow Nubilus would hear her. Each
time she received her rations, she performed the same ritual asking for Nubilus's help as tears swamped her cheeks.

She sat completely still and took a moment to reflect on her fate as she huddled her shaking limbs. Distress registered with her that her plight was sealed.

She would never feel the breeze on her face or the Father's familiar pull of the sky as she soared high.

Even if she wanted to take to the sky, she could not. Those days are now gone, gone, gone forever. She wondered if she would ever be able to mutate, it had been such a long time, she had lost the ability to do it. The betrayal had been too deep. An overwhelming panic surged through her. Her heart began to thump hard and the sweat dripped off as the fear devoured her. All her beliefs had vanished. She realised for the first time she was completely alone. No one was going to help her. Alone in the bowel of the castle, she was condemned to die a dishonourable death.

Her cell door blasted open, Riend anchored to the spot as he drummed his fingers on the wall. He stepped forward to let two guards brushed pass him into the dark damp cell.

"On your feet," he demanded.

Exhausted. She scrambled to get up. She blinked as the sudden light blared through the cell doorway. Riend swiftly launched his boot to her face sending her backwards before she had a chance to stand.

"I said, on your feet!" He screamed at her.

She ignored the taste of blood in her mouth and again she tried to stand.

Once again, Riend launched his boot as he swept her off her feet. Altaira landed hard on the floor. Pain seared through her head as it made contact with the hard surface. Huddled in a ball Altaira tried to protect herself as he followed with several vicious kicks to her ribs and one last swing with his fist to her face.

Slumped on the floor Altaira tried to focus, but darkness took hold. She could hear Riend as he spoke to the guards, but her eyes and body did not respond.

"Undo her chains," he ordered the two guards. They looked at their commander.

"Are you deaf, undo her chains?" He hollered. "The King's orders. Just do it. The King believes she is not the one he is searching for," he said with doubt in his voice.

"Do you think she is Sir?" The brave guard asked.

"It doesn't matter what I think, orders are orders. She is to be set free. But she won't get far." He sneered as he looked at his handy work that he had inflicted on her.

"She'll be dead before morning, she's not even conscious." He smiled, as the thought pleased him.

The two guards held her up under her armpits and dragged her through the winding corridors of the dungeon, once again her feet dragged behind her. Riend led them deep into the belly of the castle. She was surreptitiously hauled up a flight of steep steps to a hidden door in the ceiling. Altaira slowly opened her swollen eyes and spied a trap door. Confused, not sure where she was or what was happening, she watched as Riend took a large key from his pocket to unlock the hatch. Once again, darkness seized her as she slipped in and out of consciousness. Riend heaved her up and out through the hole. He dragged her across the grassland that was outside the curtain wall and deposited her in the woods. He took one last glance at her and smiled as he took a deeper look at her injuries. He was satisfied with what he saw. He strolled casually back to the trap door. The unknown door hidden in the ground that led to the barbarous horrors of the dark bowel of the castle. He glanced once more over his shoulder before he opened the door and quickly disappeared leaving Altaira alone, defenceless and on the brink of death.

~ Chapter Five ~

Etta and Eudora

The black and silver cloak billowed in the wind and tangled itself around Etta's limbs. She staggered towards the bleak walls that she now reluctantly called home. Lighted beacons protruded and hung from the grey, granite stone walls, lighting the mammoth fortress. The fortified colossal structure stood and dominated its surroundings. She took a deep breath, the mere sight of it made her want to vomit. If it were not for her sister Eudora, she would not have returned. She had been gone for over a month and King Ignatus would surely have noticed her absence. If he did not, she was sure his devoted guard Riend would have. Riend had a talent for noticing everything. She tucked her long blond hair inside the hood of the cloak and slowly stepped towards the castle walls. She hoped to slip inside un-noticed.

Full of self-importance, Riend stood on the tower's allure; the wall-walk gave him an excellent vantage point to survey everything that moved from within the curtain wall and everything that moved beyond it. Etta shivered as she made her way towards the north side of the outer curtain wall. Her cloak dragged through the soggy mud as she cautiously moved through the gatehouse. The gatehouse was extremely impressive with towers standing sixty feet high either side of the heavy, iron studded, wooden door that was virtually impregnable. She suddenly felt very vulnerable as she looked up at the portcullis that housed and balance sharp spikes above her head. Then, she glanced at the towers that held the oil stained hoards above her. She imagined it must have been a horrible sight to those who had previously attacked the castle. The thought of boiling oil or stones tumbling on top of her made her shudder and she was glad she was not attacking the castle. She slowly made her way through the labyrinth of shadowy corridors that made up the gatehouse and hit the cramped corridor of the barbican beyond it. She knew she was not far from where she could quietly retreat to the Keep and to her chamber. She moved with haste as she stepped on to the bailey; she did not want to be detected. She glanced up and surveyed Riend still stood on the tower's allure, but she knew it was hopeless. He had already spotted her and at a furious pace, he raced down the stone steps to reach her.

"Ah Lady Etta here you are. We have been *so* worried about you, where have you been?" he spoke in a sarcastic voice trying to sound concerned, when clearly he was not.

"Where have I been?" she questioned. "I should ask you that. Where have you been? My horse bolted in the woods. Did it not occur to you to send help, I was left for dead."

"Yet here you are, alive and well. So, where were you? I did send my men out looking for you, but, all we found was your horse... no sign of poor, little, Lady Etta. She had vanished, PUFF, into thin air." He retained his sarcastic manner trying to sound as if he cared for her safety, when it was very clear he did not. He just wanted to know where she had been as it annoyed him not knowing.

"Where were you Lady Etta?" he repeated.

"I told you, my horse bolted," she answered.

"Yes, yes it bolted, but after that, where were you?" he again insisted in a sinister voice. This time he glared straight at her waiting for her reply as he tapped his foot with an air of impatience.

"I don't know!" she confessed.

"Oh, I think you do know, you just don't want me to find out the truth, do you," he persisted.

"You want the truth? I am afraid you are going to be disappointed. You think that I am hiding something from you, don't you, and it is eating away at you because you are not getting the information from me. Am I right?"

she laughed. "I don't have to answer for you." She turned her back to walk away.

Riend was furious and grabbed her arm and pinned her up against the wall. "No, you don't have to answer to me, but you do have to answer to the King. If you are not going to tell me, then I have no choice but to take you to the King and he will not be as forgiving as I am. He will want to know everything. Do you hear what I am saying? E V E R Y T H I NG!" he emphasised each syllable.

She knew she had no choice; she had to tell him something or he would find out where she had been. "As I said, my horse bolted. Something had startled him. I felt something hard hit me in the head and the next minute I woke up and this couple and their children were taking care of me. I stayed with them until I was well enough to leave." She looked at his face and was quite sure he didn't believe her.

"How did you get back to the castle?" he quizzed.

"I walked," she answered.

"What, on your own?"

"Yes."

"Why did they not walk with you?" he continued.

"Well, I think it may have something to do with that they had very small children and they saw my black and silver cloak. For some reason that prevented them getting too close to the castle and helping me any further," she answered in an ashamed manner.

"There Lady Etta that wasn't too bad now was it. Why didn't you just tell me the truth in the first place, um," he smirked. "Now where was this place you stayed?"

"Somewhere in the woods, I couldn't even begin to tell you where. I was so dazed, I cannot help you and that is the truth Riend, I swear. Honest. I swear," she answered in a firm voice and crossed her fingers behind her back, so he couldn't see.

"Now if you don't mind, I need to see my sister. I haven't seen her for over a month," she announced as she pushed him off her and straightened up her clothes.

"No one has seen your sister for over a month. Not even the King," he declared.

"What? Why?" she gulped.

"She is not well, everyone has been forbidden to see her. She is in quarantine. She has not come out of her chamber. The King just wanted her to get well," he warned her in an unmoving voice.

"What's the matter with her?" she asked in a shaky voice.

"I have just told you. She is not well; she is in quarantine," he answered through gritted teeth.

Etta looked at him and she could see he was not impressed that he was not aware of what was wrong with the Queen. He had usually made it his business to know what was going on with everyone. But this time, the Queen's nurse refused to open the door or answer to anyone. The King had placed two guards outside her chamber. Their orders came directly from him and the King's orders were law. The King had his orders directly from the nurse. No one went in and no one came out. This enraged Riend, he was sure something sinister was afoot and it infuriated him that he was not privy to it.

The Queen had not been well for months and spent most of her time inside her chamber; locked away from view. The only person who had seen the Queen was her nurse. Even on the occasional visits from the King, she was asleep in bed and the nurse ordered her not to be disturbed. Her illness had become a mystery that was the talk of the castle. The gossip was rife inside the castle's walls. Some declared that the King had beaten her to an inch of her life, or she had been struck with a terrible illness that her fate was decided and it was only a matter of time before the darkness took her.

Etta dashed to her sister's chamber but was greeted with armed guards.

"Please, I need to see her," she pleaded as she tried to gain entry.

"Sorry Lady Etta, orders," they replied as they stood and covered the doorway that stopped her from proceeding further.

Etta moved back, she did not want to cause a scene, she curtsied and told them she understood but asked if they could inform the nurse that she desperately wanted to see the Queen. An overwhelming feeling of guilt took hold of her. She blamed herself for being in the woods and not being at her sister's side. But being away in the woods was necessary and just as important to her. She was sure her sister would agree if she told her the real reason. Not yet though, she could not trust anyone, not even her sister; just in case Riend or the King found out. She knew the consequences would mean death; after all, it was not just her life that was at risk. She sighed and took a deep breath, maybe one day she would share her secret. Her heart ached; she wiped the tears from her eyes and looked down at the floor. Silence would keep her secret safe, but it would not mend a broken heart.

Beyond the guarded door, Queen Eudora glanced at the sleeping nurse Nellie who was slumped in the chair as she took a well-earned nap. Apart from her sister Etta, she was her most trusted friend and confidant. Eudora tip toed across the cold wooden floor and tried not to disturb the snoozing woman. She slowly put on her nightgown, slipped underneath the bed sheets and pulled the heavy quilted covers up towards her neck. Her long blond hair fell over her face. Within minutes, her exhausted body was asleep. The dark, shady room was filled with rhythmic snores that echoed in unison from both women as they slumbered.

A gentle tap on the door broke the silence, as the guards knocked for the nurse's attention. She woke with a fright and quickly stood up as if she were one of the guards stood to attention. She yawned, stretched her short, plump arms high above her head, and trotted to the door.

"What!" she barked.

"We have the Queen's dinner," he informed her. "It is here for you to collect," he continued.

Nellie slowly opened the door to collect the Queen's dinner. She was greeted by Riend. He immediately shoved his large muddy boot between the door and its frame to stop the nurse from shutting the door.

"And how is the Queen today?" he sneered.

"She is sleeping. So, if you don't mind moving your bloody great big foot out of the doorway; I'd like her to continue to rest thank you," she ordered.

"Ah, but I do mind. She is my Queen and I am worried about her. I would just like a glimpse of her. You know, just to make sure," he sighed.

"Make sure of what?" she spat.

"Well, there are so many rumours. My dear, where do I to start?" he scoffed at her. "Let me see, oh yes. You have murdered her and you are trying to dupe the King into thinking she is unwell. When she is in fact, dead... or, could it be that she is so distraught with the death of Tycus," he sarcastically ridiculed her; as it was believed the Queen absolutely hated Tycus. "Maybe someone mentioned his name and she went into such a rage that for her own safety and for those around her; she has been sedated," he jeered as he tried to push his way further into the dingy dark room. "It could also be that, she is ill like you declare and that she is *SO* ill, she is unable to have visitors. Take your pick. There are so many to choose from," he said in a smug tone. "Either way, as you can see, I need proof she is alive," he snorted.

"GET OUT! NOW IS THAT PROOF ENOUGH, YOU INTERFERING, MALICIOUS MORON!" Eudora screamed, from across the room.

Riend swallowed hard and moved his foot from the doorway. He had got what he wanted and more. The nurse quickly took the plate of food and smiled with quiet delight that Riend had been put in his place.

"The King will hear about this intrusion. I am sure you were aware of his instructions," she looked at both guards and at Riend and smirked.

"Please inform the King that both the Queen and I request to see him." She shut the door with a click and grinned further. It was about time Riend was brought to face his actions and she was sure the King would be furious.

~ Chapter Six ~

The Spirits And The Shaman

The earth's lunar protection began to disappear as the dark hues of night started to fade. The red and orange shades slowly seeped through over the horizon as morning crept its way across the lowlands to greet the new day.

The occupants on the travois slept without a care in the world, as it etched its way through the dirt with the precious cargo in tow. Arms and legs dangled either side of the pony with a weary Ursus slumped on top. His head snuggled amongst the mane. His body swayed side to side with every jolting movement the pony made. The journey was slow and arduous as Dak led them home to the safety of the tribe.

"Healing Paw, Healing Paw we are here," Dak announced as he gently shook the old man on the pony. "Healing Paw, we are here," he repeated.

Ursus suddenly woke from his slumber and quickly sat upright on the animal that had carried him. His exhausted body slowly slipped off the hoofed beast. He glanced around at the faces staring at him. It had been many moons since he last stood on this spot in the company of his fellow tribesmen. He knelt and gently woke Nubilus from his snooze and leant in closely.

"Nubilus, it is important that you stay as a wolf," he whispered. "I will explain later, you need to trust me," he continued.

Nubilus put his paw on Ursus's arm to acknowledge him; even though he did not understand why, he did recognise that Ursus must have his reasons. Nubilus dragged himself off the travois and limped as he stood beside Ursus. Ursus bent down and scooped the papoose carrying the children into his arms.

"Thank you Dak. I now need to seek council and nursing mothers for the children. The children need attention, can I ask you to find suitable care for them. They need feeding. I am sure there are young mothers that can help," he spoke in a quiet, gentle tone.

"Do you want me to take the children from you?" he asked with outstretched arms.

Nubilus immediately became restless. The thought of leaving the children with Dak alarmed him. After all, the children were not Dak's responsibility. Ursus immediately declined Dak's offer and patted the wolf's head to reassure him. He held the children tight, but he knew that they would soon stir from their toxic sleep of Garchy breath and need feeding.

"Just find someone who can feed the children Dak. It has been a while since they have had nutrition, when they wake they will be screaming blue murder," Ursus advised.

Dak nodded in acknowledgement and went in search for a nursing mother to feed the younglings. He knew Ursus was right; the children would need nourishment. When under the toxic breath of a Garchy a person can lay dormant with sleep and is starved of all its needs; but when the toxin wears off, every sensation is more severe, and hunger and thirst are the two main areas that are most craved for.

Nubilus slowly followed Ursus, twisting his head around and spied at his surroundings as they moved towards a circular structure. Many faces gazed at him with open mouths. Their eyes followed every movement he and Ursus took. He then realised they were not looking at him; it was Ursus that they were staring at. A growl began to rumble in the depths of his being as he cautiously shadowed Ursus's footprints.

"It's alright, do not worry," he spoke gently as he stroked Nubilus's large head. "I did not expect a warm welcome. I have not been home since Tycus died. I think they believe me to be dishonourable," he sighed.

Nubilus observed the villagers bowing their heads to avoid eye contact as they walked passed. He noticed that they looked apprehensive as they refused to glance at the old man that he called Ursus. But, why? Why were they frightened of Ursus? Ursus lowered his hand and gently patted Nubilus's head and ran his fingers through his tangled fur.

Dak came running towards them, panting and gasping for breath.

"I have... Found... Some nursing mothers... Who have agreed to feed... The children," Dak spoke slowly; gasping to inflate his lungs with oxygen.

He lent up against a large wooden pole that had many etched faces of animals carved out of it. Behind him three nursing mothers stood waiting for Ursus to hand the children in their papoose over to them. He told them that the spirits would smile down on them for their generosity. He then reluctantly placed the children into their arms.

"Make sure you look after them or I will know and the spirits will not be happy," he barked at them.

The women cautiously nodded and turned quickly with the children and disappeared towards their dwellings.

"Dak, may I ask one more thing from you, I need to know the names of the women and what woman had what child. Please help them get what they need."

Dak nodded and swiftly turned to follow the women.

Ursus and Nubilus slowly staggered up a wooden formed slope and entered a vast room within the circular construction.

Sat cross-legged in the centre was an old man with a ring of feathers on his head that draped over his long, plaited hair. His eyes were closed as he sat in complete stillness in his meditative state. His arms hung loosely at his side as his chest rhythmically inflated then slowly deflated. The room radiated the same tranquillity and calmness that the man represented. Nubilus immediately knew the old man to be the tribal leader.

A Muto's Promise
The Guardians

Ursus sank slowly to his knees opposite the man, mirrored his pose and closed his eyes. Nubilus looked at Ursus wondering why he did not speak. He waited and waited for a response but only silence rang. Slowly, Nubilus closed his eyes as boredom and fatigue took hold. He surrendered to the realm of dreams and drifted into a peaceful slumber thinking only of the person with emerald green eyes.

Nubilus could hear muffled voices; the familiar voice of Ursus and one other that he did not recognise. Breathing heavy, Nubilus wrestled with his weighty eyelids that refused to respond and open. He continued to listen instead.

"That wasn't your fault Ursus, you didn't kill him," the voice spoke wisely.

"No, not directly at least, but …. I was given the honour of being his protector. He died. I failed in the one thing I was destined to do. Do you not see. I stopped him from living and I interfered in what the high spirits predicted. It is because of me there is now someone else on the throne. Someone, that I believe needs to be removed," Ursus whispered in a troubled voice.

The old man placed his hands on Ursus's shoulders and let out a loud sigh. "Ursus, the spirits lay many paths for us to follow. Sometimes that path will take us on many journeys beyond what we think is right. It may be a harsh journey, one fraught with danger and self-doubt. The spirits will always guide us on the way and lead us full circle in the end. It is not always the outcome of a journey that is important, but the course that we take. It is how we get there that enlightens and gives wisdom to the traveller on their journey." He spoke in hushed tones that immediately illustrated astuteness and great knowledge.

"So, are you saying this is how it is meant to be? I am worried. The land is beginning to change. Can you not sense it? Was Tycus destined to die? Is that the path the spirits intended?" he asked in a frustrated voice.

"No... No, Tycus was not supposed to die. However, he did. Not even the spirits can change that now. Nevertheless, there is another path that you must follow. You have the power to cross the bridge in between the shadows Ursus. You must enter the spirit world. Bring the world full circle and restore the balance and heal the land." He spoke in a firm voice, "you are Healing Paw, tribal healer." He handed him a small piece of carved wood with tiny pebbles inside that rattled when shook. "Now converse with the spirits and heal."

"No! I will not do it. I am not that person anymore," he protested and gave the stick back.

"Ursus you do not stop being who you are. You of all people should know that. You are not just a man. You are a Muto, and above all, you are a Shaman," he reminded him.

"And with being a Shaman there is great responsibility. It is about time you remembered that. You are not the first Muto or the first Shaman. However, you are the first and only Muto that is also a Shaman. You have a duty. You are the only one who has that gift," he hissed.

"No… I am not. There is another Shaman," Ursus confessed.

"What! Another Shaman! Who?" he asked with curiosity and in a worried tone.

"I think you know who I am referring to," he inferred.

"Surely not Ursus, are you sure?" he snapped in a shocked voice.

"Yes. I am. Unfortunately. I wish I was not, but like me they have no way of interpreting what the spirits are saying," Ursus admitted with a deflated voice.

"I cannot translate or interpret what they say without Altaira, you already know this. She's the one with foresight and she refuses to speak to me; so what is the point of me speaking to the spirits," Ursus argued impatiently as he waved his arms in the air at his tribal leader.

The tribal leader stood silent and just nodded deep in thought as if something weighed heavy on his mind. He glanced at Ursus and then looked away.

"I know she refuses to speak to you, but that is the least of our worries," he admitted, especially after learning there is another Shaman.

"What do you mean the least of our worries? Is there something bigger than that, I need to worry about?" he enquired. "Something that is more important than to try and convince Altaira to talk to us?"

"Yes Ursus there is... Altaira is missing!" he blurted out. "No-one has seen her. There have been many assaults and we are not sure if she has been captured or if she is in hiding."

This news alerted Nubilus who immediately opened his heavy eye lids and stood beside Ursus. He looked up at him and yelped as he placed his paw on Ursus's foot to get his attention and to let his feelings known.

"I need to know how many others know she is a Muto?" Ursus enquired with concern in his voice as he patted Nubilus's head to acknowledge his presence and unease.

"As far as I am aware, I am the only one who is aware there are three Muto's. You, Altaira and the dog beside you. Who by the way absolutely stinks and is now making me feel sick," he confessed.

A smirk crossed Ursus's face as he looked down at Nubilus. "Do not look at me like that; he speaks the truth. You do stink," Ursus confessed. "You stink of stale blood, and dead Garchy."

What! I stink? Outrageous, what about you, Nubilus thought as he looked up to Ursus and cocked his head to one side with utter disgust. Nubilus could smell a strong rancid odour but he thought it was Ursus. He bent his head toward his body to sniff. He realised they were right; the smell was radiating off him.

"I told you that you stink, you didn't need to check," Ursus confirmed as Nubilus held his head in shame and his tail between his legs.

"As I was saying, no one else is aware of you or the other two Mutos. And it must stay that way," the leader ordered.

"That's not true, Lord Tycus was aware of us before he died. We all swore an oath to him to protect and act as guardians to his children if he had any," Ursus warned.

"How did he find that out? Your identities have never been revealed. You know as well as I do, I have encouraged the tribes to tell stories of Muto's but as myths and legends. I did this to keep you safe. I cannot understand how he became aware you were a Muto," he stated in bewilderment.

"I have no idea how he was aware; but he told me I was a Muto and he also identified the others. He asked me to gather the other two and he requested our help. He was aware of the prophecy. How, I do not know. He made us all promise to look after each other and help to train his children; if he ever had any. Of course, we all agreed."

His tribal leader stood still, with mouth open wide staring at him in bewilderment. "Ursus this is a grave problem. Another Shaman, Altaira is missing what if Tycus told the King about you and the others being

Mutos? We must find Altaira. If someone else knows she can translate." He swallowed hard and bit his bottom lip, trying to think of a solution.

"I had a vision from her a couple of days ago. I saw her green eyes crying in the flames of a fire. She was asking for help. She said help me," Ursus informed him.

"She is in trouble and we must get her here to safety before she is introduced to the other Shaman," the tribal leader snapped.

"There is something else I need to tell you. I have in my guardianship three small infants that are now in the care of nursing mothers."

"Whose children? Please just tell me that they are some random children you came across on you way here," he pleaded fearing Ursus's reply.

"Well if I were to say that, then I would be lying."

Ursus began to retell the events of who the children were and how Nubilus had bestowed spiritual blood gifts on to them. He explained how they had fought the posse of Garchy and defeated the foul wasteland creatures. Then he confessed the details of the oath that he and his fellow Muto's had sworn to Tycus, and that they were bound to these children.

"The children's father is Lord Tycus?" the tribal leader spluttered.

"Yes."

"But Tycus is dead; who brought the children to you?" he asked

"The other Shaman brought the children to me and she knows there are three Muto's. However, she has only met two of us. She knows of Altaira but has yet to meet her. I think Altaira's identity is safe from her for now."

The tribal leader shook his head and looked upwards and mumbled incoherently asking the spirits for inspiration.

"Oh, Ursus this is getting worse. Another Shaman and she knows about the three of you. We must find Altaira. Even if it is just to warn her."

"Ursus, it is now more crucial than ever to converse with the spirits and we will try and decipher their meanings together; the two of us."

A yelp and a bark were released as Nubilus stared at the tribal leader waiting for him to admit that he had made a mistake.

"Okay, okay the two of us and the reeking half breed mongrel beside you."

Ursus nodded his head and stood up. He knew he had no choice, if he wanted to see Altaira alive. He began to sweep the floor with his foot dragging the dust in its wake to reveal a buried wooden door secretly hidden in the ground. He opened the concealed trap door. The Tribal leader offered Ursus the rattling stick once more. He stared at it. Dread began to fill his whole being. His heart thumped in his chest and pounded in his ears. His body shook with fear. He unwillingly took the carved stick that rattled. He tied it to the handle of his medicine bag and let it hang loosely by his side. He walked back and forth the room then took a long look at the open trap door. With a deep breath, he reached inside his bag and pulled out a beaded necklace and fastened it around his neck. The symbol of the Shaman hung close to his chest. Ursus stood beside the opening that would lead him into the dark underground chamber below.

The wolf also peered over the side of the hole and glanced up at the apprehensive Ursus. How am I supposed to get down there? Nubilus thought. A low grumble and a whine came from the direction of the smelly wolf as he looked up at Ursus once more. Ursus realised Nubilus was seeking permission to mutate back into a human.

"I think we have no choice, old friend, you need to mutate back to human form. I don't think you will manage the ladder on four legs and I do not have the energy or strength to carry you." He bent down to sniff him. "Besides, I don't think my nostrils and stomach will cope with you being that close," he chuckled.

From an oversize wolf, in a blink of an eye, Nubilus's human form appeared.

"Ursus, Altaira?" Nubilus uttered in a panicked voice. "We need to find her. She is in trouble. The vision. I saw her and heard her plea."

"Yes my friend we do and we will. We will find her together," Ursus promised.

Reluctantly he began to climb down the ladder into the belly of the darkness below.

The leader lit the line of beacons that protruded and hung off the walls. They flickered slowly as they gave off their wavering light that created shadows that danced across the dark cavern. Ursus let out a heavy sigh. It was peaceful underground - it reminded him of a cave. If only he could hibernate down there and forget all about what was going to happen. Ursus sat down completely still. He was hardly breathing; he needed to empty his lungs before he could cross into the spirit realm.

Gusts of winds began to encircle Ursus. He continued to shake the rattling stick as the temperature dropped to a crisp cool breeze that twisted and licked his flesh. Not knowing if he was cold or just apprehensive;

he began to feel the hairs on the back of his neck rise, followed closely by the hairs on his arms and legs. He gave a hard shudder and waited and waited. This was the bit that he hated the most. He despised waiting. Ursus slowly crossed his legs and straightened his back. The only movement he made was a slight flick of his wrist as he continued to shake the rattle. Ursus knew that it would not be long as he could feel the air beginning to thin and the shadows becoming still. Time began to slow as the oxygen was sucked from the air for the first spirit to arrive. The rattle stopped as a silver streak appeared and coiled its way around Ursus.

Ursus looked around the chamber to see his leader and Nubilus surrounded in a blanket of mist; suspended between the realms of time. An unwelcome buzzing and popping sound vibrated through his ear canals penetrating all his nerve endings as the spirit alerted him of its presence. Sharp stabbing pains pinched at his skin and his eyes began to tear. His blood began to cool pumping ice-cold plasma, slowly around his body and he was glad that he had sat down. This he had learnt the hard way. The first time he encountered a spirit, the sensation had him collapse in a dishevelled heap, shaking from head to toe. Experience had taught him to sit; before he was forced to fall. He was glad it was a silver spectre as the sensation he felt was just bearable. It was the red spectre that he disliked the most. A silver spectre usually communicated present events and the red when events were critical usually indicating war and bloodshed.

In a place where time was not important, where life died and left fragments of the sacred seeds of humankind resting until called upon - he closed his eyes. Suspended in another dimension and enclosed outside of the dominions of reality, the Shaman and the spirit began to communicate.

~ Chapter Seven ~

The Hunter And The Hawk

All was peaceful and quiet. Through the battalion of trees, a sound of rhythmic drumming echoed and suddenly interrupted this stillness. A tiny woodpecker ripped through the air as its beak vigorously tapped high up in the canopy communicating its musical message. On the ground, a herbaceous border of wild ferns blanketed the brushwood of fallen twigs and hidden from view was a broken body. From under the dense undergrowth of leaves; two blood-stained feet protruded that showed the only sign of Altaira's existence. A slight breeze ran through the blanket of green and gently swayed to reveal Altaira's fragmented body; that was discarded on an emerald sea of green. Tap...Tap... Tap, the bird continued to alert the world of its existence. It swooped elegantly through the entangled mass of branches that intertwined and looped together creating a dark encasement of foliage and landed gracefully on Altaira's head.

Altaira was motionless as she slowly began to surrender to a place of peace. She could feel the weightless tug pull her towards the heavens as her spirit began to gradually separate from her lifeless body.

A warm wetness suddenly touched her skin and sent shivers through her that momentarily awakened the essence of her soul. Sat firmly on her chest a heavy fury being lodged itself on her battered frame to stop her spirit leaving. Pain seared through her shattered body as it weighted her to the spot. Altaira gave out a faint moan as she felt the heavy, sensation press against her. Warmth radiated onto her from the resident as it heated her icy, fragile exterior. Excitement ran through the creature as it started to lick the blood off her face as she gulped and gasped for air.

A male voice drifted softly nearby that awakened her from under the cover of darkness; she struggled to open her swollen eyelids. Once again, the voice drifted toward her as it tried to rouse her. It was no good Altaira thought, please just let me go; she tried to mouth her words, but they were not audible. Suddenly her shattered body was lifted from the forest floor. Fearing that Riend had not finished with her yet, a sudden start of anxiety engulfed her as she thought it was possibly a soldier from the castle. Overwhelmed with the inability to defend herself Altaira surrendered, she could not take any more of his barbaric assaults; she just wanted to die.

Altaira felt the sudden warmth of bare skin on her; it was not the coldness of a metal breastplate. It was not a soldier, this she was sure of, but who would risk being so close to the castle? She swayed from side to side as she was carried away from what she hoped was from danger. The woodpecker continued to drum its message for the world to hear, as it kept a watchful eye on Altaira. Every opportunity it got, it swooped down and tapped on Altaira's forehead to protect her from going under the cover of darkness once more.

He carried her limp body far into the depth of the forest, away from the castle and the cruelties that its occupants had inflicted on her. The traveller stopped as he approached a large mass of brushwood. Buried amongst the undergrowth was a mound of earth. Heavy dense foliage of ferns concealed its entrance from view. Altaira felt the ferns brush her freshly torn skin as he carried her further inside the mound of earth. She could sense she was going deep underground as the air began to become stale.

"Please do not worry, I will look after you," a voice had told her in a hushed gentle tone.

Altaira let out a heavy sigh in acknowledgment as she clung on to her tears refusing to cry. Tears are for the weak she had told herself as she wrestled with her feelings and tried to hang on to her last ounce of strength.

He gently placed her fragile body on a bundle of hides and the warmth of the fury creature once more pressed up against her, offering its protection. A warm hand brushed the blood stained hair off her eyes and carefully washed her face. Altaira trembled at his touch as she struggled to focus on the blurred vision in front of her.

"Shush, I will not hurt you; please you need to drink this." He advised her as he held a vessel containing cool fresh water up to her lips.

"It's only water, you must be thirsty, here please try," he reassured her.

Altaira allowed him to hold the jug for her as she placed her swollen lips against the jug and drank greedily. A fountain of cool water travelled down her dry, sore throat and ran down her face and neck as she struggled to swallow.

"I need to wash your wounds, please try to relax, my name is Inca and this is my fury friend Lahnie," he introduced himself and the dog as he patted his faithful companion's head.

Altaira lifted her hand to touch the dog but very quickly, it fell back down. She did not have the strength to even do that. Inca grabbed her hand in his and placed it on Lahnie's head. A small smile took hold on her weary face. For the first time in a while Altaira felt hope.

"You need to rest. But - I need to wash you first, as you have blood all over you. I would like to have a look at your wounds. It will mean - em - well it will mean that- em -, I will have to undress you. I will not do this unless you give me permission. Do you understand what I am saying to you?" he asked, completely embarrassed but he knew he needed to wash her and clean her punctured flesh.

"Yes," Altaira croaked barely audible with a knot in her throat.

"Thank you, I will be as quick as possible and if you want me to stop please say so and I will," he gulped.

He knelt beside her and with a warm cloth; he gently continued to wash Altaira's face. She had several deep abrasions and he was sure her cheekbone was broken. Her eyes were severely cut and swollen. He whistled through his teeth in disgust. He lifted her hair off her shoulders that revealed a serious burn and a deep purple bruise around her neck.

"What! This looks like a burn," he gulped as he wrestled with his rage. He continued to wash her arms and he could see the same burn and purple bruise around her wrist. He quickly looked at her ankles as it suddenly emerged that she had been stretched using rope. Altaira groaned in pain as he carefully undressed her.

"I am sorry," he spoke in remorse. "But I need to help you." Inca felt sick as he continued to examine and wash her battered body. He began to wonder how she was still alive as her injuries were extremely severe. He ran his fingers along her ribs; several large bruises were visible to her abdomen and Altaira winced and called out in pain. The bruises were all different colours, black and purple showing a recent blow to older yellow bruises to her stomach and whip marks on her back. He could see several cuts that had already healed with time as the skin had knitted together, others were still fresh. Several pink scars marked her face and legs that, over time, had healed. He stood up, took a deep breath and looked at her broken frame. He knew that she had been tortured and that her suffering had been harsh and over a long time. But, why? Who was she? He wondered. She must be important, but then if she was important why did they leave her to die, Inca pondered. He placed a hide on her to keep her warm.

"I am just going outside to get a few things to help heal you, please do not worry. Lahnie will protect you," he announced.

He needed some fresh air. He needed to think how he was going to help her. He was no healer. What should he do? The site of her injuries worried him. His head began to hurt as he thought of many possible ways to help her. Perhaps he should get help. But thought that may put her in danger. He knew the least amount of people who knew about her, the safer she would be. Maybe he could help her. He had seen many healers use the shrubs and ferns to heal.

Altaira knew that she was naked and that made her feel uncomfortable, but he was trying to help heal her scars, but she knew that he was not going to be able heal all her scars. There were several that were too deep even for the greatest healer to heal. The face of Riend appeared in her thoughts and Altaira began to tremble as the vision threatened its way through the darkness. It started to suffocate and choke her. Gasping for air, she tried to sit up, but her limbs were a dead weight under her and refused her request. I need to think of something else she told herself. Lahnie's rough tongue licked her arm and snapped her out of her reverie and stopped the darkness from consuming her further. Riend's face finally disappeared.

Inca returned with a shrub of yellow flowers and an armful of lady ferns,

"Well done girl," he praised Lahnie and placed his bundle on the floor beside Altaira.

"I am not a healer and I have no idea what I have to do with these plants, but I do know they help to heal," he proclaimed with a knitted expression on his brow.

"I think, I need to get some of the oil out of these and then apply it to your cuts," he advised Altaira as he also tried to convince himself too.

Inca carefully picked the yellow flowers off the shrub, with some of the leaves he began to rub them together. He put the crumpled oily foliage on her wounds and wrapped the ferns tightly around her limbs to hold it in place.

Altaira lay motionless and surrendered her exposed body to Inca's gentle touch. Her skin began to sting as Inca applied his treatment to her lesions. One by one, Inca washed and dressed her wounds until he could see no cut that was untreated. Inca glanced at his sleeping guest; he had done all he could for her. What she needed now was sleep and plenty of it. He carefully placed several hides over her; hoping the warmth will help her doze into a deep restorative healing sleep. Inca kept a careful watch over his patient only to disturb her slumber to make her drink.

"Please, you need to drink," he whispered as he carefully embraced her as he held the container to her mouth to force her to drink. Altaira leaned heavily on Inca as she tried to complete his request. She winced in pain as she tried to sip the offered fluid. The liquid ran down her throat and reinvigorated her dehydrated body. The days passed as Inca continued to care for his frail guest, only waking her to consume fluids. Her wounds began to heal but others were too deep as the occasional scream in her sleep revealed. Inca could not heal the hidden scars; only Altaira could mend those.

Altaira slowly opened her eyes and blinked as she tried to regain focus of her surroundings. Every part of her ached, from her head to her toes. She sluggishly raised her arm to touch her face. Sharp pains ran across her cheekbones as she felt the indentations of her healing skin. Her arm was too heavy and it flopped back down on the makeshift bed with a thud. She had very little strength, her limbs were too weighty; the sharp stabbing pains radiated through her and stopped her in her tracks as she held her breath and waited for the pain to subside. She closed her eyes trying to remember where she was and how she managed to get there.

A cold wet nose brushed her arm followed with a heavy mist of panting. She felt something fury slip under her arm to raise it in the air and she remembered a man and a dog. She looked down to see the dog's head under her arm she was trying to raise her arm up to alert her she was present. A small smile creped across her face as the dog climbed up to settle beside her.

Cautiously she turned her aching head and spied at her surroundings. Sprawled on the floor was a large pile of animal hides, all different sizes. Lined against the wall, propped up like soldiers ready to be called upon and used to defend the user, were several spears with their stone arrowhead, which had been chipped then carved with accurate precision. Several shields stacked up high with their hard skin that had already been heated and stretched across the frames were left to dry.

She closed her eyes once more as her fingers tangled themselves in the dog's long fur coat. Altaira could hear the dog snoring and a continuous tapping of a woodpecker. A loud rumbling roar came from under the hide that was covering her. Lahnie's eyes opened and she immediately sat straight up as if on guard and starred at Altaira.

"Yes, it was me, I am not sure how long it has been since I had something to eat," she confessed to the dog as she clenched her rumbling stomach.

Altaira quickly sat up and immediately placed her head back down as the room began to spin in front of her. No, that was not good she had told herself and closed her eyes once more. The drumming of the woodpecker continued to beat its message as the room slowly stopped spinning. Once again, she opened her eyes, and this time slowly sat up. Her body swayed slightly and her head ached, but the room remained still. Lahnie prodded her with her wet nose and placed her paw on the covers.

"It's nice to meet you too," Altaira whispered as she grabbed her paw and shook it. "Thank you for looking after me so diligently."

"Hey, you're awake, I think you will find that I had also helped with that," Inca laughed as he entered the room and patted his faithful companions head.

"It's typical, I do all the work and you get the praise." Inca knelt on one knee and gave the dog a hug and the dog licked his face in reply.

"How are you feeling?" Inca asked Altaira.

"Aching all over and my head feels like it has been split in two and all I can hear is a bloody woodpecker hammering on the trees. At least I think it's a woodpecker I can hear, unless it is all in my imagination," Altaira moaned.

"No, it's not in your imagination; it is because of the woodpecker that Lahnie found you. She loves chasing woodpeckers; stupid I know. I keep telling her she will never catch one, as they are known to hide in the safety of the treetops. However, she noticed one flying low and watched it as it swooped through the branches. That is when she went bundling through the ferns and found you. You, with the woodpecker on your forehead. And, what's even more amazing is that very same woodpecker has not left. It tapped on your forehead all the way as I carried you. Once I got you inside it flew off up into the tree outside, where it has remained since. Every now and again it taps just to let us know he is still there," Inca informed her as she listened diligently to every word he had told her.

"Thank you for taking good care of me. If you hadn't have come when you did, I think I might be dead now. How can I ever repay you for your kindness?" Altaira enquired.

"Think nothing of it, you were in such a bad way and to be completely honest with you I didn't think you were going to make it either. You had been so badly beaten, I didn't think it was fair you should die there unprotected, half beaten to death and alone," he spoke with the deepest sincerity.

"You need to eat, I have made some soup, well it's a sort of soup."

Altaira looked at the liquid in the bowl; she could still see the bottom of the vessel. He wasn't wrong when he stated it was a sort of soup, it was completely transparent with very little substance.

"I know what you are thinking, it's very thin but I promise, you will like it," he smiled warmly at her.

Altaira dipped her spoon in the liquid and sipped it. She looked at Inca in amazement with wide-open eyes as the warmth of the broth slid down her throat. Inca smiled again at her. Altaira's eyes sparkled as the intense flavours filled her pallet. Altaira once again took another mouth full and then another until the bowl was nearly empty, she had never tasted anything like it, it was incredible.

"Family recipe," he informed her before she asked, as Altaira continued to sip her broth.

"Inca, I have never tasted anything like it, it was like an explosion of flavours all at once in my mouth, what is in it?" she asked as she continued to appreciate each mouthful.

Inca placed his finger along-side his nose and repeated that it was a family recipe that was not his to share.

"It is… Or was my mother's recipe that she used to make for us all," he declared as he looked at the floor with melancholy. "It's not as good as hers, I think I have all the ingredients but it is not quite there. Her soup is so much better, I have used what I think she used but she always added something extra and that added something is what I am missing."

"Well I think this is pretty amazing. Erm, Inca what do you mean, is or was her recipe?" Altaira asked in a confused tone and a knitted expression across her brow crinkling the healing skin.

"Well it is, if she is still alive and it was if she is dead," he answered

"What! That makes no sense at all, are you saying you don't know if your mother is alive or dead?" She looked at Inca waiting for his answer.

"Our tribe was attacked," Inca closed his eyes and took a deep breath. "I was out hunting as part of the village's hunting party but what we didn't know we were the ones being hunted. I saw two yellow eyes blinking in the bushes, I knew it was a Garchy tracking us, I also knew that we could not lead it back to the village, so we went deeper into the forest leading it further away. Then I saw the smoke and I realised it was not hunting us at all, it was a trap. We had left the village unprotected and we were too far away to help. Once we saw the smoke, we knew what fools we had been. The Garchy hooted its victory and quickly disappeared. We all ran as fast as we could but.......it was too late. Many villagers were slaughtered; blood everywhere, so much blood. Many huts were burning, men, women and children dead everywhere. I searched and searched looking for my family; they were not among the dead. I remember sitting in a pool of blood, with dead bodies around me," Inca looked at his hands and showed them to Altaira.

"You may not see the blood now but it is still there, we should not have left the village unprotected." His voice was barely audible as he spoke. "I started looking for survivors and I found one of the elders. He grabbed hold of me and told me there had been many soldiers from the castle and several Garchy. They had gathered all the boys into a cluster and let the Garchy breathe on them. The boys slumped to the ground then their unconscious bodies were tossed onto the back of a wagon. Several mothers were screaming for their boys and ran forward brandishing spears, but the Garchy chuckled and blew their toxic breath on them too. They tossed their bodies in the wagon with the boys. My mother and brother were among those on the wagon."

They stood in silence as the atmosphere plummeted and Altaira shivered. She looked at Inca not knowing how to comfort him.

"So, do you understand now why I said what I said. I really have no idea if they are alive or dead," he declared with tears in his eyes. He hung his head low, he could not look at her for fear of her misjudging his masculinity.

"You believe they are in the castle, don't you?" she asked. "That explains why you were so close when you found me." Altaira starred at him waiting for him to answer her. "How can you be so sure they are there?" she spoke in gentle tones.

"I have no idea if they are there, but I have to believe that they are somewhere and someone inside that castle knows where they are. I am not going to give up. I will find them," Inca responded as Altaira grabbed his hand in hers.

"I now know how I can repay you for saving my life, I will help you find your family," she declared in a smug tone.

"No-one can do that it will take a great warrior to help me! I am sorry but I do not see a great warrior around here - do you?" he mocked.

"Yes, I do; he is standing in front of me."

"Me?"

"Yes, you! You are stronger than you think," she reassured him. "Can I trust you?" she inquired.

"Of course, you can," he answered in a puzzled tone.

"What I am about to say must not be repeated to anyone. My life depends on it." Altaira knew she had to trust him but was still very nervous. She knew very little about him.

"You can trust me," he reassured her. She knew she had no choice but to have faith in him.

"Pledge an oath Inca and then I will believe you," she insisted.

Inca placed his blade on his hand and made a small piercing on his palm.

"Hold out you hand," he announced waiting for her to follow his command. She held out her hand for him and he pierced the skin on her palm and grabbed it. Palm to palm he spoke.

"I pledge an oath to you, I will never betray you, you can trust me. Whatever you want to entrust in me I pledge my loyalty to you," he sincerely spoke.

Altaira was deeply humbled that he had made a sacred blood oath to her. She knew he would never betray her.

"I know people. I know a great warrior that will help you," she announced. "In my opinion, the greatest warrior that has ever lived." She winked at him waiting for him to ask who.

"Alright, who? Who do you know? What is their name?" he asked.

"Altaira," she answered knowing her identity was safe with him.

"Altaira? You know Altaira?"

"Yes. I know Altaira very well in fact and I know she will help you," she smiled.

"Alright, how are we going to find her?" he asked in a disbelieving tone."

"She is standing in front of you," she answered smugly with a huge smile on her face.

"You are Altaira?" He exclaimed. "*The* Altaira? The great warrior of the Northern Tribes?" he asked in disbelief.

"Yes," Altaira confirmed with a chuckle. "And I promise I will help you," she assured him. "I just need to get my strength up first and then we can plan. Now any chance of another bowl of that so called transparent soup." She smiled sweetly at Inca as he dished another spoonful into her dish.

He shook his head and smiled, a warm feeling of optimism washed over him as he now realised whom she was and if those despots in the castle identified who she really was, they would not have let her go. He looked at Altaira as she sipped her soup. What a mistake the King had made, they had no idea who the great warrior Altaira was and what she was capable of achieving.

Altaira beamed with joy as she looked at Inca, they would make a great team. She felt a renewed feeling that she had not felt for a long time; every part of her began to tingle and she knew what that sensation was. It was the same sensation she got before she first mutated into a hawk. It is back she thought. She closed her eyes, tilted her head back, crossed her hands on her chest, and took a deep breath. Yes, it is back. She looked at the Hunter. It is now time to grow, time to see, and a time to help; it is now time for the Hawk!

~ Chapter Eight ~

The Wrath of the King

Riend's footsteps echoed through the damp corridors of hell as he completed his early rounds through the labyrinth of candlelit corridors and cells. The dungeon walls cried tears of black mucus that impregnated the very foundations of the granite structure. His daily inspection of the enslaved occupants had begun. Riend raised his sleeve swiftly to his mouth as the foul stench caught the back of his throat. The rancid particles clung and circulated its germs to each inmate caged in the overcrowded pens. Each imprisoned soul was a number, stripped of their identity, stripped of their self-worth, and stripped of their freedom. The roll call of their numbers resonated off the slime infested walls as each guard bellowed out their orders at the frail inhabitants.

"Get up scum! On your feet," they thundered in unison as the exhausted dwellers struggled to follow orders and stand.

Riend tapped the key in his pocket as he marched through the low-lit passageways and a large smirk appeared on his face as he thought of Altaira and her injuries. Yes, he thought, surely she must be dead by now. This pleased him. His favourite pass time was to inflict pain on those who were weaker than he was, and after all, Altaira was only a woman. He believed all women were weak and unimportant. They did not deserve the same consideration as men. It was a man's duty to have control and the woman's duty to follow instructions without question. Riend considered women as having one purpose in life. To have children even if they did not want too, it was not a decision that they had a choice in making. If a man made a claim on a woman, she became his property, like the captive slaves held in the cells.

"I want all the women and children up and out working," Riend screamed as he marched through.

"But Sir, they have not long come back; they have worked solid for two days. They need to rest, Sir." The guard gulped as he looked at Riend's furious expression and wished he had not made an outburst.

Riend pounced on him, pinned him up against the wall and held him up with his hand tightly gripped under his chin pressing on his windpipe.

"What?" Riend spat as he glared with contempt.

"They…um… have…not long come back from… um…working…Sir," he squeaked and gasped as Riend's grip squeezed tighter around his throat.

"WHAT!" Riend bellowed again as the guard realised he was not asking a question.

"Yes, S… Sir, I…I will, I will get them up," he nervously stammered.

"That is better, YOU are never to question me again," he announced as he brought his knee up and viciously made contact with the guard's groin.

The guard sank to his knees gasping for breath as he fought the sudden surge of pain. Riend swiftly unsheathed his knife, sliced the guard's cheek and swung his foot into the guard's face and sent him toppling backwards.

"Every time you look at that scar, I want you to remember to never question ME again!" he shouted down at the blood-stained face.

He smiled as he looked at the other guards who rapidly started to assemble the women and children up and out of their cells. One of the guards bent down to help the injured sentry up from the floor.

"Leave him there," he commanded. "If I see or hear that any one of you has given aid to this insubordinate low life.... YOU will answer to me and so will your families. Take a good look at him; all it takes is one of you to displease me and all of you will suffer the consequences. You will find it will be YOUR wife, or YOUR Mother, or sister or daughter in one of these cells." Riend pointed his finger at the petrified guards who acknowledged his threat and exerted all their energies to herd the residents as they struggled to muster their strength to stand.

"First, feed them, I do not want them to die. The Angel of Death will not save them. I want them to suffer. Dying is not a way out. Then get them working, anyone not able to work, give them to the Garchy!" Riend snarled through gritted teeth. "A Garchy slave is far worse than a King's slave," he chuckled as he continued to march his way through.

***

Eudora paced back and forth in her chamber as she twisted her hands together nervously. The plump nurse gently took Eudora's hands, raised them to her mouth, and softly kissed them.

"Please do not worry, it will be all right," Nellie reassured her as she straightened up her attire. She had taken care of her since she and Etta had been very young. She was more like a mother to her than a nursemaid.

"Do you have to go and speak with him? Can you just stay here and say I am still unwell?" Eudora pleaded with her.

"I do not think we can. You cannot hide from our King forever; after all, he is your husband. Besides, I need to inform him of how Riend barged his way in and disregarded his orders."

"Please be careful, remember not to look at him, curtsy, and wait for him to give you permission before you rise and if he offers his hand to kiss the King's stone on his finger you must…"

"Will you stop worrying," the nurse interrupted her; she smiled, squeezed her cheek and then patted it. "I will be fine; after all I am also giving him the news that you are well enough to see him."

Eudora raised her eyebrows and let out a heavy sigh as her heart sank. "Regardless of what you say... I do not feel well enough to see him," she let out a fake cough and half smiled at the nurse.

"You are hopeless child, what am I going to do with you," the nurse whispered and walked towards her.

"You will do what you always do," Eudora told the nurse.

"Yes, you are right I will, come here," Nellie put her arms around her and planted a kiss on her forehead. "You will always be my special little girl," she sniffed and wiped the tears from her eyes.

"Not so little anymore though am I?" Eudora exclaimed as Nellie continued to hold her.

"It is time. You are much stronger now remember that." The nurse enveloped her in a tight embrace, then let her go and took a step backwards and smiled.

The Queen nodded her approval as the nurse slipped out through the open door. Eudora sat on her bed, with her face in her hands and wept. The thought of seeing the King terrified her.

Two guards escorted the nurse as she slowly walked towards the North Tower.

Out of shape and out of breath she stopped to lean against the wall before she challenged herself to climb the spiral staircase. She took a deep breath to build up the courage and strength to report her news to the King. Her heart resonated loudly within her ears with each step she climbed. Beads of sweat gathered and trickled down the side of her cheek. Sharp pains ran through her muscles like hot pokers burning her flesh with every movement as she got closer to the upper chambers. Her body began to abandon her legs as she stood on the last step of the staircase. Her limbs leaden and routed to the spot. Red faced and panting for breath, she dismissed the guards.

"It is alright," she gasped and took several long deep breaths. "I will be all right to see myself in, there is no need to wait and announce me," she wheezed and placed her hands on her thighs and bent over in exhaustion.

"We have orders Mam, we are to escort all visitors to His Majesty," they advised her.

"Very well, you will have to wait a moment for me to catch my breath," she informed them as they paused for her to regain her composure. She stood still and leaned her head on the wooden door to calm her nerves. She could hear raised voices from within the chamber.

"You will have to get her back, I cannot believe you have let her go," the voice snapped.

She identified the King's voice but the other she did not recognise.

"Right, I am now ready," the nurse spoke, curious to see who the King was speaking to. She straightened her clothing and cleared her throat. The guards knocked, opened the heavy oak door and stepped into the dark chamber. Nellie looked around the room expecting to see another person but could only see the King standing in front of her.

"I am sorry Your Majesty, am I interrupting you? I can come back later," he enquired with a puzzled look as she continued to look for the owner of the other voice.

"No, you are not interrupting me. Is everything all right? Is it Eudora? I hope nothing has happened to her," he announced as he placed his wine goblet on a table next to another used glass.

The nurse noticed the two silver goblets on the table. She once more scanned the room; she was convinced there was another in there hiding.

"Your Majesty," she addressed the King and curtsied, eyes looking at the floor. It seemed a lifetime before he invited her to stand.

"Why are you here?" he asked her.

"The Queen is feeling much better and has asked me to send this news to you. She is still quite weak but she is getting stronger. She sends her sincere best wishes to you and has asked to see you when you can spare her your time."

"Yes of course, I am pleased she is recovering well. I am also thankful to you for keeping such a vigil over her and guaranteeing my orders for her solitude was carried out." He nodded at the plump lady in front of him.

"Yes, I must confess I did keep her solitude up until recently," she informed him.

"What? What do you mean up until recently?" the King's curiosity obviously piqued. "My orders were that no one, absolutely no one was to interrupt her recovery, not even I disturbed her," he stated. "Who? Tell me, WHO?" he screamed furiously at her. "I want a name, who?"

"Riend," she informed him. "And the Queen was very distressed when he rudely barged his way into her chamber without invitation. He accused me of hiding something from him and that her illness was a sham and that we had even fooled you *Your Majesty* into believing she was ill," she informed him and curtsied once more.

"Get me Riend, now!" the King bellowed at the guards. "You get back with the Queen, I will deal with Riend," he spat with fury in his voice and clenched his fist. "Someone get me RIEND!" he continued to thunder.

The nurse acknowledged that she had out stayed her welcome, and to stay would be foolish. She left the King pacing up and down screaming Riend's name.

"I am disappointed," a voice from the shadows, announced. "I will not abort my plans, I assigned this task to you; maybe I choose the wrong brother, perhaps I should have given this task to Tycus instead of you," the voice in the shadows continued. "You have amassed greatness through me and I can take it away from you. I gave you the greatest warrior that has ever lived and you let her go. YOU LET HER GO!" the voice bellowed.

"I think you are mistaken, she is not the great warrior Altaira, we broke her and still she did not admit who she was. We tortured her to the point of near death and still she had no idea of the person we were accusing her of being. She kept telling us that she did not know who Altaira was," the King corrected the stranger.

"And you believed her? She has made a fool of you. Do you think she has never been tortured? She is a warrior of war. She will never yield; death to her is her only option," the visitor snapped.

"Yes, I believed her, and if you think she *is* the 'Great Altaira,' then maybe you should interrogate her," the King said meekly as he paced back and forth.

"You know that is not possible, she knows me. You know I cannot give away my identity. No one must see me, if anyone detects me or has any inclination that I was even talking to you then our plan is ruined. RUINED, YOU KNOW THIS. Failure is not an option. You haven't even got the loyalty and respect of your chief guard, even he has made a fool of you," the transient visitor spat; but still remained within the shadows.

"I will deal with Riend," the King argued with eyes blazed with fury.

"Do you aspire to be a great King? An assertive King? A King that succeeds; or a King that is weak, overpowered, and attacked?" the unexpected visitant uttered.

"You know I do," the King acknowledged as the aggressiveness inside him began to bubble.

"Then get her back. She is the one. No more torturing her; pain will not make any difference to her. You need to work on her weaknesses. You hold many prisoners from the northern tribes, especially children. Bargain their freedom for her allegiance. She will feel it is her duty to protect her tribes," the visitor declared. "And get rid of that goblet before Riend gets here, I am sure the nurse saw it." Like a ghost, the speaker slipped away, back within the shadows.

Hurried footsteps were heard from outside the chamber, followed by a panting Riend.

"You have asked for me Your Majesty," he curiously spoke and bowed before him.

"YES," the King announced harshly as he looked upon his chief guard.

Riend stood still as he watched the King pace across the chamber floor.

"I am sorry Sire but forgive me for saying this, you seem a little agitated, is there something I can do to help you," Riend obliviously babbled with a nervousness in his voice.

"You are sorry? SORRY!" the King exploded as he sprinted across the chamber and flung Riend against the wall. Riend's terrified face looked at the Kings forbidding expression and eyes that were ablaze with rage.

"Tell me Riend, do you have any idea why I have sent for you?" the King asked in a punishing tone.

"GET UP!" the King screamed in bitterness.

Riend slowly stood and gazed at the King and was about to admit he did not.

"What are you doing?" the King questioned as he once more grabbed Riend and threw him against the hard floor. "Stay down there!" the King hollered at his disobedient servant.

"Get up!" the King once more repeated. Riend for the second time stood. The King lunged at him and hurled him against the wall. Riend slid and slumped to the floor. "What are you doing? I said stay down there." The King sneered as he swung his leg into Riend's face splattering blood on his boot. He glanced down at his foot and wiped it clean on Riend's clothes. "I said GET UP!" he spat in a repulsive attitude.

Pain seared through his body as Riend slowly struggled to focus and sluggishly stood before the King. The King pressed his face into Riend's then slammed him harshly to the floor.

"What are you doing? I said stay down there!" The King knelt on Riend's spine and compressed him further into the stone floor. "Remember your position. I am the King." The King grabbed Riend's head and suffocated his bleeding face further into the solid surface as Riend called out in pain.

"Loyalty, Riend. Respect Riend. Obedience Riend." The King continued to press on the back of Riend's head. Struggling to breathe Riend took the King's wrath. His body began to sing under the weight of the King's torso. He laid still, confused as to why the King wanted to abuse him. The King stood and looked at his intrusive servant sprawled on the floor.

"You have disappointed me; perhaps your position should go to someone else. Someone, who will obey my orders, someone, who will respect that my orders are law," he spat. "Someone who will understand that their position is below mine and will stay down there below me and not try to stand up and think they are above me. The trouble with you Riend is that you are arrogant and with arrogance, mistakes are made."

Riend did not attempt to interrupt the King. He tried to think about what he must have done to deserve this treatment. There had been so many times he had disobeyed orders, so many times, he had done what *he* had wanted to do.

"You will adhere to all the rules that I set. If you do not, then I will replace you with someone who will. You will not like it. You will join the riff raff in the dungeons. You will eat with them, sleep with them, work with them and you will be punished with them." The King knew this warning would be the cruellest punishment he could administer on Riend. "Do not become accustomed to your position. Do not annoy me further."

Riend nodded in acknowledgment, still unsure which rule or order he had broken. He decided to keep quiet and let the King rant and lecture him.

"You have been accused of disturbing the rest and healing process of the Queen. You deliberately forced your way into her chamber knowing that I gave the strictest order that she was not to be disturbed. You do not cross the threshold of the Queen's chamber, ever! That is an area of the castle that you are forbidden to enter. Forbidden, do I make myself clear?" in a raged tone the King stated more than asked. "She is your superior. You may be my Chief Guard but she is my wife, your Queen. You should remember that," the King snapped as he walked back to the table and picked up the solitary goblet and drank.

Riend remained motionless on the floor thinking about the interfering nursemaid; she must have communicated this to the King. He knew he was at a disadvantage; he would never be able to cast a shadow on her reputation with the Queen as her guardian to protect her.

"Yes, Your Majesty," Riend nodded and squeaked as the pain smarted. "I just thought I would…."

"I do not want your excuses," he interrupted him. "I am not concerned as to why. You knew my orders. I expect everyone to follow my orders. No exceptions."

"Please, Your Majesty I am sorry, let me prove to you that I am your loyal servant," Riend snivelled and bowed his head.

"Very well, I want you to bring that girl back to me. I have changed my mind. I would like to talk to her," the King insisted.

"I have let her go as Your Majesty instructed." he hesitated as he saw the disapproved look on the Kings face. "But I do not think she would have got very far as we did interrogate her within an inch of her life." Riend smirked as he remembered her covered in blood as he dumped her within the wooded area after he had tortured her further. "She could be dead now your majesty."

"I hope for your sake that she is not." He also hoped for his sake she was not dead either. He looked at Riend who sat motionless on the floor. "Well what are you waiting for you idiot, BRING HER BACK. NOW LEAVE!" he yelled at him as his face turned a puce red with anger and frustration.

Riend scrambled to his feet and with long strides hurried towards the dungeons.

~ Chapter Nine ~

The Vision

The torches flickered and created shadows that danced and dipped in different directions. Ursus struggled to sit. His head felt heavy on his shoulders and his thoughts flittered from one moment with the spirit to another. He had been in the spirit realm for a couple of days and he needed to adjust to the normality of the non-spirit world of the living. He glanced at the inquisitive faces of Nubilus and his Leader who starred silently at him.

"Water. Please can I have some water?" Ursus asked in a croaked voice as he held his hand out.

172

The Leader handed him a jug and Ursus gulped the liquid without stopping to wipe the dribbles that ran off his chin as he slurped and soothed his parched throat.

Crossed legged he placed one hand on his knee, tilted his head back further; he did not want to leave a single drop, he wanted it all. He could feel the coldness of the water as it travelled down his gullet. Finally satisfied, he dropped the jug and with the back of his hand, he wiped the drool off his chin.

Nubilus anxiously waited for Ursus to speak. He wanted to know if Altaira was safe.

"Well - what happened?" Nubilus impatiently asked.

"It is difficult to explain," he puffed as he looked at both his Leader and Nubilus.

"Well you explain and we will try to help," Nubilus continued in a frustrated voice.

"It was a silver spirit," he advised and they all sighed with relief.

"It was definitely not the red spirit," Nubilus confirmed. He now knew Altaira was alive, but he still did not know if she was safe.

Ursus took a deep breath as he thought about what the spirit had shown him and then he began to explain what he saw and felt.

"I knew the spirit had arrived. The air became still so I placed my rattling stick on the ground beside me. Soft silver streaks appeared that spiralled around licking and cleansing my spirit within. It continued to hover and twist in the air before it eventually ceased and floated before me. Three jewels appeared, an amethyst, a diamond and a sapphire. I instantly recognised them as the three gems given to the infants. I think the spirit was identifying Tycus's children. I felt warmth radiate from the spirit, I knew it approved of us taking his offspring." He smiled and looked at Nubilus who nodded in agreement, as he continued.

"It asked if I had a question and all I could think of was Altaira. I needed to know she was safe. All of a sudden, I was standing on the edge of a precipice and I could see a vast empty land surround me. It felt as if I was soaring high in the sky; the view was breath taking. I looked at my arms and I could see feathers. The spirit told me that Altaira had once again taken flight," Ursus confirmed and looked at Nubilus with watery eyes. He could feel instant relief flood from his wolf friend. After a moment of thankful stillness, he continued.

"I felt something touch my feet, something cold, wet and slippery. I looked down and I had bare feet. I was walking through long wet grass and weeds. The weeds began to tangle around my ankles stopping me in my tracks, stopping me from going any further. I tried to lift my feet but every time I tried the weeds got tighter and tighter until I was completely trapped, binding my soul to the ground," he explained in a puzzled manner and looked at his Leader who looked deep in thought.

"What about the grass, was the grass tangled around your feet or was it just the weeds?" the Leader enquired as he waited for Ursus to confirm.

"Just the weeds," Ursus replied. "Why, do you know what it means?"

"Maybe. I have a theory but I am not sure, the Earth Mother has always taught us that, if you stand still the weeds will grow and then it will be too late to do anything about the problem that has caused the weeds to grow in the first place. So, this confirms something is not right, but we have no idea what that something is. What else?" the Leader asked.

"Well, as the weeds got tighter a large snake emerged from the grass and slid over the weeds with ease. It coiled itself around me squeezing the air from my lungs. I struggled to breathe, it got tighter and tighter it felt like my chest was on fire, I thought I was going to die. The snake slid up my torso until its face was directly in line with mine. It opened its mouth and I could see a mouth full of sharp teeth; that curved towards the back of its mouth. Several times, it repeatedly opened its jaws and each time the mouth opened wider. I thought it was going to swallow me whole. From nowhere an arrow was shot at it and it recoiled to slide through the long grass from where it had appeared from, it just slipped away," Ursus explained in a bizarre tone.

"Did the arrow hit it?" Nubilus asked.

"What!"

"Did the arrow hit it."

"No," Ursus replied.

"Well I can confirm one thing and this is certain, it was not me who shot that arrow as I would not have missed," Nubilus joked.

"This is not a time for comedy," the Leader scowled. "Do not mock what the Great Spirits show us."

"Do you want to help or not?" Ursus asked Nubilus with a disapproving look.

"Sorry, I did not mean it as an insult I just wanted to lighten the tension," Nubilus explained and mouthed sorry again at the Leader, then looked at Ursus and nodded for him to continue.

"The grass disappeared. I was still barefoot, but I was standing on dry, coarse soil, the land looked parched as if there had been no rain for some time. Nothing was growing. No animals were grazing and no birds were nesting in the trees. All the trees were barren except for one. This tree was lush and green and around the trunk was an army of arrows that had formed a circle around the base. It looked as if it gave it some sort of protection from dying. At the top was a woodpecker that flew from the green tree to the barren trees. It tapped on the rotten trees then flew back to the tree with the arrows." Ursus stopped and with a confusing look, he glanced at both his Leader and Nubilus then shrugged his shoulders in complete bewilderment. "I have no idea what the spirit meant by showing me this bizarre vision."

"I told you the land is changing Ursus," Nubilus reminded him. "I told you when I bestowed the blood gifts something was not right. I could smell it then. The trees are dying from the inside. Something is poisoning the land. I did tell you this. Why do you think I imparted the gifts on the children in the first place. When the earth is sick, the rainbow warriors will heal the land. They are the rainbow warriors and we must help them protect the land and rid it of whatever evil is spreading, no matter what the cost to us. We took an oath, Ursus, a blood oath. And I endowed a blood gift from the spirits binding our oath in the eyes of the spirits too," Nubilus reminded him.

Ursus nodded to acknowledge that Nubilus was right. Whatever evil threatened the land also threatened the infants and they are the only ones that can stop it.

"Is there anything else Ursus, or is that it?" the Leader asked.

"Well there is one more image, but it is difficult to describe it was blurry. It looked like an elk standing on its hind legs with huge antlers. It was acting very peculiar it was walking like a man."

"Could it be a man with antlers on its head?" Nubilus interrupted.

"Em, well yes I suppose it could be but why would a man wear antlers? I cannot understand the purpose of this," Ursus uttered in mystification and looked at the other two hoping they could help.

They stood in silence and deep in thought, each trying to understand the last vision.

"We need Altaira," Nubilus blurted out what they were all thinking. "She would have the answers, she would know what the antler elk-man vision was about, just like that," Nubilus clicked his fingers indicating how swift she would have answered their query.

"Yes, you are right Nubilus she would have the answers, you need to find her and bring her back here to fulfil her oath with the child. It is clear they are linked to all our futures and the future of the land depends on them," the Leader uttered in hushed tones. "You must not leave together or some may suspect that you are the wolf Nubilus, do not speak of this to anyone. Is Dak aware of your name?" he asked.

"No, I told him he was called Wolfie," Ursus answered as he peeped at Nubilus's disapproving expression.

"Good, it must remain as that, no-one must know his identity, no-one must know that Nubilus has been here. Make sure people see you leave as a wolf not as a man. Ursus I want you to visit the children tonight and thank the nursing mothers," the Leader instructed.

"What do you want me to tell them?" he asked.

"Tell them to treat the children as one of their own and to speak to me, they are to be accepted as one of the tribe. Tell them the spirits will reward them for their kindness. I also want you to thank Dak and tell him you are leaving in the morning and that when the wolf is better to let him leave. Nubilus, I want you to leave a day later, which should give your wound another day to heal and another day of rest for you. Ursus when you leave in the morning you are to wait for him to join you. You can hide until you are reunited. If we can do this no one will suspect that you are the wolf." the Leader continued as he glanced at Nubilus. "I want you both to stay here while I check that no one is in the room above," he ordered as he climbed to check.

He slowly lifted the hatch, just wide enough for him to peek and scout around checking it was clear.

Daylight screamed its way through the darkness causing the Leader to squint and his eyes to water. He furiously blinked as his eyes adjusted to the natural light. He climbed out and knelt on his knees.

"All clear," he announced to the two men below who stood in anticipation waiting to be re-united with fresh air and sunshine.

Ursus climbed, first with one hand on the ladder the other shielding his eyes. His vision at first blurred and he too struggled to focus but soon adjusted. He looked down at his friend waiting for permission to leave the stifling hole in the ground.

"It is your turn my friend, but as soon as you reach the chamber ground you must mutate back," Ursus explained and Nubilus nodded showing he understood his orders.

Nubilus slowly struggled to climb the ladder, his wound on his arm had not fully healed. He stood on the last step and gulped a lung full of fresh air. With one last effort he pushed using his elbows and cleared the hole.

He rolled onto the floor and looked at them both and grinned.

"Change Nubilus, quickly you must change," Ursus whispered in a hurried tone as he was still looking at Nubilus the man not the wolf.

Nubilus swiftly mutated back into the grey oversized wolf and sat panting with his huge tongue hanging over the side of his chops.

Ursus and the leader once more dragged their feet in a sweeping motion to cover the wooden door. Nubilus tried to help and rolled ceremoniously in circles that just sent the dust everywhere, causing the two men to cough and splutter.

"Thank you, Nub...Erm I mean Wolfie," Ursus quickly corrected himself though the blanket of dust.

Ursus put his hand on Nubilus's head to stop him from rolling.

"Stop, you must stop!" Ursus bellowed at the wolf who seemed to be having far too much fun.

The wolf stopped and looked at Ursus and the Leader who both stood in a cloud of floating particles. They flapped their arms through the fog of dirt that had begun to settle on everything in the room. Through the mist of grime, the two men stared down at the producer that caused this chaos of filth.

"Honestly, you should know better, you are no longer a pup, what has got into you?" Ursus protested in a frustrated voice as he patted the dust off his clothes.

That was amazing, Nubilus thought as he looked at the two men covered from head to toe in dry soil. He felt so much better. The cloud started to clear and Nubilus spied a pile of hides to curl up on. He scampered over, sniffed, pawed at the skins, and sank his heavy, dusty frame on top. He licked his wound on his arm and drifted into a deep sleep.

****

A Muto's Promise
The Guardians

Nubilus opened his eyes, stretched his limbs, dug his nails into the soil and yawned. It was morning; he had slept through the previous day and night. He stood, stretched his neck and shook his head. He scanned the room for Ursus but could not find him. He walked to the opening and stood, letting the rays of sunshine warm his weary frame. He yawned once more.

"He has already left," the Leader whispered in a hushed tone and sat beside him. "I want you to stay one more night, then, I will ask Dak to walk you to the edge of the camp. Ursus will be waiting for you but you will not see him until he thinks it is safe. Ursus has taken two horses. He will not be far from where they are tethered. When you meet up with him, I would strongly suggest that you mutate back into a man. Now if you understood put your paw on my knee."

Nubilus placed his paw on the Leader's knee. He was anxious to leave. He wanted to find Altaira, and he realised he would not find her whilst he remained there. His body soaked up the sun's rays and he drifted once more into a quiet slumber, only to start thinking of Ursus's vision. What did the snake mean and who or what was wearing antlers? Nubilus thought of Altaira, he hoped that she was safe. They must find her...they must.

Nubilus opened one eye as he heard the laughter of children playing. He spied a woman chastising them for making too much noise as the Leader also opened his weary eyes. He too had been disturbed by their laughter. The two children sauntered up to the Leader and stopped in front of him. The Leader stood and towered over them. They gave frightened glances back at the woman who waved her hand for them to continue.

"We are sorry for disturbing you," they nervously declared as they also scanned the enormous wolf that had got up to stand beside him. With wide, open mouths and eyes darting back and forth at the Leader and the woman, they stood waiting for his forgiveness. The Wolf moved forward towards the children who were now frozen to the spot. He sniffed them and opened his mouth to yawn as the children grabbed each other for comfort.

"I think the wolf has forgiven you," the Leader chuckled. "As do I, now go and help your mother," he ordered as they scrambled away towards the safety of her arms.

Nubilus sat and watched the villagers' as they went about their daily chores. It had been such a long time since he had been part of village life. He had almost forgotten how it felt to be among a tribe all working together as one. He sensed the tribe worked and lived in close proximity, each sharing what little belongings they had. He spied many families sharing huts, all helping one another. He watched two, young women polishing shells whilst another shaped and strung them together to create a necklace. A young boy sat chipping a stone into the shape of an arrowhead. Each one had their place within the community, each with their own way of contributing to the daily running of the tribe. He watched as an elder of the tribe sat in the middle of a large open space. One by one, the children ran towards her and sat in silence in a large circle around her.

A Muto's Promise
The Guardians

Nubilus slowly got up to walk towards the circle of children. He remembered this part of life very well. He remembered the elders in his own tribe and how he also had sat in a similar circle many moons ago. A huge feeling of warmth engulfed him, a feeling that he forgot that he had. He thought about his own community, his family that he had not seen for such a long time and found that he too had joined the children in the circle. The elder looked at her new student and smiled.

The evening sky exploded with red and orange tints as the fire of gold slowly dipped behind the hills and sank from view. The spherical hunter of daylight retreated its burning harpoons; it would attack again at sunrise.

The elder waited and then in a sing-song voice she spoke. "One day Mother Earth will weep, she will discharge crimson tears of blood, she will beg for her life. You will have to make a choice," she said as she pointed her finger at every child. "Will you help her to survive or will you let her die? Remember, if you do nothing and she dies, you will die too." She looked up at the sky and then back at the children who hung on every word she spoke, "Never forget that the ground we stand on is sacred and we must protect it. Truth-Honesty-Generosity-Equality and Brotherhood," she chanted.

The children stood and chanted back. "Truth-Honesty-Generosity-Equality and Brotherhood," then they sat back down as she nodded.

"That is our way of life. Be truthful not only to those around you but to yourself. It does not require many words to speak the truth. Be honest; say how you are feeling and stand up for what is right, even if you are standing alone. Be generous, a selfish life is not a fulfilled life, you already possess everything necessary to be great. Share with others that have less than you do. Take only what you need. Recognise that everyone in this life is equal to you. Carry with you a heart that loves, a smile that is kind and a touch that heals. Show respect to all people but grovel to none. But, most of all is brotherhood, be tolerant of those who are lost on their path. Pray to the spirits that they will find guidance."

The sun had set and the stars began to sparkle in the night sky. The elder stood and quietly with the aid of two others, she slowly walked away. The children remained as they reflected on what they had been told. This time with the elder was much different. No stories about the ancestors or a story of a great battle, just the bizarre reminder of their way of life.

Nubilus could not help thinking that she was addressing him. What was it she said. "The ground is sacred and we must protect it." Perhaps that was linked to the vision. He is a protector of the forest and that is what he must do, protect. He thought about the other things she mentioned. "Stand up for what you think is right, everyone is equal, a smile that is kind, and a touch that heals."

Nubilus thought of Altaira and Ursus and realised that their way of life made sense. But he would never tell Ursus that. Night was fast approaching and Nubilus once more slumped on top of the hides and closed his eyes to world.

Morning crept over the land. Spears of light glimmered through the tiny cracks all around where Nubilus slept surrounding him in light. He could hear the Leader's voice talking to Dak.

"I am not interested if he scares you, I want you to walk him to the edge of the camp. The villagers feel uneasy that we have a wolf in the camp. They want him gone."

"But, but why me? Surely you don't need me to show him to the edge of the camp, surely you can just tell him to go," he declared in a nervous voice.

"Just tell him to go! It is a wolf Dak, do you think it can understand a command; he is a dumb animal. He does not understand what you or I are saying. You will put the rope on him and lead him away from the camp; then you will take the rope off him. He is a wild animal so once he senses his own environment, he will just take flight," the Leader announced as he walked over to fetch some twine. He made a loop and gave it to Dak.

He nervously stepped one foot at a time towards the wolf, stretched his arms out and with shaking hands went to place it around Nubilus's neck.

Nubilus thought he would have some fun, as Dak tried to loop the rope. Nubilus shook his head and twisted his body to stop him. "Dumb animal am I," Nubilus thought. "I'll show you dumb," as he cantered around the room. Dak once again moved nervously towards him. Nubilus let out a long, deep growl.

"I can't do it, he is going to bite me," he wailed as Nubilus continued to growl then showed his teeth. He was having great fun scaring Dak. Dak was so easy to frighten he thought as he barked and pretended to bite him.

"No, I am sorry I cannot do it, I can't," he muttered fighting to breathe. "He really scares me."

"Give it here," he announced as he snatched the rope out of Dak's hand and slipped it over Nubilus head.

"Honestly Dak you made such a fuss over nothing." The Leader handed him the end of the rope. "Now walk him to the edge of the camp, remove the rope and set him free."

Dak shook his head, "Nope, I'm not doing it," he dropped the rope to the floor.

"What!" he bellowed. "You will do it." The Leader picked the rope up and placed it back into Dak's hand. "Now do it!"

Dak wailed loudly and yanked the rope to lead Nubilus out of the camp. Nubilus started to walk very quickly pulling Dak with him. Then without warning, he stopped, sniffed and peed on Dak's leg.

"Argh, what," Dak shook his leg as Nubilus showed no sign of stopping.

All of a sudden, Nubilus decided that he was going to run as Dak still held on tightly to the rope. Dak started to run quicker and quicker as Nubilus pulled him. Dak suddenly twisted the rope around his wrist and began running faster than his legs could carry him when suddenly Nubilus stopped and Dak tumbled to the floor. Dak sat on the soil to catch his breath. He staggered to his feet and stood looking at the wolf. Nubilus pulled him abruptly once more and Dak's arms jerked forward, he tried to dig his heels into the ground to stop Nubilus from pulling him, but the wolf was far too strong for the feeble Dak. He once again slipped to the floor. The rope pinched and burned his skin as he travelled. Nubilus continued to run as Dak's helpless body twisted and bounced, as he was dragged through the dirt.

Nubilus stopped on the boundary of the camp. Dak quickly scrambled to his feet. His soiled body was covered in cuts and grazes.

"You can keep the rope, I'm not taking it off you," Dak hollered as he spat soil and blood on the floor. Nubilus stood on the edge of the camp and howled at Dak and then disappeared amongst the bushes. Dak turned on his heels and limped back towards camp holding his bruised and battered body.

A Muto's Promise
The Guardians

Nubilus hid amidst the bushes and waited for Dak to become a blurred figure in the distance before he mutated back into a man. He sat and giggled to himself as he recalled Dak bouncing as he dragged him. Nubilus did not like Dak. From the moment he had met him, he decided not to like him, besides he smelled. A scent he could not make out. A smell he had never sensed before and that was all he needed to make his mind up to dislike him, even though he had helped him. Even though, he had found nursing mothers, even though he gave up his pony so Ursus could rest. Even though he led them to the safety of the camp. Nubilus shook his head; maybe he had been a bit cruel to Dak. He held his head in shame thinking about all the good things Dak had done for Ursus and the children. A wide smile gathered across his face as the image of him bouncing in the dirt re-appeared, it was no good he reeked and he could not bring himself to like anyone who stank as he did.

Nubilus hid himself behind a bush and waited. Dak was now just a tiny speck in the distance. He considered mutating when he remembered his orders were to wait until Ursus had given the all clear. He lifted his paw and then replaced it on the ground. He could feel the earth vibrating. He could feel the vibrations of something approaching. He crouched to the floor and laid his frame onto the soil to get a better feel. The vibrations became clearer, maybe it was Ursus he thought and was about to play a trick and jump out on him in a surprise. He lowered the front end of his body ready to leap when suddenly, the stench hit him hard in the face. He tried to catch his breath and crawled on his belly to get a better view of the producer of the pong. A huge something was blocking his path. He stopped and held his breath when he had realised what he had stumbled upon. A singular Garchy stood before him. He quickly scrambled out of view.

Nubilus thought about the camp, he would need to go back and warn them. Firstly, he thought he would determine how many Garchies were on the boarder of the encampment. He scanned his perimeter expecting to see the rest of the pack. Usually where there was one Garchy, the others were not far behind. It was odd, there was only one Garchy this time, one solitary creature that pulled up the bushes around it and just slung them aside. It looked as if it was making a path. But... why? These actions puzzled Nubilus, he needed to return to the camp and warn them.

He turned away and was about to sprint when a hand grabbed him. Thinking it was a Garchy his heart missed a beat. "Shush, do not struggle. It is me," Ursus whispered. "Mutate Nubilus."

As soon as Ursus said it, Nubilus mutated back to his natural form.

"We must go back and warn them; Ursus, they need to be told there is a Garchy close to the camp," Nubilus whispered harshly. "We need to alert your Leader that the creature is here."

"He is already aware, he told me it was here and to be careful, that is why he wanted me to be cautious and for you only to mutate when it was safe. It has been here for some time. Our scouts have been watching it. Checking that it remains solitary," he confirmed. "Look, high up in that tree," he said as he pointed to the tree to the left of them.

Nubilus could see a man sat watching. Ursus pointed to three more trees and pointed to his fellow tribesman scrutinising the boundary, ready to report their findings to their Leader.

"Observation is the greatest source of wisdom Nubilus. They are all brothers and extremely loyal to our Leader. They are spies, they have been watching. This Garchy has been here a while, they are unsure if he is just lost or if there is a reason why he is here alone. My Leader has given me strict instructions not to aggravate it," Ursus's lips curled into a smile.

"What are you suggesting Ursus that I am a liability?" Nubilus asked with a huge grin on his face.

"Nothing of the sort.... Well may be a little of a liability," he smirked "We are to leave and head north to seek Altaira. Our horses are just through that clearing tethered to the trees," Ursus spoke as he pointed to the meadow beyond the opening.

Both men hurried towards the gap to where the majestic quadruped beasts stood grazing, oblivious to the urgency of their departure. The two splendid horses stood side by side, each had a blanket over its flank and a rope that hung over its head. One of the horses shook its head, scraped its hoof in the soil, tried to free itself from its bondage, and nervously stepped back as Nubilus approached.

Nubilus looked at the twine around the horse's neck, "I Know exactly how you feel," he muttered as he placed his hand around his own neck and rubbed where the rope had been. He placed his hand on the side of the horse's head, "Shush," he whispered softly as he gently patted the beast and placed his head on the side of horse's nose. Nubilus softly muttered to the steed and it gradually ceased panicking and gently nudged Nubilus in the chest with his nose and forehead. "Now listen, you have the pleasure of being my horse, and it is a great honour for me to be your rider. I am Nubilus," he announced and held out the palm of his hand. The horse sniffed it then snorted. "Horse, I am Nubilus, will you let me be your rider?" he asked.

The horse stood proud and immediate lifted its forearm to Nubilus giving him his consent. "Thank you," he acknowledged and patted the horse's shoulder. "You truly are a magnificent steed."

"Have you finished sweet talking it; shall I find Altaira by myself?" Ursus smirked.

"Erm, yes," he announced as he grabbed the horse's mane hopped on one foot and bounced to jump up onto his newly acquainted friend. He leant over and patted the mighty beast.

"We will head for the mountains and go from one northern tribe to the next, we need to be careful; I am not sure what we will be faced with on the way or when we reach a tribe." Ursus announced as he dug his heels into the side of the horse.

Both horses lunged forward and galloped across the meadow beyond the safety of the camp, beyond the safety of the trees and into open wasteland. A trail of dust spiralled into the air as they dashed across the arid land towards the majestic mountains in search of Altaira.

~ Chapter Ten ~

The Missing Muto

Altaira sat and hugged her knees to her chest and gave a huge smile as she looked at her host attempting to skin his freshly caught prize. Inca held on tight as he sliced through its fur. He could feel Altaira's emerald eyes spying on him as he worked. He twisted his torso to glance at her and noticed she was smiling at him with utmost delight and amusement.

"What's the matter? Have you never seen a man skin a rabbit before?" he asked her as she now started to laugh.

"Oh, that is what you are trying to do," she sniggered.

"Trying, what do you mean trying? It is called succeeding," he defended.

Altaira slowly let go of her knees, stood up and held out her hands. "May I?" she asked as she continued to hold out her outstretched arms to Inca.

"Be my guest," he announced and went to hand her his kill.

"No, not that one, that one is beyond help, you will need to continue mutilating that one to remove the fur," she smirked. "I will have a fresh one that you have not touched," she stated as she pointed to a dead rabbit on the floor beside him.

Inca scooped up the rabbit and handed it to her with his knife. She laid the rabbit on her lap and grasped the hind legs in her hand. With one quick flick of the knife, she sliced from the top of the rabbit's hind legs along its middle up to its head. She handed Inca back his knife and held the rabbit up by its back legs and let it dangle in mid-air. With one hand tightly gripped on the rabbit, the other gave a quick yank. She peeled the rabbit out of its skin. She tossed the rabbit into the pot and threw the fur at Inca.

"Now, that is how you skin a rabbit Inca, what you are doing is butchering it and getting fragments of fur everywhere," she smiled very sweetly at her host.

Inca looked at her handy work and smiled. "You made that look easy, I can find them, kill them and eat them - but skinning them, that is the bit I struggle with. In my tribe, I went out to hunt and my mother took the kill and did what she needed to do. She would skin it; take what was needed then cook the rest. That's how it was. The hunters hunted and brought it back for the women of the tribe to sort it out. I did not get involved," he sighed. "That is how my tribe worked."

Altaira starred at Inca with astonishment, "Well, that is not how it worked within my tribe. Everyone, man, woman or child learned how to hunt, how to fight and how to look after one another. Everyone was equally capable of completing any task. No-one did anything differently. At a very young age, I remember it was my mother who taught me to hunt and fight. She was an unbelievable warrior." Altaira looked at Inca with tears in her eyes.

"How did she die? Was it in battle?" he asked.

"No!" she sniffed and looked upwards trying to contain her tears. "She went into battle with Mother Nature and lost her fight giving birth to my brother. From that moment on, I decided I would never have children. My father always called her his little woodpecker he was so distraught and to this day he has never gotten over her death." she confessed and wiped the teardrops from her eyes.

"Why did he call her his woodpecker?"

"My mother had the same strengths as a woodpecker. She always provided protection for me, especially when we hunted together. She would always tell me to pay attention to my environment. How to use whatever situation or trouble I was in to my advantage. I was never allowed to give up. I remember her telling me to use my head to overcome barriers and to think of a solution. If there was an obstacle; she always showed determination, nothing stopped her. She gave me balance and taught me not to just rush in but to stop and look to consider all the options available at that time. She never gave up on me. Even when she was dying, she told me one day I would fly the nest and take her place. But remember to fly back to my roots every so often." She looked at Inca who placed his hand on her shoulder.

Silence fell between the two, neither wanted to speak first. Lahnie broke the peace as she gave a low whimper and placed her paw on Altaira as if she felt her pain. Altaira ruffled the fur on the dog's head and scratched behind the dog's ear. Altaira sat deep in thought thinking of her mother "Little Woodpecker."

"I would like it if you can take me back to where you found me. I want to examine where Riend left me to die," she said sternly.

"What! You want to go back there. Are you mad?" Inca questioned her in astonishment. "Why? Why would anyone want to go back? You were taken prisoner, badly beaten to within an inch of your life and you want to go back! Why?" he repeated as he looked at her for an answer.

"You said you found me because Lahnie was chasing a woodpecker, do you not understand my mother was known as Little Woodpecker. I think she wants me to return. Return to the same place you and Lahnie found me. It was not an accident that you found me. Everything happens for a reason. You found me for a higher cause. She led you to me. You yourself said it; the woodpecker followed us here and it would not leave me alone. The woodpecker is here for a reason. I have no idea why, but I think I need to retrace my steps and return to where fate joined us." She looked at Inca who stood staring at her with an open mouth. "Please," she asked once more.

"Alright I will take you, but I want you to know I am not happy about it and I think you are crazy," he protested. "I want you to know I think this is a bad idea."

"Thank you, I understand how crazy this seems, but I want to get a better look at the castle, I need to see what I am up against." She advised, but she also wanted to know that she had not imagined the trap door that Riend pulled her through, she was sure she did not dream it. Besides, the room was stuffy and she longed for the fresh air to fill her lungs and to feel the breeze ruffle her hair.

"We will leave after we have eaten," Inca stated as he looked at Altaira who was about to disagree. "That is my only requirement. I will not leave until we have eaten. It is nearly ready and I am not wasting my kill." Inca stipulated and then fell silent waiting for Altaira to agree to his demand. "To waste what I have taken from this world would be disrespectful to Mother Nature..."

"Fine. We will eat and then you will show me," she interrupted with an air of impatience in her voice. She was not happy about waiting, she was eager to return and get a better view of the fortress that had her in bondage and inflicted its cruelties.

Inca ladled several spoonsful of rabbit stew on her plate. She gobbled each mouthful rapidly trying to hurry

Inca into leaving. Inca glanced at her scooping heaps of stew into her mouth and swallowing almost without chewing. He on the other hand chewed each mouthful slowly, much to Altaira's annoyance. Altaira scooped the last mouthful of stew, swallowed and put her bowl on the floor.

Altaira walked around the room looking at all the clutter of shields and spears. "You have enough here to equip a whole army," she uttered as she picked up shield after shield and examined each one in detail. "I like this one, it is very light."

She lined it up against a wooden beam and picked up a spear. She ran her fingers along the shaft and gently rolled it in her palm and lifted it above her head. With all the force she could muster, she launched the spear at the shield. The spear twisted through the air and the tip slightly dented the impregnable armour.

She smiled at Inca, "I like this shield even more now," she spoke in an amazed voice and held the shield up so Inca could see that the spear had not damaged it.

"If you like it so much you can have it, you can have anything here just choose what you like apart from the armour over there," he announced and pointed to a shield and spear hidden from view. "That is mine."

"I can choose anything I like from the whole room?"

"Yes, anything from this room and the rooms beyond and from any of the rooms below us." Inca moved a long piece of animal hide that covered an entrance to a long passageway.

Altaira spied many more rooms full of weapons. Her eyes darted from the stash of spears, to shields, knives, axes, bows and quivers full of arrows stacked in piles. Inca pointed to another room that was full of animal bones and feathers, long branches, bits of flint, string and piles of fur.

"Inca this is incredible, where did you get all this?"

"Well, when I left my tribe, I was so ashamed of not protecting them I wanted to hide away from the world," he informed her in a solemn voice.

"I dug out this room first and lived in here for a while. All I did for a long time was hunt, eat, dig and sleep. I didn't want anyone to know I was here, to hide my existence I dug a big pit to bury all the animal remains. That was fine for a while but as time went on the pit was full and I started to stack a few bits in the corner. Then, I started to make myself some weapons to help me hunt. I still had many other bits all over the place that was when I decided to dig out for some more room and before long, I started to make shields, spears axes and other bits. I thought I could make them to sell. It has rather taken over the place, I didn't realise how much I have. Help yourself to what you want, you can take anything." Inca smiled as he waved his hand at all the weapons at her disposal.

Altaira placed her hand on his chest and gently patted his muscular form.

"Thank you Inca."

Altaira slowly walked towards the mountain of axes all different sizes with many different designs. She picked a small axe with a single feather lashed to its handle she smiled and looked back at Inca.

"That is a hawk's feather," he announced

"Yes, I know," she smirked as she tossed it twice into the air and caught it with ease. "I like this one," she passed it to Inca to hold.

She walked towards the spears and pulled several out to examine and hold. A tight frown appeared on her brow. None of them felt right. Her frown got tighter with each one she held. At the very back of the hoard, she spotted an ornate wooden rod. She stretched forward, her fingertips could just touch it. She moved closer until her fingers firmly wrapped them self around the pole and she yanked it out from the heap. She enclosed her hand around it and held it in the air. Her frown disappeared; this was the spear she was searching for. Decorated throughout its wooden shaft were images of tiny feathers that spiralled from bottom to tip.

"This is beautiful Inca; did you carve this?"

"Yes, but I did not finish it, I was going to add something else to it. I was just not sure what else to put on it."

"Nothing, it is perfect the way it is, may I have this one Inca?" she asked.

"You can have anything Altaira, if you like it, it is yours," he answered as he watched her press her fingertips on the carved feathers.

"Thank you, I do like it."

"Is that your weapon of choice?" he asked

"No, not really, if I had a choice it would be a bow. I find a bow is quicker and more accurate. I can reach further and it is lighter to carry," Altaira answered and looked around the room for a bow.

Inca smiled and knew immediately what she wanted and pointed to the bows. One by one, she examined as she plucked and pulled on the strings. One by one she sorted them into different piles. She had a 'definitely not' pile, a 'maybe', and a pile that held a small singular bow that was at that moment the only bow which was the 'yes' pile. With each bow she examined she held an arrow and pulled back on the string to shoot. After much deliberation, she picked up the small bow and handed it to Inca along with another from the maybe pile.

"May I will have both of these?" she asked.

"You do know that this is a bow for a child," Inca stated as he looked at Altaira.

"Yes, I know it is. A small bow is ideal when shooting in tight spaces, I still use the bow my father made me when I was a child and it has never let me down. Now, I will need arrows that fit both," she smiled as Inca pointed to what she needed.

Inca placed all her chosen items on the floor. She really had a great knowledge of weapons and she had indeed chosen wisely. Altaira grabbed a large piece of animal hide, she bundled it together and threw it at Inca.

"We will need something to sleep in, that should be large enough for two," she looked at her supplies and nodded at Inca. "Ready?" she asked.

"What about food?"

"We can get food as we travel, you can hunt and I will skin and cook what we need," she smirked as she said the word 'skin'. Inca smiled too.

Altaira strapped her axe to her waist; she hooked both bows and a quiver of arrows around her shoulder. In one hand she held her shield and in the other her spear. Inca stared in awe of her. She truly was the mighty warrior of the northern tribes. She stood in all her glory. Inca was frozen to the spot; he could not take his eyes off her. Altaira looked magnificent he had never seen anything like her before. He smiled and walked over to the corner of the room to collect his weapons.

"We are ready," he announced and whistled to Lahnie to follow as they made their way out from Inca's concealed habitat.

Altaira held her head back and took a huge lung full of fresh air. High in the tree she heard the tunes of the woodpecker. Lahnie came bundling out and started to run around in circles chasing her own tail. Altaira giggled and Inca knelt and whistled again at Lahnie. She held her head down and slowly walked to Inca.

"You are not in trouble so do not sulk, you just need to calm down and walk nicely beside me," Inca informed the sulking beast whose tail was between her legs.

"That whistle was different from the first one you used just now. Do you use certain ones for each command?"

"Yes, Lahnie helps me hunt so sometimes she needs to act in a way to help me. I have many commands that she listens for. She is a very good hunting dog; she will even let me know when there is danger. So, if you see her lie down amongst the bushes and her ears are twitching, she is telling you to hide," he advised as he patted her.

"You are very clever; I will make sure I watch you," Altaira addressed the dog.

"I still think this is a bad idea, are you sure you want to do this?" Inca said through pressed lips and a knitted expression upon his brow.

"Yes. I need to see what I am up-against; I promise we will not go too close," she smiled at her friend and placed her hand on his arm to reassure him.

"You will need to stay very close to me as I have dug several pits to ensnare larger animals. It would be unfortunate to fall into one especially if it had a wolf or bear trapped in one."

"Well if I see a wolf or a bear trust me when I say I will have no hesitation to kill it," Altaira advised in very bitter tones.

Inca lead her through the tightly packed bushes and trees. Lahnie walked a few paces ahead of them, her nose to the ground smelling all the delightful smells that a dog loves and leaving her scent whenever she could.

"We are nearly there," Inca announced as he could see some flattened ferns and the imposing grey stoned fortress in the distance. He gulped; this was far too close for his liking he thought. Maybe they could look and then leave hopefully without being spotted. He had such a bad feeling about this but all the same he placed one foot in front of the other, he had agreed to take Altaira to the place where Lahnie had found her and he never went back on his word.

Lahnie suddenly stopped and hid amongst some bushes to lie down. She had heard voices. Inca immediately followed suit and pulled Altaira under cover where they lay flat on the ground. The voices were getting nearer. Inca spotted Lahnie lying very still, her ears were constantly twitching, listening to whatever was approaching. Inca let out a soft whistle to alert the dog that they were safely hidden and that she had done her job well.

"Hurry up, just grab her," the impatient voice ordered.

Altaira's heart sank as the darkness started to take hold. She started to shake as she recognised Riend's voice. She closed her eyes; all she could think about was how Riend had tortured her. Inca felt her body shake so he placed his arm around her waist and held her close.

"Shush," he faintly whispered in her ear to comfort her and squeezed her tighter offering his protection.

"She is missing, she is not here," the guard answered with a shaky voice.

"What!" Riend screamed as he marched over to the flattened ferns. "NO!" he bellowed. "She must be near; she could not have gotten far search the place."

Riend and the two guards unsheathed their swords and frantically began chopping down the shrubs and long grass in search of the missing Muto.

"Spread out," he ordered the two guards. "We must find her," Riend said in a high tone of panic.

He knew he must return to the castle with her. To return empty handed was not an option.

"Search! Do not just stand there we must find her," he shrilled as he put his hands up to his face in fear.

"She is gone sir," the guard repeated.

"She cannot be gone you have not looked properly. Keep looking."

Altaira smiled as she saw the anguish etched on his worried face and her shaking ceased; she was no longer afraid. He had shown her his weakness. Both remained in complete stillness, Altaira knew he could still find her, but she was stronger now, she had Inca, tribe hunter with her and she knew between them Riend with only two guards were no match for them.

Suddenly there was a rustle in the trees and Riend turned around to find both of his guards missing. All that remained on the ground where they had once stood was a single boot. Riend desperately shouted for his two guards. Silence filled the air. Riend started to mutter to himself talking gibberish about how the King would be furious.

"What if she is dead? Yes. That would get me out of trouble. She could be dead, yes. Right," he paused to think about what he was going to tell the King.

"I, I will say that it looks like a wild animal found her and has had a feast on her flesh and all that remained was a mangled body. Yes. I, I will tell the King that she is dead," he stuttered. "The guards are not here to tell the truth. The King cannot blame me after all he told me to let her go."

Riend muttered hysterically as he paced back and forth on the spot. Altaira stifled a giggle she was enjoying watching Riend panic. He re-sheathed his sword, took one last glance around and sauntered towards the castle to advise the King that Altaira was dead.

Lahnie remained silent, her ears still twitching. Inca was concerned she had not moved; danger remained and Lahnie sensed it. The missing guards worried Inca - what or who had taken them? A soft whistle travelled through the air and Lahnie immediately jumped up and soared through the trees. Inca patted Altaira on the shoulder.

"It is safe, I know that whistle you can get up." Inca smiled and trailed after Lahnie through the trees.

Altaira got to her feet and glanced through the trees to where both Inca and Lahnie had disappeared. With a tight grip on her shield and her axe in the other hand, she crept through the long grass in search of her two friends.

"Well we know what happened to the guards," Inca announced as Altaira approached. He pointed to the two guards who were both tied together at the base of a tree. Four men and a boy stepped forward.

The boy who was on the cusp of becoming a man stood in front of her. She instantly recognised his goofy grin.

"Dez!" she shouted

"Altaira! I have found you!" he shouted back with excitement and ran towards her. He scooped her up in his arms and held her tight. "I cannot believe it, you are alive, is it really you?" he choked back the tears, cupped her face in his hands and kissed her cheek. "I was so worried."

Both stood in a tight embrace, there was no need for words their love for each other ran deep. He held her close; she put her arms around his waist and rested her head on his chest. She could hear the sound of his heart racing. He kissed her once more on the top of her head.

Altaira grabbed his hand and faced Inca, "Inca I would like you to meet my brother Dez," she smiled. "What are you doing here?" she asked.

"We came looking for you. After you were taken, we thought you may have been in there?" Dez pointed to the imposing structure that dominated the skyline.

"I was and it is a place I do not want to go back to," she declared with a shudder.

"We need to leave. Staying here will just put us all in danger," Dez proclaimed with a worried face.

"What about them? We cannot leave them tied to a tree," Inca announced as he knelt down beside them and glared at their frightened faces.

"Please, we must return, you do not understand what will happen if we do not go back," one of the guards pleaded as he looked at both Inca and Altaira.

"Why do you want to go back? Surely, you do not want to be in there. No one in their right mind would volunteer to be in there," Altaira asked in a baffled tone as she stared at the guard with a large scar on his cheek.

"He has our families," he blurted out. "We are forced to fight for him if we do not then it will be our families that will suffer," the guard confessed as he beseeched Altaira to let them go.

"You look as though you have already suffered," Inca acknowledged as he pointed to the guards scared face.

"This," the guard pointed to his cheek. "This is nothing, I have seen far worse than this," Inca looked at Altaira who just nodded at the guard.

"What are your names?" Altaira enquired.

"I am Orace and this is Pax," the scarred guard answered.

"Let us help you," Dez offered.

"Thank you, but no. You do not understand. Whilst we do Riend and the King's bidding our families are safe. If we are not there, our families will be of no use to them and we have seen with our own eyes what Riend will do when a family has no purpose to his cause. I will do anything to keep my family alive and out of danger. The longer we both stay here the more our families are at risk. Please. Please just let us go!" he begged as his eyes began to swell with tears.

"Alright we will, but first I want some information," Inca exclaimed.

"Anything, what do you want to know," he stammered in an anxious tone.

Inca unclipped a beaded necklace from around his neck and handed it to him. They looked at Inca with puzzled expressions.

"I want to know if there is anyone in there that has the same necklace as this one. Have you seen a young boy wearing one like this? He should be with his mother."

"No."

"Are you sure?"

"There are so many young boys and their mothers in there it is difficult to be sure. Many have died from exhaustion. I have tried to step in and help them. I received this for my trouble," he pointed to his scar.

"If we let you go back, I want you to search amongst the prisoners for a boy wearing the same necklace and you both must help to set him and his mother free. If you can swear an oath to me that you will do this then I will let you go."

Both guards nodded their heads in agreement and let out a heavy sigh. Altaira flung her axe towards the two men. It twisted and whistled through the air. With a heavy thud, it ripped through the fibres of the rope and imbedded itself into the coarse bark, leaving the twine dangling in its jaws.

Both men staggered to their feet and brushed the dirt from their uniforms.

Altaira grabbed the guard by his wrist.

"Remember your oath to Inca, find the child wearing this necklace and get him and his mother to freedom. If you can do this Orace, I promise you I will do my best to help you both and your families."

Orace held the necklace out for Inca to reclaim.

"No keep it so you can recognise what you are seeking." The guard curled the necklace into the palm of his hand and slipped it inside his pocket for safekeeping.

Pax held Inca's arm and nodded his appreciation.

"We will do our best to find them and set them free. Please do not let *us* down either. Promise you will come back and help us. There are many who need your help," Pax advised.

"Please have faith in us, I cannot say when we will help you, but we will help. You will have to give us time." Altaira addressed both guards. "I promise," she whispered.

Both guards nodded their heads and smiled at the mighty warrior who stood in front of them. Pax cupped Altaira's hand in his then kissed and squeezed it.

"Thank you," he whispered and kissed her hand once more.

Both Orace and Pax turned to face the depressive fortress and sauntered back to their depressive lives.

~ Chapter Eleven ~

The Power Of Kindness

Etta sat in her chamber alone. She longed for conversation but who was there to talk to? No-one. Her sister Eudora? No. She was unable to see her. Nelly? No. She was far too busy looking after Eudora. Etta rested her aching head on her pillow and stared up at the ceiling feeling very low. She could hear the guards shouting at the prisoners who were busy being bullied into building yet another phase of the castle.

"As if it isn't large enough," she muttered through gritted teeth.

She walked over to the window and pressed her forehead up against the glass and let out a heavy sigh. She glanced out towards the trees. She knew her happiness was beyond the forest. Her heart ached. She had a secret. A secret that she had to carry alone. A secret that she could not disclose to anyone. She glanced at the black and silver cloak that was discarded in a heap on the floor and spat on it.

"I hate that bloody cloak, and I hate bloody living here." She moaned as she screwed the cloak into a ball and threw it across the room. Her heart was elsewhere, and she knew it. Loneliness engulfed her once more and she sat on the floor and cried.

"I have no-one," she wept as the tears ran down her cheeks.

Etta sat in silence and let her emotions flow out from within her. She sniffed and sobbed until she could no longer cry. When her tears had finally ended, she wiped their remnants from her face with her hands.

She stood and straightened her clothes. She felt her chamber walls were closing in on her. Her heart began to race and her chest became tight. Tighter and

tighter, sucking the oxygen from her lungs. She needed
to escape. She needed to get out.

Etta raced towards her door, swung it wide open
and hurried along the corridor without closing it behind
her. She just wanted to run. Without even knowing where
she was heading, she continued to rush through the
labyrinth of passageways that twisted and turned from
different levels of the castle. Her chest remained tight,
her breathing was hitched and her head began to spin.

Etta stopped. She glanced around. She was lost.
This was a part of the castle that she had never visited
before. It was dark, dirty and dimly lit with lanterns that
hung loosely on the wall. Etta wanted to go back to the
comforts of her chamber. But, she had never been to this
part of the castle and she wanted to go further. She was
curious as to what was down there. She suddenly felt
alive; her adrenaline urged her to go further. Slowly she
crept forward. She felt that this section of the castle was
forbidden; a part that she was not meant to see. It didn't

matter, she needed to know what was at the end of the dark walkway.

She took one of the lanterns from the wall and cautiously proceeded. Every so often Etta stopped and wondered if she was on a foolish quest. She maintained her course regardless of her doubts.

She could see an arched doorway ahead. No turning back now she thought. The air started to become stale and her eyes began to water. The disgusting stench hit her hard and she struggled to breathe. She lifted the skirt of her dress to cover her mouth and nose. She could not stay she needed to leave. But suddenly she heard Riend's dulcet tones.

"I want to know what happened to you? One minute you were both with me and the next you had both disappeared," he asked in an unusually calm manner.

Etta could just make out that Riend was talking to two of his guards.

"Well, Sir, we were right behind you when a bear grabbed me. Pax grabbed my leg and was also pulled along with me," Orace lied and Pax just nodded.

"Pax pulled my boot right off," Orace announced as he lifted his foot in the air for Riend to acknowledge.

"Erm, well yes I can see that. It must have been the same animal that had killed that girl. The one that the King wanted me to find. All I found was a discarded carcass and the remains of her clothes," Riend lied. He knew he needed to convince the guards that Altaira was dead, so they wouldn't snitch to the King.

Etta stood and wondered - who was the girl that the King wanted to find? Etta shivered as the cold air attacked her bare arms. She had had enough and decided to return to her chamber. Etta started to walk back the same way she had come and turned her back on the arched doorway.

"Lady Etta, what are you doing down here?" Riend's voice echoed from behind.

Etta stopped in her tracks. She had been caught. She knew she would have to make up some sort of a story.

"Well, erm I came looking for you actually and then thought I should not disturb you. I decided I would speak to you later," she mumbled trying to sound convincing. He was the last person she wanted to talk to. She knew she was lonely and hungered for conversation but to converse with him would be worse than torture. She imagined even the inmates would not desire to talk to him.

"Well well well, I cannot imagine what I can help you with Lady Etta," he sneered.

"Like I said, it is not important," Etta answered and hoped he would not question her further. She quickly turned to walk away.

"Well now that you have found me what did you want to talk to me about, please enlighten me," he ushered her through the arched doorway to the dungeons.

Etta panicked and looked around wondering what to say. She glanced at a small child in a cell huddled in a ball and her heart sank. She felt the bile rise in her throat and her eyes tear. This is no place for a child. She needed to do something; she could not return to her chamber knowing he was confined in that cell under the watchful eye of Riend.

"I will not beat around the bush, I need some help. I require a servant or a maid. As you know, Nelly is busy looking after the queen and I need someone to help me. I am looking for someone who is young, so I can teach them how I expect them to behave. I was hoping that you would allow me to choose one of the low life scums in your cells. And if they fail to impress me, I will just chuck them back down here to you," Etta announced in a carefree tone that she knew would excite the unsympathetic Riend.

"Lady Etta, you do surprise me. Of course I will help you. You can choose your victim from any one of the cells. And, I will personally give you a guided tour."

Etta didn't want a tour. She didn't want to see any more. She had seen enough and the smell was far too much for her to take.

"I do not have much time. Maybe you can give me a tour another day," she advised as she walked over to the first cell.

"What about that boy there," Etta pointed to the boy huddled on the floor.

Riend took the keys off the hook and swung open the heavy cell door. He grabbed the young boy by the hair and yanked him to his feet. Etta's stomach twisted with anger as she witnessed his harsh treatment. There was a whimper from the woman behind and the boy immediately clung to her. Riend yanked him out of her arms.

"You are coming with me," he bellowed and spat then pushed the woman to the ground.

The woman rushed to her feet and tried to grab the screaming boy who struggled under Riend's grip.

Riend slammed the iron door shut ignoring the screaming woman.

Riend still held the boy by the hair and slapped him across the face. Etta struggled to remain silent. She knew she had no choice if she wanted to help him.

"Shut up now, you little scum bag or you will be given to the Garchy, and if you don't shut up I will give you both to the Garchy," Riend proclaimed as he addressed the woman and the boy.

Etta looked at their distressed faces and knew that she could not take the boy without the woman.

"I want the woman too, I will need a maid as well and I think if either one of them displeases me you can give them to the Garchy. I think that will keep both in their place. To keep each other alive they will have to do exactly what I want," Etta looked at Riend who was smiling at Etta with approval. "I want them delivered to my chamber immediately. There will be no delay. I have plenty for them to do."

Riend nodded to a guard who dragged the woman out of the cell to be reunited with the boy whom she crushed in her arms and held him tight.

"I will need an escort back to my chamber as I do not have the foggiest how to find my way back. Also, you will need to remove the shackles off my servants. I do not want to hear the constant clanging," Etta ordered. Riend nodded as he held his arm out for Etta to take. He was going to escort her personally back himself, much to her dismay.

Slowly they proceeded through the passageways. Riend continued to talk all the way back. Etta did not hear a single word that he said. What was she going to do with the woman and the boy? She had no idea. All she knew was that she could not leave them there. Riend suddenly stopped, they were at her chamber.

"Thank you Riend."

"The pleasure was all mine, Lady Etta," Riend bowed and took her hand and kissed it then turned away back down towards the dungeons.

Etta stood mortified at what Riend had done and wiped her hand in her dress with disgust. What had she done? She knew this was going to be trouble.

The boy and the women stood outside looking at the floor. Etta glanced at them both, they were filthy and in need of a bath.

"In - both of you," she ordered.

Holding hands, they entered Etta's chamber. Neither of them attempted to raise their heads and continued to glare at their feet. Etta closed her chamber door. She walked over to her window, picked up her pitcher of water and poured out two goblets of the cold fluid. She held out the chalices for them to take. They held their gazes, both were afraid to look at her.

"Please take the water, you must be thirsty," she spoke in a gentle manner.

The young boy looked at the woman who nodded her approval. He grinned at her and gulped without stopping. Etta watched; she had never seen anyone drink so fast. The woman stopped to wait for the boy to finish.

Before she even took a sip from her own goblet, she passed it to the boy.

"No, it's alright, that is yours. I have more if he wants another one." Etta held the pitcher out towards them ready to refill their goblets. The woman smiled and began to drink.

"I want you both to know that whilst you are serving me, no harm will come to you."

"You said you are going to give us to the Garchy if we disappoint you," The woman reminded her.

"Oh yes I did, didn't I. I must confess I have no idea what a Garchy is," Etta admitted. "What is a Garchy?" she asked.

"A Garchy is a night time scavenger, a foul creature that tortures its prey then eats them," the woman advised as the young boy buried his head into her side.

"Argh, how terrifying," Etta announced. She knelt beside the young boy and grabbed his hand.

"I promise I will not give you to the Garchy. If you displease me, I will just tell you and then you can put it right. You are both safe with me. I am not going to hurt you and I am not going to return you to the dungeons either," Etta promised and smiled at the pair. "What are your names?" she asked.

"I am Gaho and this is my son Shilah," the woman advised as she ruffled the boy's hair.

"It is very nice to meet you both. I am the Queen's sister. I would like you to call me Lady Etta. I would also like you both to have a bath. I can still smell the dungeon on you. Over there is a bath-tub. I will get some hot water and arrange for you to have some clean clothes and have some food brought up for you. I will be back soon I will be as quick as I can," she announced.

Etta walked over to the window and opened it wide to rid the room of the smell that radiated off the mother and son. She needed to leave and plan for the pair and left Gaho and Shilah standing alone in her chamber.

Moments later two women entered Etta's room holding a bucket in each hand. They carefully poured the hot water into the bath. Shilah had never seen a bathtub before and was not sure why they were filing it up with water. He watched as they poured a scented fragrance into the steaming mass. The bath was ready.

Gaho and Shilah stood and viewed the container that was full of water. Steam slowly emanated from the tub. It began to rise and fill the room. Neither knew its purpose.

Etta opened the door and was greeted with a mixture of scented bath oils and the rancid smell of her two servants.

"Ah they have filled it for you. I will give you some privacy whilst you both bathe," she said with a soft look in her eyes.

"Lady Etta, why is this filled with hot water?" Gaho queried. "What is it for?" she repeated as she looked at Etta who smiled at her.

Etta swallowed hard at her innocence. It took her by surprise. "I would like it very much if you got into the water and washed yourself. You are both very dirty and I can still smell the dungeon on you. I want you to rid yourselves of all connection to that dungeon. I want you to start by washing yourselves. Then, I would like it if you both put on some clean clothes," Etta softly spoke. "I have managed to get some clothes for you. Everything you need is here in your room on your beds waiting for you," Etta pointed to the adjacent room. "That is where you will both sleep," she smiled.

Gaho started to weep as she looked at the sincerity in Etta's face.

"Thank you, we have not had much kindness shown to us for a while," she squeaked as she fought back the tears.

Shilah held onto his mother as she tried to retain her emotions and he buried his face into her trying to comfort her. She held her son close, they were safe. She would no longer have to watch her son sleep on the cold, cell floor, huddled in a ball to keep warm. They would no longer have to endure the cruelties of Riend or the brutalities of the dungeons. Gaho smiled - she had forgotten what it was like to be a human. She kissed her son's head.

"Again, thank you Lady Etta, for your kindness," she whispered.

Etta nodded; she felt a warm glow bursting inside her. She now had someone who she could look after. In time they will learn to look after her. She would no longer be alone.

~ Chapter Twelve ~

The Path Of Despair

The majestic mountains graced the skylines with their jagged peaks that stretched towards the heavens. Ursus and Nubilus rode side by side towards the northern tribes to seek Altaira. The horses waded through the river; sending fragments of sediment up to the surface in their wake. Nubilus's horse carefully climbed the muddy riverbank. Its hooves slipped as it struggled to get through the slippery terrain.

"Yah," Nubilus shouted as he dug his heels into the horse's belly. "Come on you can do this," Nubilus coaxed as he leant over and patted the horse's neck.

"Yah," he shouted again.

The horse grunted, lowered his head and with all its strength dug his hooves in and slowly climbed out onto flat land.

Nubilus once again patted the horse and looked down for Ursus. He thought Ursus was behind him, but he was nowhere to be seen. Fear suddenly engulfed him. What if the current had taken him? He should have checked that Ursus had made it to the other side with him. What if his horse refused to climb the slope and they both drifted down stream? He jumped off his horse and slid feet first back down towards the water's edge. There was only one set of hooves. Ursus had not made it to the edge. He tried to look down the river, but it was flowing far too fast for him to enter and check.

"Ursus!" Nubilus screamed as panic began to consume him.

"What?" a puzzled voice answered. "Why are you down there?" Ursus asked from the top of the bank.

"What do you mean? Why am I down here? I was looking for you! You were not with me. I thought you had drowned," he shouted with relief in his voice. "How did you get up there?"

"Well, I witnessed your horse struggling. I thought you were either brave or stupid to even risk getting out from there; especially when the land is completely flat further down behind that tree," Ursus replied in a smug tone as he pointed. Ursus sniggered to himself as he saw the exasperation on Nubilus's face.

Nubilus placed his hands on his thighs and bent forward suddenly laughing.

"You mean, you watched me struggle when you knew it was much easier further downstream," Nubilus continued to laugh at his own foolishness.

"Yep," Ursus continued to chuckle.

Ursus sat on his horse and waited for Nubilus to join him. He saw a mass of black hair and a man knee high in mud.

"Ah, yes well I forgot to tell you - it is extremely muddy from where the river has burst its banks," Ursus smirked as he looked at Nubilus walking towards him.

"You don't say," Nubilus replied as he pinched the sodden clothes off his skin.

"Trust me when I say this Ursus, I will have my revenge. Just you wait and see. When you least expect it. Wham! I will strike," he smiled in a playful manner. "You have started something now."

Nubilus mounted his horse and looked at Ursus who was still smiling at him.

"After you Ursus," Nubilus smirked.

Ursus jabbed his heels into the horse and galloped. Nubilus copied and was soon at his side. Together they rode through the long grass and were at the foot of the hills. They knew that time was against them. They wanted to make it through the hills before nightfall. This was the most treacherous part of their travels. The canyons showed no mercy to travellers using its paths.

Both men jumped off their horses. It would be far easier to walk and guide the beasts through than to ride them. Slowly they continued holding the horses steady as they proceeded along the narrow tracks. They hoped and prayed that neither horse bolted or refused.

"You will have to be extra careful up here Ursus, the track is so narrow. I am not too sure if we can pass," Nubilus exclaimed with doubt in his voice.

Nubilus stopped and looked ahead at the width, then looked at the drop. His heart was thumping hard. Suddenly, his horse's nose nudged him in the back. It wanted to go on. Nubilus realised they had no choice but to press on further. There was no way the horses had enough room to turn around and return. He took a large breath and slowly placed one foot in front of the other.

"Ursus, you will need to stay in tight, away from the cliff edge. The path is very gritty and is crumbling away," Nubilus announced with concern etched in his voice.

Slowly they persevered, man and beast working together. Not a single sound was heard from the horses. It was as if they were concentrating too. Each time

Nubilus stopped the horse nudged him to go further and further into the belly of the mountains.

"Ursus, are you still with me?" Nubilus shouted.

"Yes, where did you think I was?" he answered.

"Well, I thought if you see another way that is easier, I would like you to share it with me this time," he stated.

"There is an easier way, but I thought you knew what you were doing," Ursus admitted.

"Why didn't you tell me before we got onto this ledge?"

"Because I am not sure where it begins. I have always relied on Altaira to lead the way through to the northern tribes," he confessed.

"So, you don't know the easier route?"

"No, I only know that there is an easier route, but I do not know how to get there by using that route," Ursus advised.

"So, you only know how to get to the northern tribes by going along the mountain tracks?"

"No, I am following you Nubilus. I thought you knew the way."

"What? I don't know where I am going. I thought you said we had to follow the trail through the mountains. You mean, we are risking our lives and we may not be going in the right direction," Nubilus replied through gritted teeth.

"I am joking Nubilus, we are going the right way," Ursus chuckled for the second time in the day at Nubilus's expense.

"Going the right way, you are going the right way of me pushing you off the cliff," Nubilus muttered under his breath.

The mountain path began to get wider but Nubilus stopped.

"Why are we stopping?" Ursus enquired.

"There are two paths. I am not sure which one to take. Left or Right. What one do you think Ursus?" Nubilus looked over his shoulder waiting for Ursus's advice.

"Erm, I am not sure. Try the right," he answered.

Nubilus grabbed the rope on his horse and walked towards the path on their right. Suddenly the horse stopped and refused to follow. It began to walk towards the left and tried to pull Nubilus to follow.

"Come on. We are going this way," Nubilus tried to pull the horse but it was far too strong. It was adamant that he was not going down the path on the right. "All right have it your way, we will take the path on the left," Nubilus reasoned with the stubborn horse.

The track was much wider and it seemed as if it was leading them off the mountainside. Through the tight gorge with the mountain walls either side of them the horse lead them further. Nubilus sniffed the air and halted abruptly. Ursus rode up beside him.

"What is it Nubilus?" he asked as he looked at his ashen face.

"I am not sure. There is a strange smell.... Something is not right. We need to be careful Ursus," Nubilus whispered as he reached for his bow.

"I think we should tie the horses up and proceed on foot. That way we can be quieter. If there is nothing to worry about, we can come back and get the horses," Ursus instructed.

"I can smell blood! Ursus something is seriously wrong," Nubilus grabbed his arm. "We have to check. It could be Altaira."

"And we will, but we need to be silent, not a single noise."

Both men cautiously crawled on the floor. Ahead they saw a hut. They were on the edge of a village. Nubilus wrinkled his nose; the pungent aroma of blood began to get stronger. He could also smell a sinister scent of smoke.

Ursus spotted it first and quickly got to his feet. Before him on the floor was the battered body of a young child laying in a pool of blood that had absorbed into the soil. He leant over the child and felt her cold flesh. She had been dead for a while.

The shocking scene greeted them both as they waded through a sea of carnage. Nubilus gripped Ursus's arm and groaned at the grim sight. Bodies everywhere, he looked at Ursus who had tears in his eyes. He was standing beside a young mother who still had her baby in her arms. Both dead. This left a bitter taste in his mouth. She had been bludgeoned to death. Ursus looked away with bleary eyes. Bodies grouped together in an act to protect one another.

Beads scattered in the mud. Necklaces half finished. Dyed fabrics strewn on the floor. Evidence of a village once thriving. Some of the buildings were burnt to the ground. With heavy hearts they searched for survivors.

"I don't see any of the tribal hunters. They are not amongst the dead," Nubilus announced with an enormous emptiness in his voice as he looked at the vast sight of slaughtered bodies. "Do you think they were captured?"

"Perhaps."

"This is madness. Who do you think did this Ursus?" Nubilus asked in a dumbfounded voice.

"Whoever it was I don't think they were invited," Ursus grunted. "I didn't want to believe it, but it seems that what Dak said was true. He told us there had been many raids. But who? Who is doing this? This attack was engineered to create maximum impact. It seems that they had no chance. Like you have just said Nubilus, where are their hunters? Why did they not protect them? It looks like they were ambushed."

Ursus watched as Nubilus picked up and carried the dead bodies. One by one, he placed them together in a line. He blinked furiously at the grim sight of all the deceased.

"Ursus, have you noticed there are no boys among the dead. I can see old men, but no boys and no hunters."

"What! None?"

"No, not a single one," Nubilus confirmed. "Don't you think it is curious that there are no hunters or boys?"

"I must admit I have no answer for you Nubilus. I am completely stunned. Not one? are you sure?"

Nubilus nodded his head to confirm and began to pick up the beads and dyed fabric.

"Look at this Nubilus." Ursus shouted.

Nubilus ran over to him and Ursus pointed to a group of scratches on the side of the hut.

"Garchy," they both said in unison.

"I don't think it was Garchy," Nubilus said as he took a sideway glance at the victims. "Since when have Garchy used weapons? Most of these have been killed by a tool of some sort. Also, if it was Garchy they would not have burned some of the huts. That is not their style. Kill yes. Burn the huts, no. But most of all leave the dead bodies, never. They never leave their prey. Whoever did this wanted the bodies to remain here," Nubilus proclaimed.

"To make a statement. As a sign of power. To create a sense of fear," Ursus concurred.

"Yes. There is only one person who would do this and that is King Ignatus," Nubilus spat. "I am not going to allow him to have that satisfaction. I will take away that sign of power. I will burn the bodies and all the evidence. There will be no sign of his power left here." Nubilus protested as he continued to gather all the beads and fabrics in his arms and ceremoniously positioned them on the dead.

Ursus nodded with agreement and started to make a small fire. He watched as Nubilus gathered all the evidence. Slowly Nubilus cleared all existence of the villagers. He wrapped a piece of fabric around several twigs and one by one he placed them on top of the deceased.

"Earth mother please help guide these brothers and sisters of mine and help them find peace," Nubilus whispered. "I will burn the remaining huts in the morning at first light."

Darkness began to consume the land. Ursus looked up to the stars that shone in the black sky. He took a moment and thought of the barbaric attack. He could hear Nubilus snoring. He wanted nothing more but to join his slumber. He was afraid. For the first time he had to admit, he was afraid. Altaira was missing. She was the true warrior of the north. Without her protection, the northern tribes were doomed. How many more villages have been attacked? How many more times can they witness the brutality towards their people?

He continued to stare at the stars and whispered.

"Earth Mother help! Never has the earth been in greater need of human compassion. Help guide us to put things right."

Ursus closed his eyes. Tomorrow was another day. They would continue to another northern tribe until they have found Altaira. They would never give up.

~ Chapter Thirteen ~

Free As A Bird

The hunters sat in a circle cross-legged sharing their tribal stories and laughing at each other's misfortunes. Altaira sat and listened to Inca and another hunter sniggering. Each gave their own account of the same tale.

"Do you know each other?" Altaira asked.

"Yes, I am Little Spot. But most just call me Spot, we are from the same tribe," he advised as he pointed to himself and Inca.

"Are you one of the tribe's hunters?" she queried

"Yes, I was with Inca when we were tricked into chasing the Garchy away from our tribe," he spoke in a solemn voice and looked at the floor in shame.

259

"Do you have a family Spot? Do you think they are in the castle with Inca's family? Is that why you are here?" Altaira probed. She took one look at his face and wished she had not asked if he had a family. His crest fallen face sank with sadness.

"No, my family are not in there. I have lost all my family. My wife, mother, father and two sisters were amongst the dead," his voice was barely audible. "My wife was pregnant. When I did return to the camp, I found her on the floor smothered in blood. She had gone into labour but the assault on her body was too much. She was badly beaten. She died shortly after giving birth. I held them both in my arms." Spot choked and fought back his tears as they ran down his gloomy face. "My beautiful wife was dead."

Dez looked at Altaira, bit his bottom lip and walked away. Altaira knew what he was thinking. Their mother had died in childbirth too and Dez had always blamed himself.

"My sweet innocent daughter died soon after," Spot sniffed and wiped his tears. "My whole world collapsed around me. Everyone that I had ever loved was gone. Gone forever."

The atmosphere plummeted and silence resonated in the air, even Lahnie bowed her head and whined.

"I am so sorry Spot, I didn't mean to pry. I just thought that, as you were here it must be to find your family."

"No, it is all right I can see why you thought that. I met Dez and he shared his food with me. I told him I would help him find you. Then we met some more hunters and we soon became five."

"Spot? Why are you called Spot?" Altaira asked as she tried to lighten the mood

Inca and Spot laughed. The mood lightened instantly. "I am called Little Spot because when I was born, I had a black spot on…. Well I have a spot on my…"

"On his backside," Inca interjected and laughed as Spot scornfully glanced at him.

"Yes, thank you Inca," Spot glared at him.

"Do you really. Can I see it?" Dez asked in a curious tone.

"Most certainly not Dez," Altaira shouted. And glanced at Inca who chuckled at her reaction.

Lahnie jumped and barked at Dez who tried his hardest to ignore her. He was far too busy watching Altaira who constantly looked over her shoulder.

"Are you all right Altaira? What is the matter?" Dez asked as Inca stood beside him.

"I need to do something. Please don't ask me what it is but I need to check something, and I need to do it alone."

Both Dez and Inca nodded. They promised not to ask her or interfere, but that didn't stop them both from worrying or wondering what it was she so desperately needed to do.

Altaira walked back through the trees and stopped beside the flattened ferns. Her mood plummeted as she saw scarlet blood stains splattered on the bed of squashed ferns. Her blood. Her whole body stiffened with anxiety as she wrestled with the horrors raging inside her. She stood for some time and stifled a cry. She watched as the surrounding ferns around her danced and swayed with the wind.

"Quiet the mind and my soul will speak," she whispered. Altaira slowly breathed in and out. She closed her eyes and slowly felt her body sway in time with them. Peace and tranquillity started to consume her and drive away her fears.

Her whole body tingled as she tilted her head back and lifted her arms out wide beside her. She opened her eyes and they were ablaze with an emerald glow. Within an instant Altaira lifted and took flight to the sky. Further up through the trees and above the canopy she flew.

Altaira fluttered her strong wings as she climbed to a great height. She had achieved it; her powers had returned. How she had forgotten the feeling of freedom as she twisted then hovered as she became mistress of the heavens. With little effort, she majestically circled silently high in the air; then gloriously glided on a down draft as the wind took her. Her bluish-grey plumage twinkled as the sun's rays ran along her magnificent wingspan. She truly was a noble bird. A bird sent from the heavens.

She had almost forgotten the reason why she had convinced Inca to take her back; to return to the place where fate had joined them. To where both he and Lahnie had found her. Her plan was to survey the castle and the area that surrounded it. She had after all made a promise to Inca; she promised to help find his family. Inca was convinced that they were in the jaws of the formidable castle and in the clutches of the malevolent King and his chief guard. Altaira silently sailed a little closer and discovered the true size of the daunting castle. It was enormous even from the height she flew. She knew it was going to be a hard task. She admitted, one day they would need to storm the impregnable fortress. She had only hoped it had a weakness.

"The weakness of the enemy makes our strength," Altaira thought. She quickly identified she would have to discover it. If indeed it had such a weakness.

She counted eight enormous towers, each as a pair. In total sixteen foreboding towers and a large menacing gatehouse. She looked at the solid stoned curtain wall; it must be at least twenty-feet wide. An impressive granite Keep stood alone in the middle. It too looked as if it had its own formidable gatehouse. Six tall towers with arrow slits aiding its protection. It was a fortress within a fortress. She knew it would not be easy, but she had made a promise to help free the vulnerable inside.

"Those who allow oppression share the crime," Altaira told herself. She would find a way to uphold her promises. She slowly flew around the edge of the castle and surveyed the area surrounding the colossal stone structure. She was looking for a disturbance in the appearance of the ground. Her hope was to spy the position of the trap door. The same trapdoor that she believed Riend had used on the night he dumped her to die. If she could locate it, that would be the castle's weakness. Disappointment filled Altaira; she could not see any sign of it. It was either well concealed from view or she had been mistaken. She had hoped it was the latter. She was sure she did not imagine it.

She took one more turn in the clear cerulean sky and vocalised a high plaintive whistle of satisfaction. She pressed her wings tight to her side, dived and rapidly descended towards the ground, and softly landed on the forest floor. She scraped her sharp talons into the soil. It had been such a long time she had felt the soil between her claws. She stretched her wings, gave her long tail a gentle shake and folded her large wingspan tightly to her side. She twisted her neck; her curved beak plucked a loose feather and then she discarded it on the floor.

Altaira glowed with delight inside. She swiftly changed back to her human form, she didn't want to let anyone know she was indeed a Muto. She picked up her discarded feather and beamed. She felt as if she had been reborn, she felt alive. She gave a loud whistle through the trees and Lahnie came bounding through the long grass towards her. She knelt, patted the fury animal, and followed Lahnie back to her master.

Altaira ran the feather across Dez's chin and they both smiled. Dez now understood why Altaira needed to be alone and how import this was to her. He squeezed Altaira's hand as he shared in her delight of taking flight once again. It had been such a long time since his sister soared high in the sky. Her emerald eyes twinkled and she gave him a mischievous wink. The northern warrior was getting much stronger which pleased him greatly.

"Hey that is a hawk's feather, where did you get that?" Inca enquired.

"I found it on the floor," Altaira acknowledged as she knowingly glanced at Dez who gave her a goofy smile.

"You can have it if you want it. I have quite a collection of hawk's feathers. I really don't mind if you want it," Altaira looked a Dez and they both smiled.

"I would love to have it. Just look at the colours they are beautiful. I bet the hawk whose feather this belongs to is truly magnificent to look at," Inca announced.

"Yes, truly magnificent," Dez agreed as he folded Altaira in a brotherly embrace and squeezed her tight. "Truly magnificent. Absolutely the best," he whispered to Altaira.

"You are biased," she whispered back.

"Yes, I am, but it doesn't mean I do not speak the truth," Dez whispered in return

The other hunters looked at the hawk's feather in awe and jealously. Spot even offered his knife for it, but Inca had no intention of parting with it.

"I will give you a gift," Spot announced.

"No, I do not want you to give me a gift. I know in return you will ask for the feather and I am not going to part with it," Inca advised.

"But it is custom when someone offers you a gift Inca you accept that gift and give me a gift in return of my choosing. That is the way of our tribe," Spot spoke once more.

"The way of our tribe? What tribe? We have no tribe. *We* are what is left of our tribe Spot. I don't have to trade. I do not want your gift of a knife. I already have a knife. And if I did not, I still would not accept your gift," Inca once again informed him.

Altaira looked at her brother who opened his arms and let her go. Both nodded to each other they could sense trouble. Lahnie laid on the floor and looked up at Altaira. Altaira quickly hid behind Dez and crouched amongst the foliage. She quickly returned and marched over to the two men.

"Stop it. Stop it, now," Altaira bellowed at them.

Both immediately ceased their bickering and glanced at Altaira.

"If I was aware of what nonsense a single feather would cause I would have left it where I found it. But as it happens there were more than one feather on the ground that I picked up," Altaira announced in a stern voice.

Clutched between her forefinger and thumb she held out another feather. It too was a bluish-grey.

"Now stop your squabbling. It is only a bloody feather. Here take it," she said through pressed lips.

The hunter stared at her and then at the feather. He realised just how foolish he had been.

"I said take it," she spoke with authority.

"Thank you. I have always wanted a hawk's feather," he admitted as he ran the tip of his finger up the shaft of the feather feeling its silkiness and gave a wide grin as he nodded his appreciation to Altaira.

Altaira walked over to Inca and Spot, she sat cross-legged beside them. "Spot, do you think there are any more hunters out there who have no tribe to return to?" She asked in wonder, she uncrossed her legs, wrapped her arms around them as she brought them up to her chest.

"Erm, well, yes. I suppose there are quite a few who like Inca and me are ashamed and have gone in to hiding. Why?"

"I would like to find the other hunters who are hiding. I promised those two guards I would help them. I also promised Inca I would help to find his family," Altaira announced as she dug her heels in the dirt and scraped them back and forth to create a deep crevice in the friable loam. "For me to do what I have promised, I will need help. It is going to be very difficult when it is only Dez, Inca and me. If others would join us then perhaps, we can help them," Altaira mentioned in a soft tone. "Do you think you will be able to help us Spot?" she asked.

"Help you! Help you, of course I will," Spot confirmed.

"Thank you," Altaira beamed with a cheerful smile. "We will need to move soon; before Riend returns with more men or before they are on our trail."

The wind started to swirl and launched the fallen leaves into the air. All spinning and twisting as they elevated higher off the floor. The branches began to dance and sway. The gusts of wind toiled and tormented the tiny woodpecker that clung to the branches unwilling to fly off.

Spot traipsed over to where the other hunters were resting.

"Altaira has asked if we can help track the other hunters and try to persuade them to join us. Now I am prepared to do this on my own, but I would prefer if I had company. I am asking if anyone wants to join me," Spot requested and hoped they would indeed join him on his given quest.

"There are so many hunters scattered all over, it will not be an easy task," one of the hunters advised.

"I know it will be difficult to find them but find them we must and find them we shall. We are out-numbered against the King and all his guards. You heard what the guards told Altaira, they only fight for the King because he has their families. You heard what Altaira promised them. She is not able to fulfil that promise unless we have more warriors. Some of you also have family missing and the chances are they are in there," Spot pointed to the granite structure that imposed itself on the skyline.

"You know as I do there is no prospect of freeing them today; if we did charge it is very likely we may be either be captured or even killed. And that would be of no use to your families," Spot looked at the hunters and waited for Enapay, Keme and Niyal to answer.

Keme stood and outstretched his arm and clasped Spot's shoulder. "I will help you brother. It would be foolish to storm the castle today. You are right we need to be strong before we attack. Our numbers are weak," he nodded.

"Thank you."

"I will also join you and help build our numbers," Enapay confirmed as he placed his hand on Spot's other shoulder.

273

"Me too. When do we leave?" Niyal asked as he stood and grabbed his axe, bow and quiver.

Spot looked at his fellow hunters and smiled at the loyalty. "We will need to leave soon. Altaira believes Riend may return with reinforcements."

"We will challenge him if we have to," Enapay advised in a callous tone.

"That is why we need to leave now," Altaira announced as she, Inca and Dez strutted beside them.

"We have all agreed to come with you and seek out the other hunters," Spot smiled at them.

"We are not going with you." Altaira informed them as Dez quickly glanced at his sister.

"Not going with them... Why?" Dez queried in a surprising tone.

"We need to warn the other tribes, so they don't fall into the same trap as we have," Altaira spoke with authority and held her brother's arm. "I would like you to gather as many hunters as you can and meet me at the boarder of the northern mountains. Head towards the northern tribes and we will meet you there. Tell them I sent you and I told you to say the word 'Little Woodpecker,' they will understand what it means."

"Altaira, there are no northern tribes," Dez announced in a nervous voice.

"What!... How! .... When?" Altaira blurted out in anguish.

"They have been annihilated Altaira, I thought you were aware of that," Dez replied as he looked at Altaira's distressed face.

"No... No, I cannot believe it Dez. Why have you only informed me of this now?" Altaira asked as she collapsed on her knees and cried. "Everyone, Dez?"

"Not everyone but yes most have been killed or taken prisoner. I'm sorry I thought you knew," Dez looked solemnly at his sister and watched as her distraught body shook.

"ARGHHH!" Altaira screamed at the top of her voice, she clenched her fist tight and punched the floor. "ARGHHH!" she once again screamed and held her head in her hands and sobbed. "What about father?" she stuttered through her sobs.

Silence fell. Dez walked away and looked up towards the heavens. His heart raced, and his legs became weak.

"Dez, what about father?" she enquired again as her voice trailed into a whisper.

Dez looked at his sister and his silence answered her question. Altaira held her breath and she placed her hand over her mouth to stifle her wail. The grief was too much for her to accept. She collapsed to her knees. She felt suffocated as she struggled to swallow and breathe. The pain radiated through her chest and pierced her with every heartbeat. Her heart was numb with grief, and her head hung low on her chest. Her shoulders shook through each sob.

Dez rushed towards her, he picked her up into his arms and held her shaking frame.

"I'm sorry, I'm so, so, sorry Altaira. I thought you knew."

"No, no, no," Altaira wailed. "I should have been there, I should have protected them. I should not have been so stupid to get myself captured. This is all my fault," Altaira ranted in anger and continued to sob into her hands.

Spot strolled slowly over to Altaira and knelt beside her. He grabbed both of her hands, pulled them off her face and held them in his. He gently squeezed them.

"We cannot change the past, but we have a chance to write the future. We need to gather the other hunters and you need to warn the other tribes. That is what we must do now," Spot looked at Altaira and smiled at her as he helped her to her feet. "I know how you feel. I felt responsible for the death of all my family. I felt responsible for not protecting my tribe too. I blamed myself and it hurts. But I am not to blame. You are not to blame. The King and his regime are to blame and together we need to put a stop to it. You are the one amongst us that can put a stop to it. But you know this already, don't you? You need to free those trapped inside that castle,"

Spot pointed to the dark structure. "You need to stop the persecution of our tribes and we will help you." He wiped the tears off her face with his thumb and whispered, "We will help you."

Altaira nodded and gave a huge sniff as she looked at the loyal faces staring at her.

"You are right Spot, as much as my heart aches and I want to scream with the pain that I feel, I know you are right. I want you to gather as many hunters as you can. We will warn the other tribes."

She placed her hand against her mouth to stifle another cry. Her heart was ready to burst with pain as she thought of her devoted father.

"When you have gathered as many as you can we will meet you at the foot of the northern mountains," Altaira ordered. "I swear on the memory of my father I will have justice; justice for him, justice for all of those who have suffered at the hand of the King and justice for our people who are suffering under him," Altaira promised in a stern steadfast voice. She grabbed Spot's hand. "Go, and may the spirits be with you and guide you to do right."

Altaira watched as she saw Spot, Enapay, Niyal and Keme disappear through the long grass, through the forest fauna. They went in search of fellow hunters.

Dez held his sister's hand, pulled her into a hug and held her tight. No words could explain the emotion they both felt. They stood for a while and held each other tight, both feeling each other's pain. Altaira rested her head on his shoulder. She took a deep breath, closed her swollen eyes and lost herself in her brother's embrace.

Altaira pulled away and looked at both Dez and Inca. She wiped her enflamed eyes; she knew they needed to leave. They needed to warn the other tribes. With her arm wrapped around the waist of her brother, the trio traipsed through the trees to the next tribe armed with knowledge to save them.

~ Chapter Fourteen ~

A New Friendship

Gaho sat on the edge of the bed, her small frame sank into the soft mattress as she watched Shilah slumber peacefully. She gently stroked the hair off the boy's forehead and pulled the covers up towards his chin. She could not help but smile as a warm glow travelled through her; filling her soul with hope. They were safe, and no longer a witness to the vehemence of Riend. No longer would they have to sleep amongst the rats or on the cold stone floor or in an overcrowded cell. No longer would they have to endure the damp air or fight for their share of the meagre meals that the guards threw at them. No longer would they be, just another number.

Gaho liked Etta, she was their saviour and she decided to make sure that she and Shilah would do everything possible to please her.

She glanced once more at the small sleeping child that was dwarfed in the oversized bed. His small head sank into the pillow; the covers were pulled up to his chest and tucked underneath his chin. He looked so fragile; he was after all still a young boy. A young boy that has had to endure such suffering far more than any child should ever deserve. But, a boy never the less.

Just a little more sleep she thought as she glanced at the exhausted child. This was the first time in a long while Shilah had slept all night. She did not have the heart to wake him. But, wake him she must.

She sat in silence… She watched the rise and fall of his chest underneath the heavy covers. Suddenly her solitude was broken with a gentle knock on the door that startled her and made her jump to her feet in panic.

"Hello," Gaho answered in a shaky voice.

Etta peered her head around the door and greeted Gaho with an enormous smile.

"Hello to you Gaho, how did you sleep?" Etta asked. "I can see someone has had a good night sleep." Etta smirked as she looked at the unconscious child slumbering.

"We slept very well, it has been such a long time I had forgotten what it was like to sleep on such a soft surface. I was tempted to put the covers on the floor and sleep down there," Gaho pointed to the space on the floor beside the bed. "But I realised I don't need to do that anymore. Shilah is exhausted it has been a couple of days since we had any sleep. If possible Lady Etta can he have just a little more," Gaho pleaded.

"Of course he can, you both can. I only came in today to check you had a good sleep."

"Thank you," Gaho acknowledged as tears began to flow.

Etta put her arms around the woman and gave her a warm embrace. Gaho wept uncontrollably, her body shook as she sobbed with relief - at last she felt safe.

"How long have you both been down in the dungeons?" Etta asked as she grabbed a jug of water, dipped the corner of a handkerchief in and dabbed the tears off Gaho's face.

"I am not sure. Shilah was much smaller when we first got there. He has grown about this much," Gaho raised her hands and parted them to show the child's growth rate.

"What did you both do in the dungeons?"

"We did many things. The guards would line all the boys up together and march them out of the castle's grounds. Shilah was forced to crawl into caves in search of a yellow rock. They were not allowed to come back out unless they found it. Shilah has spent many days underground digging for this," she whimpered and put her hand up to her mouth to stifle a cry.

"What about you Gaho? What did you have to do?"

Gaho glanced at the floor then at her child to check he was still sleeping.

"I…" she paused. Gaho wondered how much she should tell her. Could she trust Etta? She looked at Etta's innocent face as it eagerly waited for her to answer. Her heart raced. She looked upwards and took a deep breath as she tried to stop the tears from falling.

"I, like all the other women was told to make sure the men were happy," she put her hands swiftly to her face. Her eyes began to fill and once again, tracks of salty residue took residence upon her face.

"If we failed or refused, Riend would beat us. Even some of the men didn't want us. They knew what they were doing was not right, but they had no choice either. Riend would tell them if they didn't, he would use their wives or daughters instead." Gaho clutched her dress and pulled it tight then wrapped her arms around herself for protection.

Etta gasped with shock at the horrors Gaho had told her. She stood silently and gazed open mouthed at her newly acquainted maid. Etta held her hands out and grabbed Gaho's hands in hers. The two women stood in silence, neither needed to speak. The bond of friendship was forged.

Shilah began to stir, the two women smiled at each other and Gaho wiped away her tears as Shilah sat up.

"What I would like you both to do is to rest for the next couple of days. I want you both fit and well. I have already arranged for some food to be brought up for you both."

"Does that mean I don't have to dig today?" Shilah asked.

"Yes Shilah, no digging today or the next or even the day after that. Your digging days are over," Etta announced as she ruffled the boy's hair.

"Really? Are they really over?"

"Yes, you both work for me now and I want you to rest."

"Can I stay in bed?"

"Yes," Etta chuckled as she glanced at Gaho who gave her son a motherly smile.

Shilah peeked at his mother and watched as she mouthed "thank you" at Etta. Etta stretched her arm out towards Gaho in friendship, she placed her hand on her shoulder and gently squeezed. Etta nodded in reply.

Gaho felt the warmth and goodness as it sang from every one of Etta's pores. She was a true spirit of compassion, everything about her radiated kindness. She was beautiful on the outside as well as beautiful within. She shone as their beacon of hope and faith in humanity. Gaho recognized that she stood in the presence of no ordinary human.

Shilah sat up in bed. He raised his hands up high above his head, exposing his bare chest. He stretched and yawned that caused the others to yawn too.

"Oh dear, now I am yawning," Etta announced as she watched Gaho do the same. Both women giggled and yawned once more.

"That's a nice necklace Shilah," Etta announced as she gazed at the string of beads that hung loosely on his torso.

"They are not mine. I am looking after them," he advised her as he pressed his chin on his chest so he could also view them.

Gaho smiled at the child and looked mournful as she thought about the rightful owner of the beads. She walked over to her son's side and stroked his rosy cheek.

"You are looking after them?"

"Yes, I will give them back. But mother has told me to wear them and never forget the person who gave them to me. He told me to look after them and to give them back to him when I next saw him. But the problem is that was the last time I saw him. Mother thinks he might be dead." Shilah stopped as he looked up at his mother's forlorn expression. He knelt up on the bed, wrapped his arms around her waist and buried his face into her side.

Gaho ran her fingers through the boy's hair and held him tight; with the other arm firmly swathed around him.

"Shush now, it's all right my son. Your brother was a great warrior and you will meet him again one day," Gaho advised in a shaky voice as she swallowed hard.

Etta watched as the pair held each other close. Their love for each other radiated into the air. Neither of them wanted to be the first to let go.

"Erm," Etta quickly paused. She wanted to enquire about the brother but thought this was not the right time to ask.

"I will leave you both to get some rest."

Gaho nodded her appreciation.

"I only ask one thing from you both and that is not to leave this chamber without me. The castle is enormous. I don't want either of you to get lost and find yourselves returned to the dungeons in error," she warned. "Get some rest," she ordered as she closed the door behind her.

Etta paced around her chamber and thought about what Gaho had told her. Anger and bile raised inside her. How could anyone want to hurt another human being? She questioned. She looked at the dividing door that partitioned the adjoining rooms and thought of the two on the other side. They were so fragile, yet so resilient. Etta knew she did not have Gaho's strength. Gaho was amazing and Etta was in awe of her. It was clear the bond between her and Shilah was strong and she would endure anything for her son.

Etta smiled to herself; she did not feel so lonely now. A renewed feeling engulfed her. A feeling of optimism, she was no longer alone, once again she had someone whom she could talk to. Someone who would help her and she could help them in return.

Etta's thoughts quickly turned to the dungeons. How many children have there been forced into hard labour and suffered exhaustion? How many other women have been subjected to the same abuse at the hands of Riend? Etta had never liked Riend but now it was more than dislike, she despised him. She loathed everything about him, just thinking of him made her furious. Etta needed to talk to Eudora, she was sure if Eudora was aware of what was happening, she would want to help to put a stop to it.

Etta opened her chamber door and shut it firmly behind her. She hurried towards the Queen's chamber and hoped her sister was well enough to see her. There was so much that she wanted to tell her. She marched through the corridor and suddenly stopped as Nellie ambled towards her.

"Nellie!" Etta screamed with excitement.

"Oh, my goodness child is it really you?" the nurse replied.

Nellie rushed towards her and Etta flung her arms around the plump nurse.

"Let me look at you?" the nurse demanded in a high pitched squeal as she held Etta at arm's length and looked her up and down.

"Nellie," Etta chuckled at the nurse. "I am no longer a baby"

"You will always be my baby. You forget - I delivered you; I was the first person in the world to hold you. There is something different about you," the nurse stated. "You have a secret my child, don't you?"

"What... How do you know that?"

"I know you better than you know yourself. I am right, am I not?" the nurse gazed at Etta and smiled.

"Nellie, I," she paused. "So much has happened to me, I need to confide in someone. I..."

"Stop!" the nurse ordered. "First you speak with your sister and tell her your secret, if she agrees, then you can tell me."

"But I...,"

"Shush." Nellie interrupted her and pressed her finger up against Etta's lips. "Shush, you need to stop.

The King is in there with your sister," Nellie pointed sharply to her sister's chamber. "Whatever is on your mind child, you need to keep it to yourself for the time being."

Etta nodded, the nurse was right; she had always confided in her sister before anyone else and she certainly did not want the King to know. That would be very foolish if he ever found out. The nurse held her tight and kissed her forehead.

"I have neglected you these past few months." Nellie admitted. "I am sorry, but your sister needed me more, I could not leave her in her time of need she would have died."

"It's all right Nellie, I understand my sister was unwell," Etta looked at the floor and moved from one foot to the other. "Thank you for looking after her."

"She is still unwell Etta, she may look better but her mind is still very weak, she needs a great deal of care."

The door behind them suddenly opened and interrupted their conversation.

"Ah, Lady Etta," the King greeted his wife's sister. "Are you here to visit the Queen? Good luck, maybe you can cheer her up." The King addressed her in a tone of utmost exasperation as he marched away with lengthy strides and an air of self-importance.

Etta rushed into her sister's chamber and immediately embraced her. They both held each other tight.

"Oh Etta I have really missed you. You don't know how much I wanted you by my side. The last few months have been so dark and at times I thought the darkness was going to swallow me whole," she admitted in a sombre tone.

Etta got in her sister's bed and immediately rested her head on Eudora's shoulder.

"Just like old times," Etta announced as she wrapped her arm around her back and clung to her.

"Not quite," Eudora whispered. "So many things have happened. So many things have changed."

"Yes, they have," Etta spoke softly as she thought of how her own heart was aching and how she was unable to mend it. "Eudora, I have a secret and I need to share it with someone," Etta blurted out in frustration as she glared at her sister and gave out a heavy sigh.

"Does your secret only involve you or does it involve others?" Eudora probed.

"It's not just me, there...."

"Then it is not just your secret and you should not tell it to anyone as it doesn't just belong to you," Eudora advised.

"But Eudora, I need to tell someone," Etta blurted out in exasperation.

"If you told me and others found out will it place you or anyone else in danger?" Eudora probed further.

"Yes," Etta confirmed.

"Then that secret must stay with you. If it involves the safety of you or others, I do not want you to speak of it to anyone. No-one Etta, do you understand? You do not risk it," Eudora ordered her sister in a firm but caring voice.

Etta knew her sister spoke wisely. She would not speak of her secret; she must bury it deep down inside her. Maybe one day she could reveal it but until that time, she must not think of it, ever.

Eudora squinted and raised her hand up to cover her eyes as Nellie pulled back the heavy drapes at the window. Shards of light twinkled and lit even the darkest of corners in the stuffy chamber.

"Ignatus didn't seem happy when he left," Etta acknowledged.

"He is never happy," Eudora answered and gave a fake smile.

"Are you happy Eudora?" this was a question that Etta had wanted to ask Eudora for such a long time but did not have the courage to do so.

"That is difficult to answer. I am happy with some things and unhappy with others," Eudora replied and ignored answering the question properly.

Etta got out of her sister's bed and strolled around the room picking up different objects off the floor. Etta suddenly stopped as she stood on a mound of crumpled black velvet fabric. She stooped down, grabbed it with her thumb and forefinger and held it up in the air like a dirty rag.

"I hate this bloody cloak. We should be wearing a red cloak, not black," Etta threw her sister's cloak across the room. "Things would have been so different if Tycus was King," Etta spat.

"Stop. It. Stop. Just stop Etta. Do you hear yourself? Tycus is dead and Ignatus is King. He is our King. We don't know if things would have been different if Tycus had not died. You have put Tycus up on some golden pedestal, but you didn't really know him, he also had his faults," Eudora cursed in anger.

"Well even if he did have his faults, I don't think he would have been as wicked as Ignatus. I have seen the depth of his power. I have been in the dungeons. I know what he and his little puppet Riend are capable of doing and how they are both abusing people. Not only to those inside of the castle walls; but to those outside of them too," Etta cried as she paced back and forward across Eudora's chamber in fury.

"Etta please stop. I am aware of what Ignatus is doing."

"And you are happy with that?" Etta screamed.

"No, I didn't say I was happy about it. I just said I am aware of it. What can we do about it? Nothing. Absolutely nothing," Eudora implored and then shrugged her shoulders as she gazed at Etta's frustrated face.

"I know you looked up to Tycus, Etta, and I know you dislike Ignatus but you need to understand Ignatus is my husband and my place is at his side."

"I understand where your loyalties must be, but I cannot help but wish Tycus was King instead," Etta looked at the anguish that was written across her sister's face. Just the mere mention of Tycus and her sister exploded.

"I am sorry Eudora. I know you and Tycus disliked each other. But you need to let go of your feelings for him after all he is dead," Etta pleaded.

"Let go of my feelings. Let go of my feelings for Tycus. I can assure you one thing is certain I will never let go of my feelings for that man. My feelings for him will haunt me to the day I die," Eudora confessed.

"Why won't you confide in me Eudora, what was it that Tycus did to you to make you dislike him so much?" Etta pleaded her sister. She desperately wanted to understand.

Eudora shook her head.

"No, that is something you do not need to know. It will change your view of him forever," Eudora advised.

"Will you tell me about it one day?" Etta pleaded.

"Maybe... one day," Eudora answered in a weary tone.

"I think you need to leave now Etta. Your sister needs her rest," The nurse walked towards Etta and guided her towards the door.

Etta stopped and looked at her sister. A halo of sunshine shone hints of golden beams around Eudora as she rested. Etta could not think of anything so beautiful as it lit Eudora up like an angel from heaven.

"I am sorry if I have upset you Eudora, and I promise I will not mention Tycus to you again."

Nellie gave Etta a tight hug and kissed her on the forehead. Then shut the door.

Etta stood in the cold corridor, once again alone. This time she was neither sad nor felt lonely. She knew she would never be completely alone - not now anyway. She skipped and hummed down the corridor to her new friends, Gaho and Shilah.

~ Chapter Fifteen ~

The Last Northern Tribe

The icy wind whistled through the trees, it secreted a strange eeriness that enveloped and suffocated the cold, crisp northern air. Snow-capped mountain peaks jutted high in the ragged skyline. These silent onlookers towered over the ferocious terrain of the north and the grasslands below. The rough territory of the harsh northern terrain and its remoteness invaded the landscape like a plague. Huge trees and brushwood dominated the acreage of backcountry, it was certainly a land for survival of the fittest. The ground now laid untouched for some time by human hands. Briar strangled the once cultivated land that had thrived with crops from a bygone era. Hemlock now stood in its place, evil had stretched its fingers and the contamination ran deep into the biome.

Eight hooves thundered across the wilderness sending clouds of dust in the air as they hurried towards yet another northern tribe. Time was against them, they were coming to the end of their search. They had gone as far North as they could. They needed to find Altaira and find her fast, this was their last hope of finding the great Northern Warrior.

Nubilus abruptly pulled his horse's harness and forced the beast to halt. He raised his hand swiftly in the air for Ursus to immediately follow his lead. He sat on his horse, straightened his spine and spied at his harsh location. He tilted his head back and sniffed the stench that lingered in the air. Nubilus glanced at Ursus, he pressed his lips firmly together and shook his head from side to side.

"I can smell blood, I think we are too late," Nubilus announced in a sombre tone.

"We still need to check for survivors," Ursus replied in a tone that mirrored Nubilus's.

Both men dismounted and tethered their friends tightly to a tree. Nubilus gently patted his strong steed.

"You need to be quiet my four-legged friend," Nubilus whispered as the horse nudged him in the chest and scraped his hoof into the soil in acknowledgement. "I will come back for you," Nubilus patted the horse for a second time.

Slowly and carefully they proceeded through the weeds and long grass towards the last northern village. Nubilus suddenly stopped and put his hand on Ursus's shoulder to stop him from continuing further.

"What is it Nubilus?" Ursus enquired.

"I'm not sure, I just," he paused.

"Just what."

"I don't know how to explain it, I feel as if someone or something is watching us," Nubilus explained as he looked over his shoulder and glanced around from where they stood.

The two men stood still to listen. Silence. Complete silence. Nothing! Not even the melodies of birds. Complete stillness, not even a breath of wind.

"It is far too quiet," Nubilus spoke cautiously.

"I think you are just a bit jittery Nubilus, I'm pretty sure it is nothing."

"Jittery? What do you expect after what we have been through these last few months? Every time we reach a tribe we are greeted with complete carnage. So many have been slaughtered Ursus. How many more lives?" Nubilus voiced in a melancholic tone and dipped his head low.

Ursus was lost for words, he simply nodded his agreement and continued to stare at Nubilus as he slowly walked with small steps still sniffing the air.

"I can smell something, but I don't know what it is," he whispered as he still felt they were being watched.

With an air of caution the two companions carefully crept light-footed towards the village. The pungent pong pierced its way through the dense green foliage. With small sideway steps Nubilus swung his axe at the undergrowth and dented his way through the thick undergrowth towards the village. Ursus followed in the wake of Nubilus's footsteps. He bowed his head and let out a heavy sigh as he once again looked upon another grimacing scene. They had stumbled on yet another massacre of a northern tribe. He clambered over a sea of bludgeoned figures. The stench radiated off the battered bodies and flies had now taken up residence on their flesh.

A trail of black charcoal stained and marked a path of destruction. Remnants of a dilapidated structure remained as evidence that a wild hungry beast had swallowed it and belched out an amber river of scorching flames that had licked the very heart of the village. A sad reminder of the ferocious slaughter of the people who had once lived there. The heart of the village had stopped beating and was now left in a state of annihilation and arrest.

Nubilus took huge gulps as he sucked in the air around him. He strangled a cry and pointed to a broken body that hung from a tree.

"NO, NO, NO! I cannot accept this Ursus," Nubilus cried as he stretched to cut the man down.

Nubilus collapsed to his knees. He cradled the man in his arms and screamed until all the breath had left his lungs. He rocked backwards and forwards as he clutched the dead body close to his chest and surrendered to his pain.

"Nubilus do you know this man?" Ursus asked with a puzzled expression as he witnessed the devastation etched on Nubilus's face.

Nubilus nodded as a loud painful wail escaped his throat. He swallowed hard and wiped the bloodstains off the man's face.

"He is Altaira's father," he proclaimed in a hushed tone as he wrestled with his feelings. "This is Altaira's home tribe," he advised as he wiped his eyes with the back of his hand.

Ursus stood still in silence as he watched Nubilus carefully place Altaira's father on the ground. Around him he placed an axe, knife and a bow and arrow.

"Your spirit will continue to walk the land, my wise friend," Nubilus whispered and kissed the man on the forehead. He grabbed the man's plaited braid and cut it off and handed it to Ursus.

"That is for Altaira, please put it in your bag for safe keeping. If she is still alive, she deserves to have something of her father," he said in an embittered tone.

Ursus nodded and placed it inside his bag. A strange feeling washed over him as he stood rooted to the spot. This was the last great northern tribe left. He realised the days of peace were now over. They needed Altaira more than ever now.

Nubilus remained on his knees, his head bowed low, and his arms dangled by his side. Everything around him mingled into one big blurred vision as grief saturated his soul. He blinked hard but all he could see was a distorted view of haze around him. The hardest task was yet to be carried out. He knew he needed to check if Altaira was amongst the dead. His heart raced as his chest bore the heavy weight of apprehension. He was eager to find Altaira, but to find her alive. What if she was dead? No, he didn't want to think about it. A world without Altaira was unbearable to think about. His heart belonged to her, it had always done. With leaden legs he stooped on one knee and bowed his head towards the deceased. With a deep breath he took one more glance at Altaira's father. He felt a loud pulsating beat pounding in his ears as he fought against the melancholic numbness of death that surrounded him.

He slowly raised to his feet and began to line the dead up into a row. He carried a young girl and moved the thread-like strands of hair that splayed across her face that hid her identity and placed her with the rest of her tribe.

"Altaira is not here," Ursus blurted from the other side of the camp.

"What? Are you sure?"

"Yes, I have checked all the bodies and she is not here," Ursus once again confirmed.

Nubilus released a huge sigh of relief, there was still a glimmer of hope that Ursus's vision with the spirits was correct and Altaira was indeed still alive.

Hidden from view, two yellow eyes silently lurked in the shadows. It gave a demonic smile as it witnessed their grief. It watched Ursus and Nubilus carry the deceased and pile them in a ceremonious line. Within an instant it knew it could ambush the pair and slaughter them. But it had its orders to remain still, to remain concealed and undetected.

"Ursus, once again no boys," Nubilus observed.

"Or hunters," Ursus replied.

Nubilus gathered the scattered beads and sprinkled them over the deceased. Any tools he could find he also placed them on the bodies.

"Ursus, just look at all this carnage," Nubilus waved his hands at the dead. "This tribe has been completely destroyed and we have no idea why or who is behind it."

"I share your concerns Nubilus, I do. I must admit I am worried. We do need to act, and we need to do this sooner rather than later. The problem is like you have just said; we have *no* idea who is instigating these attacks and for what purpose," Ursus spoke and shrugged his shoulders at the same time in bewilderment and concern.

"I can answer that," a voice whispered.

"Did you hear that Nubilus or am I now hearing voices," Ursus spoke.

"I heard it too," he replied as he looked around for the owner of the voice.

"Shush. Very quietly walk towards the hut in front of you. Do not make it obvious as you are both being watched," the mysterious speaker advised.

Ursus and Nubilus naturally looked around. Who or what was watching them?

"I said do not make it obvious, stop looking around and just come to the hut and I will explain," it whispered in a hurried tone.

Nubilus took a step towards the ram shackled hut and Ursus immediately grabbed his arm.

"Wait! It could be a trap," Ursus announced in a cautious manner.

Nubilus stopped, "I didn't think of that, what if whoever did this is still here? First, you show yourself. How do we know we can trust you?" Nubilus whispered with an air of uncertainty.

"I cannot. Please, you have just got to trust me. I know who you both are, you are Ursus and Nubilus. I cannot tell you how pleased I am you are here," he was still whispering.

"Will someone tell me why we are whispering," Ursus asked in an impatient tone.

"Garchy!" Nubilus advised through gritted teeth. "There is a Garchy watching us, I have just caught a whiff of its odour."

"Yes, it has its orders to make sure no one survives. I am not alone, I have others here. If it discovers us it will hoot and more will arrive to make sure that there are no survivors. Now do you understand why I cannot show myself to you," the voice declared.

"So, what now?" Ursus asked.

"We kill it. We have no choice do we," Nubilus advised him as he drummed his fingers on his chin for inspiration.

"Well, first we need to know where it is," Ursus pondered out loud.

"That is easy; I can smell him, he is just behind those bushes," Nubilus pointed discretely with a slight nod of the head. Two yellow eyes blinked and confirmed its exact position.

"How are we going to trick it to show itself?" Ursus asked Nubilus.

"That bit is easy. We pretend to leave, and we outflank it by coming up behind. You get its attention and

I will hide. Once it spots you, I will come out of hiding and kill it. Agreed?"

"What! You mean use me as bait?" Ursus queried.

"Yep. You are going to be a nice juicy bit of fresh meat. Ir-re-sis-tible, yum," Nubilus announced as he licked his lips and a wide smile crossed his face as he looked at Ursus's ashen expression.

"Nubilus, I know you said you would get your own back on me, but don't you think you are taking this a bit far?" Ursus declared.

"Oh no I'm not getting my own back, I'm saving that for *another* time," Nubilus advised with a smirk on his face.

"What! What do you mean - saving it, are you planning something worse than me risking my life?"

"Um yep," he laughed and patted Ursus on the back. "Come on we can do this."

"Please be careful, it is a very large Garchy," the mystery voice warned.

Sat on the soil hidden by the trees, the beast of eternal darkness watched both men slowly walk towards the edge of the camp. It stripped a small bush of its berries. It longed to hunt for its true dietary needs it would much rather have the taste of fresh meat.

Without a sound Ursus and Nubilus crept up behind the Garchy. Nubilus knelt on one knee and carefully pulled an arrow out of its quiver and placed it on his bow. He glanced at Ursus and nodded. Ursus inhaled deeply, he knew it was now up to him to sound the alarm and alert the Garchy of his presence. He just hoped Nubilus was a good shot with the bow. He would have preferred Nubilus to use his knife as he knew what he could do with a knife.

Ursus with an air of apprehension, ambled out from the bushes into the company of the soon to be doomed creature. Ursus silently stood behind it, unable to make a noise. It was huge. Much bigger than the other Garchy he had met. He looked at Nubilus and shook his head as Nubilus mouth the words,

"Go on."

"No, it's huge," he mouthed back and turned to walk back to Nubilus and the safety of the bushes. He wanted to rethink the plan; a single arrow would not take this monster out. Without warning Nubilus picked up a stone and blasted it through the air towards the Garchy. Smack! And another. Smack! Both had landed on the Garchy's head. It moaned and looked around to see Ursus stood in horror, his mouth wide open as he gazed at the mammoth size of it. They had got its attention. Fresh meat it thought. It licked its lips and stomped towards Ursus who now began to nervously back away.

"Now Nubilus!" he shouted.

"Not… Yet," he replied. "Just a bit closer."

"Any closer and we will both be dead. NOW!" he bellowed with an air of panic in his voice.

The Garchy chuckled. "Now Nubilus, NOW."

Over the bushes an arrow screamed through the air and pierced the monster's membrane between its eyes. Two more arrows followed hitting the gigantic Garchy in the sockets causing it to stumble. It frantically, fell to its knees waving its arms and writhing in pain from the pointed arrow-heads that had embedded in its eyes.

Nubilus hurried out from the trees and leapt into the air with his knife in his hand and ploughed it deep into the neck of the foul beast. It stopped. It had been silenced.

"Chuckle on that," Nubilus spat. He pulled the arrows and the knife out of the fallen creature of darkness and grinned.

"Chuckle on that! Chuckle on that," Ursus gave a nervous laugh. "I thought I was going to die, look at the size of it. Have you *ever* seen anything so disgusting and huge? We will need to burn it and then bury the remains so its clan will think it just wondered off."

Ursus took the flints out from his bag and lit a small piece of dried grass and placed it on the Garchy. A slight red spark glowed as it ignited the fabric that began to smoulder and shrivel as the embers took hold. Toxic

Garchy fumes spilled from the corpse, contaminating the surrounding fresh air.

"What a stink! I thought that it was smelly when it was alive, but this stench is beyond anything I have ever known before," Nubilus coughed and backed away covering his mouth and nose.

"I've known worse," Ursus winked.

"What, me? I can't believe you have said I smell worse than that," he pointed to the dead mass that was now burning bright. He laughed as he knew Ursus was just joking. Well… he *hoped* he was joking.

"We cannot allow it to burn for too long as the smoke may alert others that we are here," Ursus spoke with caution in his voice.

Nubilus held his axe high and took a heavy swing as it made a huge thud on the ground to loosen the soil. He repeated this action several times until the soil had been loosely disturbed. He quickly mutated into a wolf and started to dig a pit large enough to hide the remains of the Garchy. With his front paws, he scraped rapidly flicking the soft soil upwards and with his back paws, he kicked the soil out from the freshly dug pile of earth leaving a carefully crafted crater.

"I think that is big enough now," Ursus advised as he patted the wolf on the head.

Nubilus mutated back into his human form. "Are you sure? I could go a bit deeper if you want me too."

"No that is big enough," Ursus announced as he picked up some of the soil from the waste heap and began to throw it on the burning Garchy.

"Sure?"

"Yes."

Tight tresses of smoke slowly curled aloft in to the air as both men continued to scatter some of the surplus soil on the flames. Gradually the red roaring blaze was extinguished into a slight smouldering cinder. They sat and watched. Ursus's shoulders started to shake as he tried to stifle a giggle.

"What's so funny?" Nubilus asked.

Ursus shook his head and answered, "Nothing."

"No, tell me. What's so funny?" he enquired again.

"You. You came charging out and stabbed the Garchy in the neck and said, 'chuckle on that,' he now began to roar with laughter.

Nubilus also began to giggle. "It was because you said, '*now Nubilus, it's starting to chuckle,*' and I saw the look on your face." Nubilus mimicked Ursus's reaction and began to hoot with laughter as he clutched his sides.

It had been such a long time since the two friends had sat down with each other and laughed. For the last couple of months, there was nothing to laugh about.

Ursus stood and walked over to the heap of Garchy cinders. He waded through the sea of ash and pulled out the remains of the demonic beast and dragged it towards the freshly dug crater and tossed it in with a thud. Both men scrambled on the floor. With their hands they shovelled the earth back on top of the shallow grave and concealed the remains.

Ursus pulled some shrubs out of the ground and planted them in the mound of earth to hide the fallen Garchy's whereabouts.

"There. No one will ever know," Ursus said as he patted and compressed the soil further.

Both men stood and looked down at the slight mound of earth.

"Well done Nubilus," Ursus patted him on the back as they began to make their way back to the mysterious voice in camp. "That will be a brilliant story to tell. The *Great Warrior Nubilus;*" he lifted his hands in the air and then pointed to Nubilus who began to smirk. "Our very own warrior; who brought down a colossal Garchy all on his own." Ursus clapped and cheered.

Nubilus continued to smirk, "I could get use to that, Great Warrior! I think you should call me that from now on."

Their joyous moods soon evaporated as they strolled back into the camp to be reminded of the vicious attack. An elder stood beside the hut and nodded his appreciation.

"Thank you, that was very heroic of you both. I will certainly tell that tale," the Elder smiled as he twisted his torso to reveal a gathering of survivors behind him.

Huddled together were a mixture of adults and children. Ursus immediately noticed the boys and smiled at Nubilus. One by one they stepped forward from inside the protection of the hut. The Elder gasped and swallowed hard as he looked more closely upon the dead.

A commotion of screams shrieked high and touched the heavens as the newly orphaned children peered on with horror in their eyes as they glared at their motionless families. Their swollen faces stared up at the Elder who struggled to give a suitable explanation.

Nubilus wrestled with his tears and shuffled the distraught younglings back in to the hut, away from the distressing scenes. He took a deep breath...he felt completely useless. He could only imagine how they must be feeling.

A Muto's Promise
The Guardians

Grief consumed the survivors as they sank to the floor, their chests heaved as they tried to contain their sobs. Their hollers echoed and grew louder and louder. Recoiled into tiny balls, they brought their knees up high to their chest; then wrapped their arms around their limbs and gently rocked backwards and forwards through each sob.

Ursus slowly bent forward and picked up some flints and tossed them in the air and caught them in one hand. He knelt before the silent villagers and pulled a braid of sage from his bag and placed it on the floor beside his knees. He quickly rubbed the flints together creating a red and amber spark. Each time the flints sparked he held them over the sage. A grey serpent of smoke coiled into the air as the sage began to smoulder. Ursus picked the sage up, he held it at arms-length and began to perform a ritual ceremony to honour the fallen.

He slowly waved the burning braid over the bodies and muttered a spiritual prayer.

"Earth mother; support us to do right by the spirits we send to live by your guided hand," Ursus prayed and dropped the flints into his bag.

Nubilus looked once more at Altaira's father. He sat on the floor with his elbows rested on his knees and his head in his hands as he tried to contain his emotions. He had known Altaira's father since he was a young boy. Nubilus sniffed back his tears and frowned.

"Where is she?" Nubilus asked through clenched teeth and in an exasperated tone as he raised his arms into the air with frustration. "I know the spirits advised she was alive, but was that before this attack on her tribe or after? Ursus I fear the worse. All the northern tribes have been slaughtered. Our people are being eradicated; our culture disintegrated, our way of life is at risk. If we are to survive, we need to act now. I know we need to find Altaira, but we can't carry on searching for her when this is happening," Nubilus spoke in a heavy voice and a hard look reflected in his dark eyes.

Ursus remained silent and deep in thought as he listened to Nubilus's concerns.

"We need to help rebuild this tribe Nubilus, they must have food and shelter," Ursus advised. "Their food supplies have been ransacked and taken. They will starve if will do not help."

"We have food, it is just the rebuilding of a shelter that you can help with," the Elder commented. "Altaira had always insisted that we have additional food stores for the winter months. It is stored underground where we were all hiding. We have only eaten a tiny bit of it."

Ursus and Nubilus began to clear the village camp of its debris. Any surplus wood that was not scorched they stacked in one pile. Wood that was beyond saving was discarded in another to use as fire wood. Many of the young women left the camp to bring back a supply of water from the nearby stream and a stash of pine branches. The needled branches were ideal to construct a covering for the roof. With the help of the survivors both Ursus and Nubilus started to rebuild a communal hut.

Night was fast approaching and the hut was close to completion. The last branch was lashed tightly and secured in place. The elder stood back and smiled as he admired the building. He nodded at their exhausted tear stained faces that eagerly waited for his permission to stop and rest. One by one they found a vacant spot and curled into a ball to snooze. Children snuggled together for comfort and warmth.

Ursus held the Elder's arm and helped him to sit and rest his weary frame. "Thank you for helping us," the Elder spoke in an exhausted tone. "Now I believe you have questions that I have the knowledge to answer," he panted as he tried to sit comfortably.

Both Ursus and Nubilus nodded, they wanted to know everything.

"We knew there was a Garchy on the edge of the camp. The very same one that you managed to kill," he nodded to Nubilus. "It was there on its own for weeks and nothing happened. But then one Garchy soon turned into a posse of Garchy. Many of the hunters chased them deep into the forest. That was our downfall, our tactics were wrong. As our hunters left to chase them away so did our only protection." He closed his eyes and tried to recall the moment he knew they were going to be attacked. "First, they set fire to one of the huts, this was their signal to alert their forces that our village was left unprotected. Then came all the hooting from Garchy after Garchy as they stormed towards us. Then the King's Guards marched in with horses and wagons. The older hunters tried to protect us, but it was too late," he paused. They um… they already had the upper hand and we were outnumbered," he sniffed and tried to recompose himself. "The guards raided our food supply whilst the Garchy began to breathe their toxins on the boys," he paused as his lips began to wobble and his voice wavered. "Erm," he paused again as he tried to continue. "They just threw them on the wagons like pieces of meat. That was when I knew I had to gather as many people as I could. I managed to gather most of the children and many of the young mothers, and I hid them below the hut. I told them no matter what they heard or how they felt they were not to leave without my permission and that they needed to be in complete silence," he whispered softly. "I heard one of the guards hollering his orders to take only the boys."

"Just the boys? Why?" Nubilus asked in a puzzled voice. "I don't understand what the King would benefit from by taking just the boys.""Well that is something we need to work on answering," Ursus replied.

The Elder shrugged his shoulders. "The guard that was doing all the talking told us that Altaira had abandoned them to save herself and that she did not care if they lived or died as long as she was safe."

"Did you believe that!" Nubilus shouted in outrage.

"Of course not. None of us believed it. Altaira's father was furious saying she would never abandon her tribe and charged at the guard, wrestled him to the floor and cut his tongue out. He held it up in the air for everyone to see and shouted, "Now we will have no more lies from you, then they hung him." The elder tried to hold his tears back but failed miserably. "You both need to know that I am no coward, and I am no longer useful in battle, but I knew I needed to save some of my tribe if I possibly could."

Ursus nodded, "And what a wonderful job you did. None of them would be here if it wasn't for you," Ursus swung his arm to acknowledge the sleeping survivors. "Your tribe exists because of you; it is because of your quick thinking and passion that they are still alive. You can rebuild and survive," Ursus smiled and patted him on his bony back.

"What about Altaira, do you know where she is? Do you think they have captured her?" Nubilus anxiously asked.

"No, I don't think they have her, he answered.

"That could explain why they came here. They were looking for her, that explains why all the Northern Tribes have been wiped out. They were hoping to draw her out and capture her," Nubilus spoke as he looked at Ursus.

"Did you say all the Northern Tribes have gone? Are we the only tribe left?" the Elder questioned in a shocked tone.

"Yes," they both answered in unison.

"Then you are right Ursus, we will rebuild and survive. What about the tribes in the other regions?" The Elder asked in a curious tone.

"Some have suffered, some not," Ursus advised.

"Yours?" the Elder enquired.

"No, but," he paused as an ashen look crossed his face.

"What? What is it?"

"There is a Garchy on the edge of my camp. It means that they are planning to attack. What do we do? We are so far away," Ursus panicked.

"You leave, and you leave now," the Elder ordered. "You need to warn your tribe before it is too late, and your tribe suffers the same fate. GO," the Elder ordered. "We will be fine now, thanks to you two. We will rebuild, and we will be waiting for you to return. You are both very welcome here." The elder smiled and watched as both men scrambled through the bushes and left the Last Northern Tribe behind them.

~ Chapter Sixteen ~

The Pit of Doom

Dawn crept its way through the arrow slits of the dungeon wall, it was eager to scream and wake those residing within. It was awake so everyone else should be too. Loud penetrating shouts from the guards echoed and bounced off the fortified structure as they yelled their orders with military precision.

"GET UP!" a guard yelled at a sleepy boy as he struggled to stand up quickly enough for the guard.

"ON YOUR FEET, MOVE IT!" another yelled at a woman as she tried to help a child beside her to stand.

"LINE UP, NOW!" the third guard bellowed in their faces as they rushed to stand and line up.

One by one the occupants left their slumber behind them as they stood in line. The rattling of chains could be heard as they were dragged along the stone floor towards their destination and fed through the manacles that dug into their already ulcerated skin. All looped together in one long train. On one side, the young boys stood; on the other were the women. Soon they would have to march out beyond the castle's walls to the pit of doom.

Pax and Orace walked the entire length of the line looking for a child that fitted Inca's description. Pax shook his head at Orace.

"I can't see any child wearing a necklace, do you?" Pax asked Orace as he stretched his arm high above his head in the air and held the necklace up that Inca had given to him so Orace could recall it to memory once more.

A boy stood at the back of the line, starred at the beaded necklace and smirked; they weren't likely to find him either, he thought. He knew the guards must be thinking of Shilah. And he was no longer down in the gloomy dungeons. Shilah and his mother were taken some time ago now. They were the lucky ones, he thought.

Pax looked at the boy as he caught him staring at the necklace and watched as the boy smiled.

"Have you seen this before, boy," he asked as he dangled it in front of his face.

The boy shook his head, he had but he was not telling him that.

"Are you sure? I think you have, where! Tell me!" he demanded. The boy shook his head. His lips were sealed. He would not be the one to betray Shilah.

"What, no you have not seen it before, or you refuse to tell me? Which one is it, answer me,"

"I have never seen it before," the boy lied.

A voice further along the corridor shouted, "SIT!"

Like a pack of dogs obeying a command; they immediately sat on the cold stone floor. Each person was given two small stale pieces of bread for their breakfast. The hungry mouths stuffed it in, chewed twice and swallowed hard. A small jug of water was handed down the line; each boy took a huge swig; that would be the only fluids that they would get for a while.

"Right, on your feet... MARCH!" the voice roared. All immediately stood on their feet and began to march slowly placing one foot in front of the other as they proceeded to leave the darkness of the dungeons to the fresh world outside.

Shilah got out of his bath and wrapped himself in the cloth that his mother had left for him and patted himself dry.

He could hear the guards shouting their orders as the prisoners were marched out of the castle's grounds.

"May I? Please, can I," he pleaded.

"If Lady Etta agrees to letting you watch them march off then it will be alright by me," Gaho confirmed.

Shilah rushed to get dressed, he needed to see his friends. He had saved some food for them and he stuffed it into his pockets. He walked into Lady Etta's chamber to seek permission.

"My Lady, sorry for disturbing you," he hesitated. "But I was wondering if I may see the other boys leave before they start digging," he asked.

"Shilah, why would you want to do that? You do not have that life anymore. Why?" she asked with curiosity.

"Because they are my friends. I may never see them again. It is certain that someone will die," he looked at Lady Etta's shocked expression. "And I will never be able to see that person again," he argued.

"That is a very good point," she acknowledged "But I don't think that that tiny crumb of bread that you have in your pocket will feed all of them." She picked up the un-touched loaf on her tray and tossed it towards Shilah. "There, that will feed more. Alright you can go but only if I can come with you. That way I know you are safe," she addressed Shilah.

He rushed into where his mother was sitting and beamed a wide smile.

"Lady Etta said I can go, and she will come with me. Isn't that great," he squealed as he rushed to finish getting dressed.

Lady Etta waited for the eager boy to knock on her chamber door.

"You may enter," she spoke as she looked at the boy.

They left the chamber hand in hand as she escorted him down the corridor.

"Wait! Wait!" Gaho shouted as she held his necklace in her hand. "Shilah your necklace, wait," she tried to shout louder but it was too late.

With the mad rush of getting dressed he forgot to pick up his beloved beads. She walked back inside the chamber and placed them inside her pocket for safekeeping ready for his return.

Etta held his hand all the way through the unoccupied lower corridors that winded and twisted until they reached the large Bailey below. He could hear the chains rattling together in synchronised steps as they each mirrored one another's pace. Heads bobbed up and down in front of him as the crowd stretched to get a better view of what the King called, 'low life scum.' His heart raced and bile brewed in his throat. He had never viewed the situation from this side of the castle before. He had only experienced it as a link in the chain; all strapped together as he struggled to keep up with the older children. He shuddered at the thought of entering that dark cavern. Etta felt his body shake uncontrollably beside her. She firmly wrapped her arm around his shoulder and pulled him close. Immediately, Shilah's shaking began to subside as he felt the warmth of her body and experienced the warmth of her heart. He knew she would protect him and that he had nothing to fear.

With every beating moment the line drew closer and Shilah let out a squeak of fear. His whole frame shook from head to toe and he quickly placed his hand over his mouth to stop himself from calling out their names. He so desperately wanted to see his friends; he needed to know who was still alive. Guilt began to consume his thoughts like wild fire burning his very soul. He should also be part of that train and on his way to the place they boys called the, 'Pit Of Doom.' He shuddered, he felt relieved and grateful but at the same time angry that his friends were in that position. Everyone deserved freedom not just the select few.

"Shush, it's all right I will not let any harm come to you," Etta whispered in a comforting tone. The line advanced quickly and Etta screamed at the top of her voice. "STOP!"

The guard at the front raised his arm in the air and bowed at Lady Etta.

"I would like to take a look at these foul little creatures," she winked at Shilah.

Shilah followed his mistress as she walked up and down the line.

"What is your name?" she asked the guard at the end of the line.

"Pax, my Lady," he answered as he bowed.

"I know I cannot stop you from marching these children to hard labour, but I would like it if you would allow me and my young servant to give them some bread."

"Erm, well yes, my Lady, I suppose it will be alright," he confirmed in a shocked tone and looked at Orace who just shrugged his shoulders. No-one had ever shown the boys any compassion before, it had startled him.

Etta and Shilah tore off chunks of bread. They walked up and down the line and handed out their offerings. Pax followed and looked carefully at Shilah as many of the children grabbed his arm and patted him as he walked by.

"Do you know these boys?" Pax asked Shilah.

"It is possible that he will know some of them as he himself was one of them up until a few months ago until I took him away from that nightmare," Etta announced as she placed her body between Shilah and the guard like a Mother protecting her young pup.

"Yes Lady Etta, I agree," he hesitated as he wanted to choose his words wisely. "It is a nightmare for them, but who are we to bring an end to it, we are powerless," he gave a sincere nod and a tight smile.

"I wish I could," she whispered.

"Me too," he whispered back.

Etta stepped away; she knew this guard would not harm Shilah. Pax nodded and immediately looked the boy up and down from head to toe. Nope, he is not the one I am searching for; no necklace on him either, Pax thought as he shook his head at Orace.

Pax smiled, and walked back to his position at the end of the line, he raised his arm high in the air to signal that they were ready to proceed.

Gradually each chain began to pull until it rippled through to the boy on the end. Shilah stood and watched as they slowly left the Bailey. Many of those boys were his friends. Etta sensed his anguish and ruffled his hair.

"I cannot help everyone Shilah, you must understand that. I wish I could," she knelt on one knee and grabbed his hands in hers and smiled. "May be one day things will be different."

Etta stood up and pulled Shilah to her where she held him tight. She did not like seeing him upset, he had become very important to her and she felt it was her responsibility to ensure he was happy as well as safe. The pair slowly walked back through the labyrinth of twisting corridors towards Etta's chamber. At the door waiting for them was Gaho who greeted them with a warm smile. In her hand she dangled Shilah's necklace for him to see.

"You were in such a rush my son that you forgot to put this on."

Shilah gave half a smile; he walked towards his Mother and buried his face into her side and began to cry.

"Hey, what's brought this on?" she asked

"Seeing them all marching off to…" he paused.

"I know my son, it is not easy to understand but for now you just have to accept what is happening. It will not be like this forever, everything will come in the right moment, be patient," Gaho kissed his forehead. "Why don't you go and lie down and get some rest."

Shilah glanced at Etta who nodded in agreement. He dragged his feet across the room and plonked his melancholic frame across the bed. He laid in silence as he stared up at the vaulted ceiling. His thoughts soon turned dark as he fell asleep and was forced to relive his time in the pit of doom.

Shilah could feel the cold metal manacles dig in around the flesh of his ankles as he marched towards the pit with the other boys from the dungeon. The trek was slow and arduous as each boy took tiny steps forward as they shuffled their feet into the dirt. The heat from the late morning sun scorched their shoulders. Hungry and thirsty they continued to march without rest as the morning sun disappeared and the mid-afternoon sun blared upon the exhausted younglings. They had been marching since daylight and they were now in great need of a rest. Shilah was hoping for someone to fall to their knees, at least that would give him a momentary rest whilst they stopped to sort it out.

A voice up ahead bellowed, "Stop!"

All the boys stopped and instantly fell to their knees with exhaustion. Shilah desperately needed a drink. His throat hurt and his tongue was stuck to the roof of his mouth. Gasping for breath he took a huge lung full of fresh air. He knew his time in the outside world was now about to come to an end. He could see the entrance of the tunnel that he knew he would be forced to enter.

Two boys at a time were released from their manacles only to find that a rope was tied around their waist lashing them together as a pair. Each pair walked towards the tunnel, not even sure if they would ever see daylight again. Their prospects were not good.

Next it was Shilah's turn as he was paired and lashed with another boy.

"Move," the guard shouted as he pushed the boys towards the foreboding entrance.

"I'm Shilah," he addressed the boy.

"Erm, I'm Kezi," he replied in a nervous voice. "Where are we going?"

"Into the hillside, just in there," Shilah pointed to a large doorway in the side of the rock face.

"Is this your first time?" Shilah asked thinking that it was as Kezi's body began to shake.

"Yes. I'm afraid," Kezi admitted to Shilah.

"It's nothing. You will be alright," he lied as he could not guarantee he would be alright. "I will look after you," that was one thing Shilah did not lie about - he would do his best anyway. "Just stay in tight to the wall when you get out of the bucket. There's very little room and you will need to lean your back up against the back of the crag."

Together they walked into the portal of doom. They climbed into the bucket and gradually, they were lowered on to the narrow ledge that was just wide enough for them to fit their small feet. Darkness had immediately consumed their sight. Both boys stood with their backs up against the cavern wall and slowly took small side

343

steps. Shilah knew if either of them slipped they would both die. He could hear Kezi beside him snivelling with fear.

Hearts drumming in their chest and their breathing hitched they gradually felt their way along the ledge to the gap in the wall.

"You will need to crawl along this bit." Shilah dropped to his knees. He pulled Kezi down with him and crawled along the narrow passageway with Kezi closely at his heels. The hard surface tore their already calloused knees as they continued further and deeper into the belly of the mountain.

They continued to crawl like rats in search of food. They had reached the end of the narrow ledge. It was now time to dangle off the edge to swing and jump over to the other side. The air began to get thin and the temperature suddenly dropped. Swirls of wind travelled up through the cavern and nipped at their bare skin. Shilah knew they were now at the end of the ledge. He suddenly stopped and Kezi bumped into him.

"What's the matter? Why have we stopped? Kezi enquired.

"We have reached the end of the ledge; we will need to jump over the everlasting pit to get to the next passageway."

"The what?" Kezi panicked.

"The everlasting pit, or you may have heard of it as the bottomless pit, no one knows how far down it goes," Shilah advised. He heard Kezi squeal.

Shilah glanced upwards to the very top of the mammoth shaft. He prayed that the sun was still shining. He needed to see the tiny sliver of light that shone through the crack from the outside world. Shilah felt that Kezi was shaking; this was not good for either of them. He was not sure if it was through the cold, or from fear. He hoped it was through the cold, as he knew that they both needed to stay calm.

"Are you ready?" he asked him.

"What if one of us misses? I don't even know how far I have to jump or where to jump," he uttered with a panicked tone.

"We are not going to miss. I have done this a hundred times, trust me." Shilah grabbed his hand and pulled him close so he was now stood right in front him.

"Now, look up. Do you see the light?"

"Yes."

"Well, follow that light all the way down to where it stops. Are you following it? Do you see where it stops?"

"Yes."

"Good, because that is how far we have got to jump. We need to sit on the edge and slowly move our body, so it dangles over the edge and hold on with one arm. Try and bring your knees up high to your chest so you can push off. That will make you jump that little bit further. Make a little dip with your hand in the floor and use that to grip with as you dangle," Shilah instructed.

Both boys sat on the edge and lowered themselves off the ledge and scrambled to raise their legs up towards their chest.

"Right, are you ready?" Shilah asked.

"I think so," he answered.

"Right hold on with one hand, lean forward slightly and when I say, 'Mother Nature go,' we jump straight after I say go. Alright are you ready."

"Yes."

"One hand. Lean out. Mother, Nature, GO!" Shilah bellowed as it echoed up through the shaft.

Both boys leapt into the air across and immediately landed on the floor on the other side.

"Yes, we made it," Kezi screamed with delight.

Shilah let out a soft giggle.

"What is so funny?"

"That *was* your first time wasn't it?"

"Yes."

"Come with me." Shilah grabbed his wrist and took a few steps back towards the edge that they had just dangled from. "Here, give me your hand."

The boy gave Shilah his hand and Shilah pressed it up against the side of the shaft.

"That is the edge we have just dangled from. I'm sorry it's more of a step than a ledge."

"You mean there was no pit to jump over?"

"No. All we needed to do was jump down off the ledge," he now roared with laughter.

"That was not funny, all I kept thinking about was even if I made it across, how I was going to make it back," he too began to giggle, more with relief than anything else.

"You will have to be careful in here as it can be very tricky. In places you will need to lie flat on your tummy just to get through." Shilah advised.

Both boys continued along the narrow passage way until their way became blocked.

"This is where we need to lie on our bellies," Shilah advised as they both lay on their torsos. "It's not far."

They carefully leaned up on their elbows. Both tried not to bang their heads or scrape their spines on the sharp peaks of rock that jutted down from above them. Slowly and carefully they crawled and slithered like a snake. They pushed on all four of their limbs through the confined space to the other side.

They could hear the rumbling of wheels ahead of them from the carts and the voices of many other boys who were hard at work. Suddenly there was a rumble and the passage floor started to vibrate. Many screams were heard, followed by a huge cloud of dust as it swept the boys off their feet.

"The roof has collapsed," a boy shouted further ahead. "HELP! HELP US! WE ARE TRAPPED!" the voiced shrilled in a high pitch tone of desperation.

Shilah shouted, "WE ARE COMINING, and WE ARE COMING!" he repeated.

Both boys hurried through the darkness towards the voices of the trapped boys. The air was thick with dust as the particles floated in the only breathable air the boys had. Suddenly another roar of rocks was heard ahead as they thundered to the floor. The whole tunnel once more shook and knocked the boys off their feet.

"Are you alright?" Kezi asked Shilah.

"Yes, what about you, are you alright?" Shilah asked.

"Yeah, I think so," he coughed and spluttered through the fragments of the pyroclastic blast.

"HELLO!" Shilah shouted as he bumped into what seemed like another person.

"We are trapped," the panicked voice declared. "He is on the other side and I am here on this side. I can't move as the rope between us is buried deep underneath the rocks. I don't even know if he is still alive."

"We will need to move some of the rocks," Kezi announced as he immediately began to shift the debris.

Both boys worked tirelessly to remove as many boulders as they could. Their hands were raw as the blood dripped off each finger. Their backs were breaking but they were determined not to give up. Finally, the trapped boy wriggled free. His rope had been severed by a sharp falling stone. There was no-one on the other side of it. The boy had vanished, or had he escaped?

Kezi walked a little further. "There is no one here Shilah, all those voices we heard…"

Shilah immediately opened his eyes as he saw Gaho starring at him. His hair was stuck to his face and his clothes were soaking from sweat.

With watery eyes he looked at his mother and sought comfort from her.

"Bad dream," Shilah told her as he could see the worry on her face.

"I know, that is why I have made you one of these," Gaho presented him with a dream catcher. "Your bad dreams are becoming more frequent." She held him in a tight embrace and Shilah shook.

"I saw Kezi in that line today. It reminded me of the first time we met. And I am here, and he is… well he will be in that pit now." Shilah looked up at his mother who could only manage a smile as she continued to hold her son.

"You cannot blame yourself or feel guilty for not being with him, we will see him again. You have taught him well."

"Will I? Or will he be just another one who gets lost and disappears in the Pit of Doom, like all the others?"

Etta walked in and stood by the door, "When you say they disappeared, what do you mean by that. Do you mean disappeared as in vanished or disappeared as in dead?"

"Disappeared, vanished," he confirmed as he explained about the boy that should have been trapped on the other side of the rock fall. He had simply vanished without a trace.

"Has there been many that have disappeared in there?" Etta asked.

"Yes lots, some say there is a Garchy that lives in there and it has taken the boys," he answered.

Silence filled the room as both Gaho and Shilah watched Etta pace up and down the room as her finger tapped on her chin.

"Was the boy who vanished tied to you?"

"No. I was paired with another boy called Kezi."

"What did the guards say when the other boy returned to the surface on his own," Etta probed.

"Nothing."

"Nothing. Absolutely nothing, did they ask where he was?"

"Yes, but we explained that there was a rock fall and he was killed."

Etta continued to pace backwards and forwards across the room as she continued to ponder on what Shilah had said.

"You told me this morning that you wanted to see your friends because you feared that you may not have the opportunity to see them again. Are there many that come back up to surface on their own, or would you say that it was a rare occurrence?"

"No, many come back on their own," Shilah informed her.

"Do the guards ever want to see the proof that the boys are dead?"

"No, they take our word for it. Especially if we tell them that the body is trapped under a pile of rubble and to remove the rubble would cause more damage."

Etta stopped her pacing. "I have an idea Shilah. But it may take time. When the boys return, I think I will have a very nice conversation with that lovely guard I was talking to this morning. Oh, what was his name, what was he called?" she questioned herself as she placed her hand on hip for inspiration.

"Pax," he reminded her.

"Yes! That was it. Pax, well done. I will have a nice quiet word with that lovely guard and hopefully he will be able to help me with my plan and turn the 'Pit Of Doom' to our advantage." She chuckled and walked out of the room leaving both Gaho and Shilah speechless and wondering what she was planning.

~ Chapter Seventeen ~

The Ohme Gully Tribe

High in the sky Altaira soared and surveyed the expansive territory below her. A gentle breeze ruffled through her feathers as she glided and circled on the down draught through the crystal-clear cerulean sky. A sea of green grasslands stretched as far as she could see. Suddenly her gaze spotted an area of grass that had been flattened. She swiftly swooped closer to investigate why. Hidden from view amongst the high grass she spied a single Garchy that had taken up residence on the border of the Ohme Gully tribe. She knew that that tribe was doomed if she didn't put a stop to it. She needed to warn them that the Garchy was hiding and about its intentions. Altaira flapped her powerful wings and accelerated high up towards the heavens for one last time before she suddenly stopped and dropped forwards, free falling through the air. She stretched her sharp talons out wide as she swooped and let her claws brush through the meadow of green. Silently without a sound she landed softly on the soil beside Dez and mutated back into her human form.

"There is a Garchy just over there," she pointed. "As far as I can see it is alone. It's not very big, but it's not the size that worries me it's just the fact it is there. We will need to warn the Ohme Gully tribe," she whispered so the Garchy would not hear her.

"What! A Garchy?" Inca whispered through gritted teeth as he walked through the long grass to meet them. Inca stood beside them in complete silence and deep in thought. A forlorn expression etched across his face as he remembered his family. What if this Garchy helped to kill my family he thought? A pressing lump held his vocal cords silent. His tongue too numb to speak. He knew what he wanted to do.

"Well, we kill it," Inca suddenly announced in a vengeful voice.

"No," Altaira stated as she shook her head. "No," she repeated. "That will ruin my plan."

"What plan?" Dez asked

"We must have an alliance with the Ohme Gully tribe. We need as many people as possible to help our cause."

Carefully and quietly they traipsed through the high grass towards the village. Inca towered over the grass in some parts and was forced to stoop low as he walked. Altaira suddenly raised her hand in the air for her two companions to stop.

"I think it will be best if I went on my own," she advised with an air of caution in her voice. "This is not a very friendly tribe, they have been known to be extremely hostile. Make sure you stay here, do not approach unless I call for you. Do you both understand?" Altaira asked in a manner of authority. Both nodded their replies.

Altaira removed her weapons and placed them in a heap on the floor beside her brother and placed her arm gently on his shoulder.

"I think it would be better if I were to leave these behind," Altaira gave a slight nervous smile.

"What!" Dez exclaimed in a confused voice. "Why? How will you protect yourself? You have just said they can be volatile." Dez stared at his sister with disbelief and grabbed her weapons and held them out for her to take. "Please take them Altaira, you need some sort of protection. Please."

"I think it wise not to take any weapons," Inca interjected as he looked at Dez and took the weapons from him and placed them back on the ground. "From the stories I have heard about the Ohme Gully tribe they will see it as a threat. If you do take weapons," he gazed at Altaira. "They will see it as an act of hostility and they will respond in that way. They are a very hostile tribe, you have no choice but to enter without any weapons but please be very careful." Inca nodded his approval at

Altaira. He placed his hand on Dez's shoulder and gave him a reassuring pat.

Altaira stared at Inca with surprise and nodded her thanks for his loyal support. She knew if anything did happen to her, Dez would be alright with Inca's hand to guide him.

"Don't worry about me little brother," she whispered closely into his ear. "Stay with Inca, I will be fine. I will come back for you."

Dez held his head low, his eyes looked up to hers. He opened his mouth. He was about to argue but closed it. Dez paused for a moment he did not like this at all but respected her enough not to question her judgment. He held her gaze and nodded.

Slowly Altaira proceeded forward through the grass alone. She stopped to turn and looked at both Inca and Dez who stared at her with apprehension imprinted on their faces. With one foot in front of the other she walked away from their safety towards the most hostile tribe in the region.

Carefully she advanced, her eyes spied the roof of a building. She could hear the laughter of children playing and mothers shouting. All the right sounds of village life. She stopped to take a deep breath before she proceeded to gain her alliance. She began to ponder how to enter the camp. She knew she couldn't just walk straight in. They would be embarrassed that their hunters had not heard or seen her coming. They would immediately become hostile to protect their tribe. She would have to get caught and enter as a prisoner. She hoped they would allow her to speak and not see her as a threat.

On the boundary of the camp she could see several hunters holding spears, she would have to make sure they heard her. She stomped her foot harshly on the grass with a loud crunch. That should alert them she thought. With the other foot she repeated and stomped it loudly with another crunch as it tightly pressed the grass beneath her. Suddenly she felt the tip of a spear press up against her skin on the side of her neck. Brilliant she thought as she felt another spear press on her shoulder blade and another pointed at her face. Three hunters had heard her clumsiness, this was better than she could have hoped for.

She was surrounded, outnumbered and defenceless. She held her hands in the air as a gesture of peace.

"I mean no harm, I am here to help your tribe. I urgently seek counsel with your Leader," she spoke softly but also with an air of authority in her voice. She watched their expressions expecting them to soften. But their gazes remained the same: harsh and foreboding. She began to worry, what if they would not allow her to enter the camp? They could kill her right on this spot, after all, she had no weapons to help her. Maybe Dez was right, maybe it was foolish to enter without any weapons to defend herself.

"I am here to seek counsel with your Leader. It is extremely important," she repeated. "I mean no harm, I have no weapons, the only thing that I carry is knowledge and it is important your Leader hears of this."

The hunters looked at each other and grunted. They prodded their spears into her to step forward. They had decided to give Altaira rite of passage to their tribe and to their Leader. But they were going to escort her.

"Hands!" one of them demanded.

Altaira immediately dropped her hands from above her head and held them out in front of her. A sigh of relief washed over her, she was going to be taken into their tribe as a prisoner. A hunter jabbed his spear into the ground and tied some twine around her wrist binding her hands securely together. He held the end of the twine tightly in his hand and swiftly tugged, forcing her to step clumsily forward. He tugged it once more and picked up his spear as she quickly fell into step with the hunter's pace as they entered the Ohme Gully village. She could still feel the sharp spears pressing on her neck and shoulder as they occasionally jabbed her as a warning to remind her that they were still there.

Suddenly they stopped. She was in the centre of the village. With a sharp tug on the twine she was forced onto her knees. Altaira bowed her head and tried to remain calm. Slight apprehension tried to force its way through her thoughts, she had no idea what was going to happen to her, but she knew she need to be strong, she needed that alliance. She knelt back onto her feet and placed her bounded hands on her lap.

Altaira slowly lifted her head and gazed at the villagers as they started to leave their dwellings to see what the hunters had snared. All were brandishing spears. Men, women and children stepped forward towards her and enclosed her into a tight circle. She was completely trapped. Their outstretched arms all waving and pointing a spear in her direction.

Altaira looked at their intimidating faces, "I mean you no harm. I come to seek counsel, I come to give you important information," she looked at their faces. This was not going to work she thought. "I am Altaira from the Northern Tribes," she informed them.

She could hear whispers through the crowd, as they all repeated her name. They had all heard of the great warrior named Altaira, but none had seen her.

"How do we know you are the Great Altaira?" one shouted from the crowd. A muttering of agreement rattled through.

An elder stepped forward, he placed one hand on her head and forced her chin to touch her chest. With the other he held her long locks in his hand exposing her neck. This is it Altaira thought, they are going to chop my head off or scalp me.

"If she is Altaira of the Northern Tribes she will have a mark on the nape of her neck. A mark of three arrow heads burnt into her skin," he declared. "You!" he shouted at one of the hunters who had captured her. "Take a look, my eyes are old and unable to detect it. Yours are young and if it is indeed there, you should see it," the Elder stated. The hunter gazed at her neck and swiftly looked at the Elder.

"Well. Is it there or not?" the Elder mumbled.

365

The hunter looked at the crowd as they also waited in anticipation.

"Yes, three arrow heads burnt into the skin," he replied as a gasped was heard from the villagers.

The Elder smiled.

"What? I have what," Altaira asked.

"You have the marks of three arrow heads on the nape of your neck," he casually answered. "I think you better untie her," he stated as he looked at the three hunters who captured her. They immediately untied the binding.

"How did you know I had those marks, I didn't even know they were there," Altaira asked as she stood and rubbed her wrist.

"Ah, my child that is something I cannot tell you, so please do not ask me again."

"But…."

"No! Do not ask me. If I decide to tell you one day I may, if I think you need to know."

"I do need to know, and I choose to know now!" she demanded and placed her hands on her hips then glared at the Elder and waited.

"No. You do not. We will leave it as that," the Elder spoke sternly. "Now, if I am not mistaken you seek counsel do you not?" he spoke to avoid any further probing from Altaira. He led her to a small hut and ordered her to enter and sit.

Altaira sat on the floor thinking about the mark on her neck and how did he know she had it when she didn't even know it was there. She wanted answers and she knew that she was not going to get them. Her parents would have known but they are now both dead. The only person who could answer her refused to discuss it. She huffed in frustration and waited and waited and waited.

"I understand you seek counsel, Altaira, Warrior of the Northern Tribes," a soft voice was heard from behind her.

She immediately stood and bowed her head as a sign of respect for the Ohme Gully Leader. "Yes," she answered.

"Chaska our Elder has insisted I speak with you. He believes you have great knowledge to part with and that I must listen to what you have to say," he spoke in a soft voice that reminded her of her father. She nodded her reply.

"I need to advise that I am not alone, my brother and a hunter from another tribe wait for me just outside the village," she admitted.

The Leader stood and smiled. A brother he thought. He shouted for the hunter outside to enter. "Go, on the border of our camp you will find two more. Tell them to join us they are not to be harmed. Tell them Altaira is with me and I request that they join us," he ordered, the hunter nodded.

"Why did they not join you?"

"I thought it would be better for us if I came on my own. I did not want to show any disrespect or cause any of your tribe any un-necessary worry. I thought you may have seen it as a threat, so I convinced them to stay there and I would go unarmed and alone."

The Leader laughed, "You are very wise Altaira. It is your wisdom as to why you are still alive. Not many have entered our tribe and lived."

"Thank you," she nodded her civilities. "But I came here for a reason. I need to warn you of a great danger to you and your tribe," she uttered urgently.

The Leader shifted his stance and looked gravely at her. "What danger?"

On the outskirts of your village there is a Garchy, and…."

"Yes, we know," he interrupted her.

"You do?"

"Yes, it has been there for some time. It has never attempted to come any closer, so we have chosen to leave it alone."

"What if I told you it is not completely alone. It

is there for a reason and it will place your whole tribe at risk," Altaira counselled with an air of passion to save his tribe.

"What do you mean?"

"It is there for a reason, when the time is right it will hoot and holler for re-enforcements," Altaira advised. "Then one Garchy on the edge of your village will soon be three or four."

"Well if that does happen, I will order the hunters to make chase and kill. I will protect the tribe," he spoke with an air of annoyance.

"And that will be the wrong decision. That is just what it wants you to do. Whilst you send your hunters after the Garchy you leave your whole village unprotected."

The Leader looked at Altaira and frowned. "How do you know all this?"

"Because all the Northern Tribes have been annihilated and killed. Including my father," she sniffed and held her breath to maintain her composure. "My brother managed to escape and is travelling with me and a hunter. A hunter from another tribe that fell into that trap. When he returned, he found all his tribe dead," she paused to look at the Leader who continued to stare at her and waited for her to continue. "They had been slaughtered. His wife and new born daughter were among the dead. All the tribes that have been attacked had a single Garchy on the edge of camp. They were tricked into sending their hunters to chase the Garchy away from the village. This left the village un-protected. It is a trap. Once all the hunters are far enough from the camp and unable to quickly return, the King's guards will attack with more re-enforcements of Garchy killing everyone in sight."

"All the Northern Tribes are gone?" he asked in bewilderment.

"Yes," she replied with a huge lump in her throat. "I think they are targeting the tribes that are more of a threat. The North is gone? Your tribe is one of the strongest in the South. You need to protect it."

"Yes, and I will. I will select some of our finest hunters to kill it," he spoke in a worried tone.

"No, you cannot send more than one person. If you send more it will immediately feel threatened and hoot for re-enforcements or it will run and get them. Do you have anyone skilled enough to kill a Garchy on their own?" Altaira asked hoping that he did not.

The Leader knew he did not. Not one person amongst his tribe was strong enough to kill a Garchy on their own. A long time ago he would have had the perfect person to do it but not any longer. He looked at the Northern Warrior and frowned.

"I need to think," he gave a half smile and stepped outside of the hut and felt the breeze lick his bare skin. He looked at the children playing, he could hear their carefree laughter, and he knew the responsibility was his to protect every living soul in his village. He knew what he had to do, he had no doubt but... two hunters interrupted his thoughts as they approached him with Dez and Inca at their sides. "She is in there," he gazed at Dez and pointed to the hut as the two scrambled inside to join her. He could hear voices from inside. He knew he needed them, but he was the tribe's Leader he should have all the answers he told himself.

"You need them," the Elder softly spoke, telling him what he already knew. "I did tell you one day she would return. One foe is too many and a hundred friends are too few. You need to forgive; she is not the one who deserves to be punished. You need to remember that your children are not your own but are lent to you by the creator, and so was her mother. She chose her own path. You need to respect that it was her decision to leave. Listen to her or your tongue will make you deaf," the Elder smiled and placed his hand on his shoulder and squeezed.

"She had a son too," the Leader spoke with tears in his eyes.

"Yes, and if they are anything like their mother, they will be a force to be reckoned with."

The Leader nodded. He had received the counsel he so very much needed. He watched as Chaska walked slowly away. He stepped back inside the hut and gazed at Altaira and Dez. He so wanted to tell them who he was.

"Well do you? Do you have anyone who has the skill to kill the Garchy?" Altaira asked.

"No, we do not. Do you have any ideas?" he asked as he looked at her knowing she did. He had seen that look so many times before in her mother.

"Yes, I will kill it," she smiled. "In exchange for an alliance."

"No, I cannot allow you to do it. No, absolutely no," he said sternly.

"Why?"

"Because, because you are a woman," he lied. He could not tell her the truth. He had once lost her mother and the thought of losing her would be too much especially after just meeting her again after all those years apart.

"Trust me, she is more than capable of killing a Garchy," Dez interrupted. You should see her she is amazing," he glanced at Altaira who held him with a beaming smile.

The Leader interrupted, "That may be true, but a Garchy on your own," he paused and remembered what Chaska the Elder had said. His tongue was making him deaf and he did need to listen to her. He needed to listen to them both. "All right," he looked at the floor. "All right," he repeated. He knew he didn't have much choice but to give her the honour of killing the Garchy. There was no one else who was capable to complete such a deed. "Are you sure you can do this, and tell me more about that alliance? What are you talking about, why would we need an alliance?"

"It is very clear to me that the King is trying to eradicate the tribes. I have sent men to search for all the hunters that went after the Garchy. I am trying to gather as many forces as possible. Inside the castle walls are many of our people that he has enslaved. I want to free them," she looked at the Leader who just smiled at her. "If I kill the Garchy I want an alliance with you. I want the Ohme Gully tribe to join our cause when the time comes. I also want it to be a public alliance where everyone in the tribe agrees," she spoke sternly.

"And this is because if I die the alliance lives on, I suppose," the Leader gave a slight chuckle.

"Em, yes, exactly. Forgive me for saying you are not much younger than the Elder, so naturally I need it to be agreed publicly. So, it will be honoured after your death if you do indeed die before," Altaira stopped talking - this was difficult to say without sounding disrespectful.

The Leader smiled at her and then gave a slight chuckle.

"I must say you seem very relaxed about all of this, knowing there is a Garchy on the edge of the village and why it is there," Dez announced.

"Well yes I am. We have the Great Northern Warrior who is going to slaughter it for us. I agree to a public meeting after I have met with the Elders who will discuss your offer and if we should enter in to such an alliance. Then we will announce the outcome to the whole village." The Leader sounded the village horn to gather all Elders to counsel. One by one they entered the hut.

***

Altaira paced outside the hut where the Leader and Elders had gathered to discuss her proposal. Several of the villagers had gathered, it was not often that all the Elders and the Leader held counsel. The last time was when they declared war on the Northern Tribes many years ago. Several villagers stared at Altaira, not sure if they trusted her; she was after all from a Northern Tribe. She heard more whisperings of her name and spotted a mother with a young baby in her arms walk towards her. She stopped in front of her and held her arms out wide offering Altaira to take the child.

"What?" Altaira asked. "What do you want me to do?" she asked, as she took the child and held it in her arms.

"Maybe it is an offering, she is giving you her baby," Dez laughed and Altaira panicked. Her heart began to race and beat in her ears as her stomach threatened to reach her mouth.

"No, No No, I do not want to have any babies. Thank you, but no," Altaira handed the child back to its mother. There was nothing in this world that would make her want to raise a baby.

"I am not giving you my child to keep, I would like you to bless her," she smiled.

"Oh," she looked at Dez and smiled. "I freaked out a bit then, didn't I? Just the thought of even holding one sent shivers down my spine. "That was a close one," she giggled with relief. "Bless it! How?" she looked at the young mother.

"A kiss on the forehead, that is all I ask from you," she went to hand the child back to Altaira.

"No, it's all right I can bless her in your arms," Altaira confirmed.

"No, it doesn't work that way. The blessing is only complete if you are holding her when you kiss her, that way the positive energy from you is transferred to her sealing the blessing," she announced.

"Oh dear," she muttered. "You mean I have to hold her." She glanced at Dez and watched his smile get wider and wider as more mothers joined the queue for their children to receive their blessings too. "All right I can do this, how hard can it be to hold a baby anyway."

She took the child and held her under the armpits and let her dangle in the air.

"What is her name?" Altaira asked.

"My daughter is called Enna," she replied.

Altaira kissed Enna on the forehead and uttered the words her mother had always told her. "Fly high Enna and let the stars guide you."

There was a sudden gasp from the women and Dez immediately stood beside her. He was worried, he didn't know why they had gasped. Altaira had heard it too.

"What, what did I say that was wrong?" she asked as she looked at the young mother.

"You didn't say anything wrong," the mother reassured her. "You said what we were expected you to say, Great Warrior."

Dez saw their smiles and realised his sister was not in any immediate danger. They touched her arm and continued to hand her their babies for her to bless.

Altaira reached the end of the line and blessed the last child and looked at Dez who was still smiling at her.

"Well I must admit you are a natural, I think you should have at least ten children," he smirked.

"Stop it! You know that babies are my worst nightmare, they frighten me more than a Garchy," she admonished her brother with a grimaced look.

"That was fun, I think you should do that at every tribe we visit," Inca announced and smiled.

"I'm just glad I was able to hand them back. I must admit I did at one time think she was gifting me her child. It was such a relief when she said she only wanted me to kiss it."

All three of them began to laugh. "You should have seen your face Altaira, I have never seen you so frightened. It was brilliant, I think I will never forget that for as long as I shall live," Dez giggled.

"Well if you continue to tease me you will not live for much longer," she too giggled but more with relief than anything else.

Their good humour was suddenly interrupted as a loud horn was sounded throughout the tribe. Families left their huts to gather in the centre of the camp to await the deliberation of why their Leader and Elders were in counsel. All the villagers had huddled together when suddenly they separated to allow their Leader and Elders through.

"As you know we have been in counsel and some of you may be wondering why," the Leader paused. "You are also aware that we have three visitors to our village. I want you all to know that they came here with knowledge that will put our village in danger," he paused and raised his arms as he heard the mumblings of concern. "Please, listen when I tell you that you are not in any danger yet. But we could be if we do not take the advice of our friends here today," he waved his arms in the direction of Altaira, Dez and Inca.

The villagers stepped back from the three visitors.

"As you already know on the outskirts of our border is a Garchy. It is believed that it is there waiting for re-enforcements to lure our hunters away and leave our village unprotected," he glanced at the hunters as they all held their spears high. "We know we must kill the Garchy and at the same time protect our tribe. Many tribes have been killed because their hunters had left. We will not fall into that trap," he looked directly at the hunters. "We cannot send more than one person to kill it as it will feel threatened and either hoot for more re-enforcements or run to gather them," he paused as he watched and listen to them panic. "Altaira came here to warn us that this will happen and that the King is behind it. She believes the King is trying to eradicate the tribes one by one and that we could be next. We have no reason to doubt her word. She has offered to kill the Garchy for us," he once again paused as the crowd mumbled. "All she has asked in return is an alliance, an agreement between the North and South. It is important that we stand together as one tribe when the time comes."

The villagers became restless; an alliance with the North was something that they thought was impossible. They had been enemies for too long.

"If Altaira succeeds and kills the Garchy the Elders have agreed to an alliance. The Northern Tribes are no longer our enemy, Altaira and her Brother Dez are evidence of that. They have come at great personal risk to themselves to warn us and offer their assistance; we would be very foolish to refuse. Someone very wise once told me that one foe is too many and a hundred friends are too few," he smiled at Chaska. "The North are no longer our foe."

The Leader finished his speech and walked towards Altaira, "Now, you have your alliance, my tribe is completely in your hands," the Leader said grimly. He had heard of her greatness as a warrior but never seen it. He was hoping the rumours about her were true. "When are you planning to carry out your deed?"

"Right now, there is no time like the present," Altaira announced in a firm voice.

"Do you want me to come with you?" Inca asked with a crooked smile. He too had heard of her greatness but was yet to see it. He was extremely curious to see if she was as truly magnificent as Dez had reported her to be.

"Yes, but you mustn't let it know you are with me or it will know it is a trap. So, stay well hidden."

Inca smiled as he handed Altaira back her weapons as they walked towards the bringer of death.

Slowly and carefully they waded through the ocean of green and then stopped.

"Stay here," she whispered. "If anything happens to me you must make sure you kill the Garchy. We need that alliance so make sure we get it," Altaira urged.

Inca nodded, he was sure it would not come to that, or more that he had hoped it wouldn't. He watched Altaira take a deep breath and stretch her arms and jump up and down on the spot.

"Right, I'm ready now," she gripped Inca's shoulder and smiled and stepped out from the protection of the tall grass and stormed towards the foul beast.

"OI, UGLY," she bellowed at the Garchy.

The Garchy twisted its hideous body to see what had disturbed him. He looked at the Northern Warrior and licked the drool from its lips.

"Phew, perhaps I should have said oi smelly. You really do stink," she continued to insult it.

"I am Altaira, from the Northern Tribes and I am going to kill you," she advised him as she grasped the handle of her axe that was safely hidden behind her back.

The Garchy chuckled. It laughed that hard it sat on the floor with a hard thud rocking backwards and forwards. Altaira smiled, it had fallen into her trap and was now at a more manageable height.

"I am Altaira, from the Northern Tribes and I am going to kill you," she repeated once more.

The Garchy continued to chuckle and rock backwards and forwards. Altaira gripped her fingers tightly around the axe's handle; within a flash and without hesitating she swung the axe. The axe twisted and whistled in the air towards the producer of pong and embedded itself between the eyes splitting the Garchy's head in two. Its grotesque body immediately slumped to the ground with a crash. DEAD!

Altaira casually sauntered towards the fallen creature to retrieve her axe. She yanked the axe and wiped the sinew sludge in its clothes.

"That's for my father," she spat.

"That was amazing," Inca shouted as he ran towards her. He grabbed her and gave her a tight embrace. "You are amazing," he repeated. "You didn't even flinch, I can't believe it. I have never seen anything so incredible as that. You truly are the Great Warrior," he stood in awe of her.

Altaira smiled at Inca. "We need to return to the village quickly and tell them the deed has been done," Altaira announced as she made her way towards the long grass.

Dez paced back and forth waiting for a glimpse of his sister, hoping she would return soon. The longer she took the more concerned he became. From the curtain of grass; she peeked her head through the blades of green and was greeted by a very relieved brother who immediately held her in a hug and swung her around with jubilation.

The Leader stood and watched the two siblings hold each other in a warm embrace. He could not contain his joy when he discovered she had returned unharmed.

"I take it that your return is the sign that your mission was successful," he smiled.

"Yes, you will need some men to drag it into camp and burn it before it releases his toxic gases. If you don't do this quickly the smell will linger," Altaira advised.

The Leader ordered four hunters to quickly retrieve the vulgar creature as its gases already began to radiate and contaminate the surrounding air. With two ponies the dedicated hunters disappeared to recover the wasteland scavenger. The sound of rustling got louder as the hunters hauled their vile package of pong and dumped the foul beast in the center of the village for all the tribe to see.

The young children gasped at the grotesque Garchy with open mouths. Although it was dead it still had an overwhelming presence to those who looked on.

The Leader watched as the villagers one by one lit a piece of kindling and threw it onto the smouldering carcass.

"Our work is done," Altaira announced. "We need to leave.

"You can always stay, you do not have to move on," the Leader advised.

"Thank you, but we need to leave and warn other tribes, and we need to leave soon," Altaira addressed Dez and Inca.

"If what you have said is true Altaira and the King is targeting the strongest tribes then you need to head towards the Ulhra Tribe next," the Leader advised.

Altaira bowed her head and nodded. She knew he was right, they also deserved to be warned just like all the other tribes, but it was not going to be easy for her.

"Something tells me you know this already," the Leader spoke with a soft tone. "I sense you do not want to go there do you?"

"It's complicated," she spoke and looked to the floor. "It is the home tribe of someone I no longer wish to see."

"Don't let yesterday use up too much of today," the Leader counselled. "You need to warn as many tribes as you can and put your own feelings to one side."

Altaira nodded she knew what she had to do, but it was not going to be easy; she had not seen Ursus since he betrayed her and let Lord Tycus die.

One by one the hunters threw a burning ember at the dead Garchy. Slowly the amber flames twisted and consumed the colossal giant of darkness. A loud pop and crack sounded and vibrated on the floor as the gases escaped from the captured beast.

Altaira, Dez and Inca watched as the tribe danced around the inferno structure, mesmerised as the flames flickered, all celebrating the victory. A cacophony of ambers and oranges all mingled together as it devoured its prey.

A Muto's Promise
The Guardians

Suddenly one of the hunters tapped Altaira on the shoulder and caused her to jump with unexpected fright.

"I am sorry, I didn't mean to scare you," he said sincerely and bowed his head in respect. "I would like you to have this as a gift."

Altaira looked at what he was holding, she couldn't believe her eyes. "Are you sure," she asked in a disbelieving tone.

"Yes," the hunter confirmed.

"Then I must give you a gift in return," she smiled.

"You already have given me and my family a gift, the gift of life," he answered.

"I would still like it if you chose something, it is custom to give a gift of your choosing in return. Please anything," she ordered.

The hunter hesitated, "Alright then I will have your axe."

The deed was done. Altaira handed him her beautiful axe that Inca had made and in return he gave

391

her a piece of twine to hold and on the end of that twine was a magnificent white horse.

The Leader nodded his approval and smiled at the hunter for his initiative to help them.

Two more horses were brought forward and they were given to Dez and Inca. All three of them looked at each other and beamed from ear to ear; no more walking from tribe to tribe. Their faces all carried a look of relief.

"These horses are mine and I want that," the Leader pointed to the towering inferno that encased a dead Garchy in its claws.

"But you already have it," Altaira advised.

"No, I don't, this creature is your kill and it therefore belongs to you. And I would like to have it in exchange for those," he pointed to the horses.

"Well of course you have it, but I think we have the better gift," Altaira patted her snow-white steed.

The villagers gathered around their three visitors and handed them food supplies for their journey.

"Thank you, you wise and brave warriors from the North," the Leader smiled and placed a necklace around Altaira's neck. "You are now our loyal friend and are part of the Ohme Gully tribe. As soon as they see your necklace, they will know exactly who you are," he announced and handed Dez a decorative tribal horn.

"Thank you," Dez answered as he examined his gift.

"When the time comes you will both need to return back to us. You will need to blow the horn of honour before you enter and then you will both have safe passage," the Leader said as he patted Dez on the shoulder and smiled.

The three visitors mounted their quadrupled beast and bowed their heads and placed their hand on their hearts.

"Thank you. We will return when the time calls," Altaira confirmed.

"And we will be waiting," he smiled.

Twelve hooves slowly trotted through the grasslands away from the Ohme Gully tribe to the next strongest tribe of the South, the Ulhra tribe. The home of Ursus.

~ Chapter Eighteen ~

The Guardians

Travelling for several days and nights, eight hooves raced from the North and twelve hooves thundered from the South; all heading to the Ulhra Tribe.

High amongst the tree tops the Ulhra watchers gazed at the Garchy below in its solitude. It continued to rip bushes up as if it was preparing a pathway. It pulled up the largest of bushes with incredible ease and tossed it aside into a heap. It sat its oversize frame on the soil and gave a soft hoot. In the distance it heard a soft hoot in reply, then silence. Then a slight chuckle was sounded from the foul beast.

Two hoots echoed in the distance. The Garchy immediately stood and hooted two back. Finally, it thought, finally they were coming. Soon it would feast upon a proper meal, soon it would feast on meat.

Within a few moments the Garchy was joined by another Garchy twice its size, then another and another each overpowering the first in size. Eight yellow eyes blinked and all four gave soft hoots and a little chuckle as they all glared in the same direction down the newly built pathway.

The watchers in the trees all lit a burning arrow and fired them high into the sky to warn the tribe. One of the watchers slowly descended from his branch, he knew he needed to run back to the tribe and warn them. A race against time had now begun. With his heart pounding in his chest and ears he raced through the village to seek counsel with his Leader.

His Leader stood in front of him with a worried face. "I saw the arrows. What is it? Tell me," the Leader spoke with a concerned voice.

"Garchy," he spluttered. "Garchy. There are now four," he spoke as he tried to catch his breath.

"What, four Garchy?" Ursus's Leader bellowed and threw him a horn. "Sound the alarm," he shouted.

The watcher looked at the horn, the last time the horn was blown was before he was born. He placed the horn up to his mouth, took a deep breath and blew with all his might. The tone echoed through the village as it called to its people to assemble. From all directions the villagers left their homes and gathered outside the Leaders hut.

The Leader stood in front of his tribe, he knew he needed to warn them.

"The alarm has been raised to advise you that on the outskirts of our village is a Garchy. It seems that it has taken up residence," he announced as he looked at all their nervous faces.

"A Garchy," the crowd mumbled in panic as they all looked at each other with fright.

The leader stood in front of them with his arms outstretched and open wide. "Our watchers have informed me that up until this morning it was on its own, but now it seems there are four."

The panic amongst the crowd escalated as they tried to digest the news.

"I want all the hunters to gather their weapons and meet me immediately. Everyone else - go back to your homes and stay indoors," he paused as he looked at the crowd who nodded their replies. "Do not panic, our hunters' will either make chase and move them from our borders or kill them."

One by one the hunters arrived in full war dress and armed with their weapons.

"We will creep up and take them by surprise and give chase, that should stop them from entering the village," the Leader announced.

The hunters looked at their Leader with disbelief on their faces as he picked up his weapons to join them.

"Are you going with them?" One of the Elders asked.

"Yes, why?"

"Well, I don't want to upset you but...,"

"You think I am too old don't you," the Leader interrupted. "Well you may be right, but I am a former hunter and I will be going with them. I want you to make sure our people are safe," the Leader ordered.

"Are you sure this is the right thing to do?"

"No, I'm not sure but I am going with them none the less," he said as a matter of fact as he began to walk out of the village with the hunters beside him.

They walked to the edge of the boundary and stopped, they could smell them but not see them. The Leader looked up to the trees and spotted the two remaining watchers who pointed the direction of the smelly giants. The Leader nodded his thanks.

"They are just through those trees," he advised. "We will charge at them and then kill them," he ordered.

The hunters took a deep breath and screamed at the top of their lungs as they flung their bodies forwards at the shocked Garchy who immediately hooted and let out a high pitched shrill. They instantly turned and started to run. The chase had started, and the hunters had fallen straight into their trap.

The Garchy ran through the bushes leading the hunters further from protecting their tribe and from the Kings guard that was marching towards the village. Marching to destroy yet another tribe.

The elder blew the horn to assemble the villagers and to get them to safety. Dak ran, screaming, towards the Elder.

"We are all going to die, we are going to die," he shouted as he began to run around. "We have no protection, all our hunters have left, what the hell are we going to do," he snivelled.

"We are going to fight," a voice from behind interrupted. "We may be old and no longer able to hunt but we can still shoot our arrows, maybe we can hold them off, we were successful hunters once," an elder hunter spoke as he stood by the other elderly hunters.

"What? You think you can protect us, just look at yourselves you are old and useless there is not a chance that you will defeat that," Dak pointed to the oncoming invaders and once again screamed.

"Dak, you are not helping," the Elder said through gritted teeth. "Build a barricade on that side there," the Elder pointed to a spot that was in the same direction as the invaders were advancing. "Grab your weapons and start to protect the tribe the best as you can," he addressed the elder hunters. "You will come with me," he ordered Dak to follow him.

"Dak, get as many of our people as you can and lead them to the elders hut. Inside, you will find a trap door in the floor. There is enough room to hide our people. Now go! I'm afraid I think we are on our own. It is up to us now."

The Elder spoke the truth - they were on their own. Their hunters were too far away to be able to get back in time.

"Halt!" the Leader bellowed. "Halt," he repeated, as all the hunters stopped. "Garchy are known for their speed yet we can still see them. They could easily out run us. Yet we are keeping up with them. Why?" the Leader began to question his judgement. "I think they wanted us to chase them. They knew we would chase them. And by doing so we have left our tribe and our families unprotected. I am such a fool. We must return, and return quickly," the Leader proclaimed. "I want the two of you to keep up the pretence of the chase and the rest of us will return," he ordered.

The two hunters nodded and continued their chase, whilst the rest changed direction to return to their unprotected community.

The dust clouds began to swirl as twelve hooves raced from the South to the Ulhra Tribe. Altaira could see the Kings guards and a posse of Garchy ascending on the tribe. This was going to be a challenge she thought. Their horses entered the centre of the village and she quickly jumped off her horse before it had chance to stop. She swiftly ran to the Elder that was standing with a group of elderly hunters.

"Where is your Leader?" she asked.

"He has left," he bowed his head.

"What? Then where are your hunters?"

"With our Leader. They have left to chase a posse of Garchy off the border."

"It is a trap," she cried.

"Yes, we are aware of that now," he said as he pointed to the hostile crowd that marched towards them. "Can you help us?" he enquired.

"We will try our best," she answered as she looked at Inca and Dez who nodded their acceptance at her and the Elder as they too jumped off their horses to join her.

"I see you have made preparations," she pointed to the heap that they were standing behind. "Right are you all ready? Everyone behind the barricade," Altaira shouted as the Kings guards were nearly in range. "Aim for the horses first, if we maim them it will force the guards to fight on the ground," Altaira bellowed her orders. "Once the horses are down aim for the Garchy. Once they reach us, they will try to breathe their toxic breath on us," Altaira glanced at the older hunters, who nodded to confirm that they accepted her orders.

"Altaira! They are getting closer," Inca spoke in a nervous tone. "Altaira!"

"Not yet. I want them to think that we are defenceless. If we attack now, they will send the rest of the guards that are waiting in the trees," Altaira pointed to the re-enforcements that were just visible and waiting further back. "If we defeat those outside; we will then be able to kill the rest. Now are you all ready?"

They all nodded.

"Remember, maim the horses, kill the Garchy but you must aim for their eyes, if they have no sight, they are useless and no threat to us," Altaira reminded them. "There are ten Garchies and about thirty guards. Inca, Dez we will take the Garchies. I want you four to aim for the horses. The rest of you aim for the guards. Everyone got that?"

Everyone nodded once again and waited for her to give the order to fire their arrows.

"Wait… Wait…Wait,"

Inca looked at the enemy charging and getting closer, his heart began to beat faster and faster. He had a strange twist in his stomach. This is what his tribe must have faced. He knew he needed to be quick, he took several arrows out of his quiver and laid them on the floor beside him. Within an instant all the elder hunters copied and smiled at Inca with respect as they now realised; he was a hunter too, he was one of them.

"Altaira, when?" Dez bellowed. "They are nearly upon us."

"NOW!"

Dez pulled back the string and let go. Two arrows whizzed through the air and landed in the eye sockets of a Garchy, with accurate precision.

"What? How did you manage that?" Inca acknowledged in awe.

"One down, nine to go," Dez bellowed and smiled then winked at Inca.

"Did you just wink at me?"

"Boys!" Altaira shrieked. "Concentrate we have a job to do."

Inca mouthed sorry. He loaded his bow, pulled back the bowstring and fired his arrow through the air. He watched with anticipation as the arrow narrowly missed a Garchy but caught the horse behind him instead. The horse bucked its hind legs causing its rider to fall and the horse quickly toppled on top of him breaking his body.

Altaira pulled on her bow and fired several arrows in quick succession, each arrow screamed through the air and embedded themselves into two of the   Garchies eye sockets - blinding them. They instantly began screaming and flapping their arms about killing several of the King's guards as they aimlessly stomped before crashing into one another. They eventually fell to the floor with a loud crash.

"Seven to go," she shouted. Dez you take the one on the right and Inca you take the one on the left. I will take the one in the middle. Ready, NOW!"

A further six arrows whistled as they travelled each hitting their targets.

"Six," Dez shouted.

"Right same again. Ready GO!"

Six arrows once again found their target and sent three more Garchies crashing to the ground screaming and shouting as their sight was destroyed. The elder hunters maimed all the horses forcing the guard to the floor.

"Right, everyone, aim for the last three Garchies," Altaira ordered.

An army of arrows and spears all aimed for the last remaining Garchy. One by one they toppled. The hunters cheered in jubilation at the sight.

"Charge!" Altaira bellowed at the top of her voice. Over the barricade they climbed towards the King's guards. Altaira ran at top speed as she skidded on the floor and buried her knife into a guard and sliced him from groin to neck. He spat globules of blood and crashed to the floor. She quickly grabbed the dead man's spear and ploughed it swiftly into the guard that was approaching behind her without hesitation. Inca swung his axe and left it in the back of a guard as he tackled another who lunged at him. Inca grabbed the guard and quickly pushed him forward to Dez who stabbed his knife into his back and pierced his kidneys.

Time seemed as if it had stood still as they continued to fight. Only one guard stood. He looked around at his fallen comrades in fear of his own life. He lifted his arms in the air and waved frantically for re-enforcements. Without warning the re-enforcements left the safety of the trees and ascended forward towards the Ulhra Tribe charging at full speed.

"Here we go again, are you ready?" Altaira shouted. She knelt as she picked up two axes off a dead hunter, Dez tutted.

"What, it's not as if he is going to use them," she frowned.

"That's not the point you don't steal off a dead man," Dez reminded her.

"I am not stealing I am borrowing," she answered in an annoyed voice.

"Same thing."

"No, it is not. Stealing is taking, whereas borrowing, is still taking but I plan to return them to him afterwards," she spoke as she gripped the handles tightly. "Now are you bloody ready or not?"

The elder hunters struggled to breathe, and some knelt to the ground in exhaustion.

"You have all fought very bravely, do not feel ashamed if you want to return to your village," Altaira announced as she looked upon the blood-stained men in front of her.

"No, we will not give up, we will fight until the last drop of blood leaves our bodies, or until our last breath," one of them stated.

Inca stared at them and smiled, he felt it was an honour to stand along such brave souls.

"TO THE END!" Altaira shouted as she sprinted towards the re-enforcements taking them by surprise. All followed suit and charged hollering and screaming as they ran. This caused the re-enforcements to also charge bringing them closer and closer.

Contact was made as Altaira brandished the axes and swung in several directions slicing through their skin. Inca knelt to the ground on one Knee and fired his arrows at anyone who came near her. Spears rained upon Altaira who held her shield in the air causing them to bounce off. She knew that she had picked her shield wisely.

From behind the King's guards, four horses thundered closely. Nubilus quickly stood on his horse and leapt into the air, with his arms open wide. He jumped onto two guards causing them to topple to the floor. He stood still as four guards charged at him. He quickly grabbed the handle of a spear and yanked it out from a dead body beside him. He stood still and beckoned three guards towards him. The guards smiled - there were three of them and he was alone. With their swords raised by their chest they charged.

Nubilus twisted the spear in his hands and with the blunt end poked it at one of their faces causing them to drop the sword. As his hands came up to cover his face, Nubilus drove the spear into the guard's chest.

"COME ON!" he bellowed at the remaining two.

Both guards glared at him and charged. He swung the spear swiftly at their legs and caused both men to lift off the floor and land on their backs with a thud. He quickly cut their throats and spat.

Altaira had spotted Nubilus as he single handily worked his way through several guards. She was furious at the mere sight of him but also relieved that he was at their aide. Then she turned her head and spotted Ursus. Fury bubbled up inside her. Both, here together she thought. Have they formed an alliance? This fuelled her anger more as she slashed her way through several guards. Her feelings for them were less than friendly.

Loud hollers were heard from the trees as the Ulhra hunters returned shouting and screaming. The King's guards were surrounded they knew they had lost but continued to fight regardless. The Ulhra hunters made short work of it with the help of Nubilus, Altaira, Dez and Inca. One guard remained; he slumped to his knees too exhausted to care and completely out of breath.

Altaira held her spear in her hand and pointed it at his throat. Inca and Dez did the same.

"No," Ursus shouted.

"Why not? He could have been the one who killed my father," Altaira spat with venom in her voice.

"Or my wife and child," Inca growled through gritted teeth.

"Never the less you will not kill him," the Leader spoke.

"No, please just kill me. I'm dead anyway. If I return, they will just kill me," he spoke and lowered his gaze.

"No, you will return and give the King a message. You tell him he may have slaughtered the Northern tribes and tried to bury us but what he doesn't understand is that we are the seeds," Altaira grabbed her brother's arm.

412

"And we will grow. Now get up, on your feet and run back and tell him and his weasel of a guard Riend that they should have killed me when they had the chance." She grabbed him by the scruff of his neck and kicked him hard. "Run, go on, run."

The guard staggered and tried to run but his legs kept slipping from under him and once again he fell to the ground. Altaira watched as he meandered to the trees and disappeared. She swiftly grabbed two spears and swiped both Ursus's and Nubilus's legs from under them causing them both to crash heavily to the floor. She held them both with a spear head pointing at their chest.

"Give me one good reason why I shouldn't kill you both," she cried. "GO ON, ONE REASON, ONE!" she screamed as she pressed down on their chest.

"I will give you a reason," the leader spoke softly. "You are on Ulhra land and as I am leader of this land; I forbid it. Especially as one of them is of the Ulhra tribe."

Altaira looked at the Leader who waited for her to yield. She knew the Leader was right this was Ursus's home tribe and to anger them would be foolish especially as she knew she would eventually need an alliance. She reluctantly lifted the spears off their chests.

Ursus got to his feet and went to check on the elder hunters. Miraculously only a handful had died.

"Your bravery has saved the tribe," he spoke.

"No, it was Altaira that has saved us," he smiled his thanks in her direction. "I have never seen anyone like her. She is incredible. Without her we would be dead and the rest of the tribe with us."

The Leader walked around to check on his elder hunters and to thank them. Each one pointed to Altaira, Dez and Inca and confessed the victory was theirs to celebrate.

Nubilus got to his feet. His heart began to beat heavy in his chest. His whole being smiled as he looked upon Altaira. His heart was hers it always had been. He rubbed his chest. His fingertips touched the indentation from the spear. He knew it was not going to be easy to approach her. He looked around and noticed Ursus stood staring at him. Ursus smiled and nodded his approval to approach her.

He slowly walked towards her. He had a strange twist in his stomach. His heart raced and the sound of drumming filled his ears. Be brave, he told himself. He knew he needed to speak to her sooner rather than later. Hopefully the battle may have tired her a little, he told himself. Altaira's back stood in front of him, it's now or never, he thought. He sucked in his cheeks and took a huge breath and tapped her on the shoulder.

Altaira swung around and stood directly in front of him.

"What!" Altaira screamed as fury bubbled inside as she looked at him. She had no desire to talk to them.

"Altaira it is really important, we need to talk with you."

"WE, WE. Who are WE. Oh yes that WE must be YOU and URSUS!" she shrieked. "You two best buds again now eh? Is that it? What has that crazy fool convinced you to do now? No don't tell me, I don't want to know. Whatever he wants the answer is NO!"

"It is not that easy my child," the Leader spoke in gentle tones. "You need to listen, if you will not hear it from them then you must hear it from me."

She looked at the Leader with surprise. "What, what do I need to listen to? There is nothing that I want to hear from those two traitors."

"I understand you are angry with them. But this is far more important than your disagreement or how you feel about them. It is about the survival of our people. The survival of our culture and beliefs. You need to help our people and to do that you need to listen to them." The Leader grabbed her arm. "Come, please listen to what they have to say." The Leader escorted her to his hut and to where Ursus and Nubilus waited for her.

She stood outside and hesitated. She didn't want to go in. She didn't want to speak to them. She didn't want to let her people down either. She reluctantly entered. Inside the other of the two Muto's sat.

"I want you both to know that I despise you and if it wasn't for your leader Ursus, I would have had no hesitation in killing you both here and now. Alright what is it that you both desperately need me to know.

"Do you remember that day Lord Tycus told us we were all Muto's?" Ursus asked.

"Erm, yes."

"Can you remember we made an oath to him, a promise to look after his children if he died." Nubilus interjected.

"Yes, I remember. Why?"

"Well, a couple of months ago I was fooled into entering a particular home that was cooking porridge. And you know I cannot resist it, but it was a trap to lure me inside. I discovered in a crib three small children," Ursus advised.

"And what has that got to do with me?" she asked.

"Well those three children are in fact the offspring of Lord Tycus," Ursus stopped as he looked at the horror on Altaira's face.

"What. He had children?" Altaira gasped.

"Yes, and this means that…."

"No, no, no," Altaira cried with panic as she finally realised the implication this had on her. "No."

"Yes, Altaira, I'm afraid so," the Leader spoke as he held her hand. "You made an oath child, a blood oath if I am not mistaken. You have no choice. You will leave here tonight under the cover of darkness with a child."

Altaira looked at all three of them completely speechless. I cannot do it. She told herself. She would rather be chained back in the castle then look after a child.

The Leader pulled back the door covering and in walked three nursing mothers who held the children close. One by one they handed a child over to Ursus and Nubilus who naturally took the offered children and held them in their arms. The third nursing mother held the child out to Altaira to take. Altaira took one look at the child and scampered away in fear.

"Get that thing away from me," she screamed.

The nursing mother looked at their leader for reassurance. She didn't know whether to stay or go or what to do with the child. The Leader held his arms out to the woman and willingly took the child off her.

"Altaira hold out your arms," the Leader advised.

"No," Altaira stated as she shook her head and moved further away.

The Leader moved closer, so close that Altaira could not back away any further. He quickly placed the child in her lap and walked away.

The whole of Altaira's body went rigid with fright. A high pitched wail was sounded as she closed her eyes.

"Altaira just open your eyes and take a look at how beautiful she is," Nubilus suggested.

Ever so slowly she opened her eyes and glanced at the child. The tiny child looked up at Altaira and gave her a smile, cooed and blew a bubble at her. Altaira let out a soft giggle as the child continued to babble.

"What is her name?"

"May," Ursus answered. "We have been charged to care for these children Altaira."

"Do you remember the prophecy the spirit showed Ursus? The very same one you foreseen," Nubilus reminded her.

"Yes, I remember."

"Well, take a look at these three children," Ursus pointed to them. "It foretold us about them. With our help and guidance; we will help them to make the right decisions. No one is aware that these children are the offspring of Lord Tycus and it must remain that way," Ursus advised.

"What am I supposed to tell my brother? He knows exactly how I feel about children. Am I to lie?"

"Yes, you are. You have no choice. No one must know, if someone found out it would put their lives in danger and risk the prophecy from coming true." Nubilus spoke softly.

"Well what now?" she asked.

"We give the children back to the nursing mothers for tonight we feast and celebrate our victory," the Leader cheered and clapped his hands together. "It is to honour all those who saved our village. Now come!" he ordered.

All three Guardians sat and watched as many of the tribe danced and celebrated their victory. Nubilus watched as Altaira got up and moved away from him and sat the other side of Ursus.

"What, what have I done," he asked her.

"Nothing, it's not what you *have* done, but more what you *haven't* done," she smiled politely at him.

"And what is that?" he asked.

"WASHED!" she giggled, you really do stink.

Ursus looked at Nubilus. "I did try to tell you, but you still didn't believe me."

The celebration festivities began to end and the crowd slowly thinned as they each left to settle down for the night. The three nursing mothers approached with their precious cargo. Ursus and Nubilus willingly took the children from their arms.

Inca and Dez stood with Altaira and watched as she held her arms out to receive the child.

"Have you been asked to bless this one too?" they both sniggered.

Altaira twisted around to face the pair. "No, this one is coming with us. No questions please," she looked at them as they both starred at her in utter confusion.

"Don't," she spoke. "I am her guardian, which is all you need to know.

Altaira, Nubilus and Ursus stood together in harmony for the first time since the children's father died. It was his death that separated them, but it was his children that had reunited them.

"I am sorry Ursus, you did make the right decision after all," Altaira smiled as she cuddled May close to her.

"What now?" Nubilus asked.

"We each teach them, I will train her to be a mighty warrior. When she has all the knowledge and skill that I can give her I will bring her back here to reunite her with her brothers. We will reunite them to fulfil the prophecy," Altaira spoke quietly.

Ursus and Nubilus nodded as they held their precious load close to their chest. Each Muto walked away to fulfil their promise and become a guardian. A guardian that will teach each child their culture, their beliefs and their strengths until the time comes to reunite and fight.

This was to be a fight for survival that would be in the hands of three small children and their trusted Guardians.

No one could be certain of the future. This was not the end. It was just the beginning.

Printed in Poland
by Amazon Fulfillment
Poland Sp. z o.o., Wrocław